kweli

The Truth Unmasked

Joseph & Jane Matthews

Double Edge Press

Scenery Hill, Pennsylvania

Double Edge Press

ISBN 978-1-938002-03-8

This novel is a work of fiction. Names, characters, places, and incidents either are the product of the author's imagination or are used fictitiously.

Dedication

We dedicate this book, *Kweli*, to all individuals who seek the truth. Acting on your fundamental beliefs isn't always easy, but it molds character and produces core values: trushworthiness, loyalty, honesty and sincerity.

Our uniqueness and different approaches to discovering truth doesn't alter the reality that truth can be verified and always stands the test of time. The truth is rock-solid and unchangeable. For those of us who embrace it, our lives are transformed by a divine purpose.

We acknowledge all those brave souls who dare to take a stand for what is right, especially when it's not politically correct.

"We hold these truths to be self-evident, that all men are created equal, that they are endowed by their Creator with certain unalienable Rights that among these are Life, Liberty, and the Pursuit of Happiness."

~The Declartion of
Independence

Other Titles by Joseph and Jane Matthews:

Janjaweed – Devils on Horseback

\

kweli

The Truth Unmasked

Joseph & Jane Matthews

Acknowledgements

We thank God for inspiring us to write an action fiction about social and political injustices that can be overcome by the positive actions of caring individuals and concerned citizens.

We thank our family and friends for their encouragement. Joan Mclean, twin sister of Jane, suggested the name for the title of our book and the idea of using a ceremonial mask for the cover. Nikki Choi extended her expertise with the grammatical edits. Kaye Coppersmith provided professional critique of our first book, *Janjaweed - Devils on Horseback*, and suggested we tighten *Kweli, the Truth Unmasked*. Our friends at the Melbourne Florida Writers Association group offered good recommendations on the first chapter of this book.

We're also grateful for Rebecca Melvin, our publisher. To all of our friends and acquaintances who shared their time and talents, may you receive a double portion of God's blessing.

"I think we have a little voice inside that guides us…if we shut out all the noise and clutter from our lives and listen to that voice, it will tell us the right thing to do."

~ Christopher Reeves

Prologue: The Mask

The marriage of Travis Martin and Karasa took place in the open-sided church in a small village in Kenya. Jim Anderson, their friend and pastor of the local mission, presided over the wedding ceremony. Karasa looked radiant. A long, linen pastel gown gently caressed her slim, athletic frame. A shimmering veil hid her attractive, angular ebony face and dangling, copper earrings reflected the light of the setting sun. She carried a beautiful bouquet of fresh flowers. Travis and his best man, Jeshi, dressed in cotton suits and decorative ties for the occasion. The song leader sang a wedding melody accompanied by a chorus of vocalists singing the harmony.

When the nuptails concluded, the couple joined their

family, friends, and the villagers to indulge in a bountiful banquet in their honor. After the feast, the joyful pair led the dance to the rhythmic drums.

"I am so happy to be your wife," Karasa fingered her gold wedding band as they swayed to the music. "I like your American custom of exchanging vows. My favorite is the meaning of the rings... a circle of love that never ends."

Travis embraced her and kissed her.

"Yes, until death do us part, and I don't plan for that to happen anytime soon."

While the entertainment proceeded, Travis and Karasa mingled with their guests. Each guest presented them with a small gift of flowers, fruits or nuts, or homemade household items. Karasa's family, members of the Dinka Tribe, traveled from Sudan and presented them with two goats, male and female.

Moran, a Maasai Warrior, honored them with his gift, the Tribal Wedding Mask. A one-of-a-kind piece of art, crafted from local wood, this unique mask depicted two small profiles that faced each other. Each profile appeared over the brow of a full face mask that featured slits where the mouth and eyes should be. It symbolized the union and friendship between two people who cared for each other.

Following the ceremony, they were invited to reside in a small Christian community of the local Kikuyu Tribe in Kenya. Like their neighbors, they lived in a thatched roof hut. These round mud huts were constructed so the interior would be warm in the cold season and cool in the hot season. Their cherished Maasai wedding mask now hung on the wall where it would be visible upon entry to the Martin's home. For Karasa, just glancing upon it always elicited beautiful memories of that special occasion.

kweli

The Truth Unmasked

"All of us who professionally use the mass media are shapers of society. We can vulgarize that society. We can brutalize it. Or we can help lift it onto a higher level."

~ William Bernbach

"Life is not about waiting for the storms to pass . . .

it's about learning how to dance in the rain!"

~ Vivian Greene

CHAPTER ONE

Kenya, Africa
Summer, 1997

"Oh, Dear God, please help me!" Travis gasped. He felt like he'd been kicked in the stomach by an ill-tempered mule. He gripped his gut, dropping the envelope's contents to the dirt floor as if it burned his fingers.

Travis struggled for breath.

This sudden bash at his life chilled his body and clawed at his soul, ripping apart the essential elements of his world - the people who gave it meaning. His entire world tilted over a meat grinder, precariously hanging over grating teeth.

No way am I going to be shred into sausage, he

thought. His face contorted in pain, but his eyes steeled in determination.

Kookie craned his head to the side so that he could see the dropped photograph. Travis followed his gaze to the dirt floor. The young African male in the photo showed signs of malnutrition. Rusty colored hair framed his thin face. Numerous scars covered his body. His skin stretched across his bony frame and protruding belly. An ugly knobby lump protruded above his knee where his leg had been broken and not properly set or healed.

Recovering slightly, Travis' hand shook as he picked up the fallen items. He glanced again at the photograph before shuffling it behind the letter. He read it in silence.

Mr. Travis Martin,

This memo relates to a matter of mutual interest.I am a freelance Foreign Correspondent and represent an international news agency. We understand that your wife has searched for a number of years for her son, Twangi. We know his present whereabouts. We also have the ability to purchase him from slavery and to relocate him to whatever country you desire.

In return, we want to feature you in a human interest story that will appeal to our readers. During your reunion with your stepson, reporters will interview you and a photographer will take pictures to record the event.

Please contact me at the Nairobi Hilton at your earliest convenience. I will be available for one week. If I do not hear from you within the specified time, I will assume you have no interest, and will offer our services to his mother.

Ms. Desmonica Houston,
Agent at Large

When the shock cleared, Travis' cheeks burned and he felt his face turn shades of scarlet. A rage welled up that he had not known for years. His fists clenched and his arm muscles tensed and bulged. He wanted to throttle the person responsible for this. He glared at Kookie, but reconsidered.

I can't hurt the Aussie; he's only the messenger.

"What's wrong, Mate?" Kookie leaned forward to look at the paper.

Travis stared at Kookie and perceived genuine concern in the Aussie's eyes. His friend worked odd jobs, such as delivering this message to this remote African village, due to slackening trade in his import-export business.

The Aussie stood about a half inch taller than Travis'

five-ten. Kookie pulled off his brimmed bush hat, and uneven lengths of dirty blond hair hung about of their own
accord, as if they'd been trimmed with a bush knife.

"About ten years ago, the Janjaweed raided my wife's
village in Sudan and killed her first husband. Their son and
daughter were taken for slaves," Travis said.

"Are they the slavers who kidnapped the missionary
kids you went over the border to rescue?" Kookie asked.

"Could be," Travis answered. "I teamed up with the
Sudan Peoples' Liberation Army to locate the enslaved
missionary children. My wife, Karasa, fought with the
SPLA rebels. We've both been tried in absentia in Sudan
and sentenced to death if we return. The government of
Kenya has refused to extradite us, but we're both dead meat
if we cross the border and get caught."

Travis handed the paper to the Aussie. After quickly
scanning the letter, Kookie shook his head back and forth
in disbelief.

"Sorry, Mate, I had no idea that mongrel was using me
for something like this. If I had known," he waved the paper, "I would have clobbered him T over A".

"It's not your fault," Travis said. As he calmed, he began to think straight. "Who hired you to drive all the way
out here to my neck of the woods and deliver this?" Travis
asked. Kookie's Landrover stood outdoors, engine still
pinging from the heat.

"Some British bloke in Nairobi paid me to drive out here and hand-deliver it."

Travis sat back a minute to ponder. Life had chiseled strong international features into his tanned face. In his early forties with dark brown hair and eyes, of average appearance with a solid muscular frame, he could easily blend into most cultural surroundings. When his wife, Karasa, had asked him about his ancestors he had referred to himself as a 'Heinz 57', an American cliché that he had to explain to her. She was of the Dinka tribe of Sudan, but to them the difference in their races did not exist.

"What you gonna do? Even if they tell the missus, you can still send someone else to go after him."

"No, she's a fighter. She'll never forgive herself if she doesn't go. I'd wake up one morning to find her sleeping mat empty," Travis sighed.

After years of futile searching for her lost son, Karasa had found him on a farm while rescuing the kidnapped American children. Her son, Twangi, stood less than a meter away, and she hadn't recognized him at first. It broke her heart.

"We had to leave Twangi in Sudan. Being crippled and mentally challenged, he couldn't have kept up. He'd have jeopardized the safe return of the other children. We returned like we promised, but he had disappeared again."

Kookie started to respond but Travis quickly motioned

for quiet. He listened and heard a faint musical humming. Recognizing Karasa's quick steps approaching on the path, his mouth tensed to a thin line and his eyebrows furrowed.

"I need to keep this from Karasa. She knows I'm scheduled to leave on a twenty-three day *safari* next Monday. I'll just tell her that you've come to pick me up early because there's been a change of plans. You'll back me up?" Travis whispered and waited in anticipation.

"Bloody oath!" Kookie said with assurance.

"Thanks."

Following protocol, Karasa stopped just outside the threshold and waited to be invited in. She adhered to this custom of the Kikuyu tribe who befriended them and allowed her and her family to reside in their village.

"Come in, Karasa," Travis called.

She stooped as she came in through the low doorway, carrying their eighteen month old daughter Tamara.

Karasa's attractive, ebony face showed no notable signs of middle age. A traditional multi-colored *kanga* draped and contoured to her tall, lithe figure. She wore a matching scarf tied behind her head.

Travis greeted her with a kiss.

"Hi, Princess," Travis tickled Tamara, who laughed at his touch.

"*Baba,*" Tamara stretched out her arms to her father.

Travis grabbed his daughter and gave her a hug.

Tamara responded in kind and giggled.

"Karasa, there's someone I want you to meet," Travis nodded toward his guest.

"G'day, Ma'am. I'm Kookaburra Jack Burkes. But..."

". . . his friends call him Kookie," Travis finished the sentence.

"Are you from Australia?" Karasa asked.

"Sure am. O'im frum Sidney," Kookie answered.

"You know each other?" she asked.

"Yes. I took your husband's first *safari* tour three years ago after reading about your exploits saving those slave kids in *Soldier of Fortune* magazine. That was a fair dinkum piece of work," Kookie affirmed.

After introductions, Karasa said, "I have made *ugali*. Please come for breakfast."

"Thank you. It's one of my favorite dishes," Kookie replied.

Travis stretched as he stepped outdoors past the threshold of his round, thatch-roof *thingira*. A traditional structure of the Kikuyu Tribe, a *thingira* provided privacy for a man to conduct his family affairs or to hang out with friends his age, his *riikas*.

He savored this time of day, breathing in the clean fresh air and drinking in the warm rays of the rising sun. Streams of sunlight had transformed the Kenyan veldt into a sea of golden hues as the morning breezes had raced across miles of grasslands.

Travis basked in the quiet before the annual convergence of tourists on the wildlife preserves. With the arrival of the dry season, the travelers of the world would descend on this paradise. As their tour guide for *Simba Safari Adventures, Ltd.,* he'd ensure that they experienced the expedition of a lifetime. His clients would view Africa's splendid scenery, observe migrating herds in search of water and savor the heady scent of the wild. Best of all, Travis got paid to make it all happen. Would these *safaris* soon be memories of the past?

As they walked the seven meters to Karasa's hut, despair flooded his heart. Now, only an hour after his habitual morning stroll, his world appeared beaten down by a heavy sun, and the savannah's grasses flattened as if by a huge blacksmith's hammer on an anvil. Scattered trees dotting the savannah that once provided an oasis for travelers, at this moment mirrored ticks on the back of a mangy brown dog.

When they arrived at Karasa's hut, Travis forced a smile.

Karasa served goat's milk and fresh fruit with the *ugali,* Kenya's national dish of cornmeal porridge.

"Mmmm, that was ace," Kookie licked his lips.

"Kookie is a new hire," Travis lied.

Kookie nodded in agreement and a hint of guilt crossed

his face. Travis hoped Karasa hadn't notice.

Travis weaved a convincing tale, explaining that Kookie had come early so they could begin to prepare their itineraries for the photo *safari.*

"You are leaving today?" Karasa asked, looking back and forth between Travis and Kookie as though she had surely misunderstood.

"Yes, I'll gather my gear and say good-bye to your father before I go."

"So soon? I will miss you." She hurried over to embrace him.

Travis reached out to catch her and gave her a lingering kiss.

"That was for good luck on the hunt."

"*Mimi panda ku,* I love you," Karasa whispered in his ear.

He caught a single tear that swept down her cheek and turned to go.

"Wisdom is not a product of schooling

but the lifelong attempt

to acquire it."

~ Albert Einstein

CHAPTER TWO

"Give me ten more minutes," Travis said.

"No worries," Kookie walked toward his Land Rover.

Moving with rapid steps, Travis approached his father-in-law's *thingira* and entered.

"Jambo."

Bahrundi's intelligent eyes peered from beneath his bushy grayish eyebrows. Short white hair crowned his head. Reclining on a straw mat, he wore traditional Dinka garb.

"Father," Travis sat beside him and spoke in Swahili with a quiet urgency. "I must speak to you about a serious matter."

Travis felt genuine affection for Karasa's parents. In their culture, he'd become an adopted son when he married their daughter.

"What is wrong, my son?" Concern etched his brow.

Travis showed him the photograph.

"Who is this?"

Travis didn't know how to soften the blow so he just stated the fact, "That is your grandson, Twangi. Let me read this letter to you."

Although Bahrundi possessed timeless wisdom, he'd received no formal education. Travis translated the words into Swahili.

"My son, a hunter's trap is set and is waiting to snare its quarry." The old man placed his hand on Travis' arm. "Do not go."

"I must."

"I love my grandson, Twangi. Even though he suffers, they will not allow you to bring him back here. We have lost one. If you go to the enemy's stronghold, we will lose two." Mist clouded Bahrundi's eyes.

"Father, if I don't show up, they'll approach my wife."

"Have you told my daughter?"

"No, my wife thinks that I'm going on a twenty-three day *safari*," Travis said.

The muscles around Bahrundi's mouth tightened. "A husband should not tell lies or hide the truth from his wife. Without *kweli*, there can be no lasting trust between you."

"She'll insist on coming with me. Worse, she wouldn't

hesitate to go in my place even though Tamara needs her."

"*Kweli* will be revealed, either now or in the future."

"Not now; I'll explain it to her later," Travis said.

"You are the husband; you have authority over your wife. She must listen or suffer the consequence."

"What consequence?"

"She would be publicly shamed before our relatives and the village."

"I can't do that to her."

"You mean that you will not do it. You are afraid to war with words, even though you have the final say. A battle not fought, cannot be won."

Travis' jaw dropped slightly. His father-in-law's insight touched on his fear of confrontation with Karasa. It would have been their first serious verbal barrage. He chose not to respond to it.

"If I don't return, please use your authority to prevent her from following me."

"My daughter is strong willed. She may choose not to respect my counsel and to suffer a punishment afterwards," Bahrundi continued. "You must be shrewd. The lion makes the kill, but often the hyenas take it away."

"I don't understand."

"Do not trust these people of the Press. Be alert and act quickly when the time is right."

"If you don't get a message from me after thirty days,

I'm dead. My last request is that you all are to go to America. My friend, George Mitchell, is a lawyer, and he can arrange your trip. I'll contact him before I leave."

"I do not know, my son; this land is all that my wife and I have ever known. We would not be happy in such a strange country."

"There's a settlement of Dinka refugees in southern California. My friend can help you relocate," Travis explained.

"I will meditate on it. When are you leaving?"

"Now."

"Come, receive my blessing," He motioned to Travis.

Bahrundi placed his hand on top of Travis' bowed head and spoke with authority.

"Father God, your loving kindness is greater than life. Your ways are higher than our ways, and we seek to walk in your will. We ask you to blind the eyes of the enemy and cause confusion to stop their wicked plans. Protect Travis and Twangi. We believe your mighty arm will carry them both back home again because we serve a mighty God. Praise the name of Jesus."

"Amen," Travis whispered.

"Go with God."

Travis took one last look at this beloved, wise man as if memorizing his features.

After retrieving his gear, Travis hurried down the path.

He turned his head toward home for one more glance. His eyes widened when he caught sight of Karasa holding Tamara.

"*Mimi panda ku.* I'll be back in thirty days," Travis yelled as he waved a final goodbye.

This may be the last time I'll ever see her, but she must not suspect it.

"*Kwaheri,* my love, good-bye," Karasa called.

When Travis approached the Land Rover, he threw his duffle bag and gear into the back seat and slid into the passenger seat beside Kookie. He couldn't look back.

"Thanks for waiting," he said.

"Ready?" Kookie asked.

"Yes, I'll need a ride to Lapaki to talk with my boss before we go to Nairobi."

"Okay, let's hit the frog."

"Let's what?" Travis asked.

"Frog and toad. Toad rhymes with road. It means 'let's get on down the road'."

"Every issue, belief, attitude or assumption is precisely
the issue that stands between you and your relationship
to another human being; and
between you and yourself."

~ Anonymous

CHAPTER THREE

Khartoum, Sudan

The Minister of Defense, Dr. Mansoor Huzang, leaned over his oak desk in his office, examining several legal documents. Referencing the *Qur'an,* Koran, as his standard, he contemplated a pending course of action. As he reached for his pen to jot down some notes, the phone rang.

"Yes, of course, send him in," said Dr. Huzang upon answering it. After hanging up the receiver, he concealed the documents and rose in anticipation of his visitor.

The commander of the president's personal guard, dressed in a dark green beret and matching military attire, entered the office. The insignia of his rank on his shoulder boards glistened of gold. He wore his personal weapon holstered at his side. Stepping to Huzang's left; he knuckled his forehead in salute, and announced, "The President of Sudan."

The guard dropped his salute and Dr. Huzang bowed to President Omar al-Bashir. In spite of the summer's heat, the president dressed in a deluxe Arabian, an unbuttoned knee length suit-style jacket, worn over a traditional ivory *dishadasha* robe. His white *turban,* studded with a diamond wing, lent the entire ensemble an elegant, formal appearance.

"*al Salamu Alaykum,* peace be with you, Mr. President. I am honored by your presence. How can I be of assistance?" Huzang touched his head and heart and bowed again.

The president turned to his officer and commanded. "You are dismissed. Wait outside and guard this door."

"Yes, sir."

When the officer left, the president's countenance changed. He reached over, pulled Dr. Huzang toward him, kissed him on each cheek and said, "My good friend. We need to talk."

Dr. Huzang bent to receive the greeting because he stood slightly over an inch taller. He wore a tan *turban* and a matching *kurta* with embroidered collar, and a short sleeve shirt over traditional elastic waist cotton pants. His tan face showed a full set of smiling teeth which appeared less prominent than his hooked nose. A brown goatee covered his distinctive narrow chin.

"Come, please sit down," Huzang pointed to a comfortable arm chair beside his desk.

"Your political council has served me well these past eight years," the president reminisced.

Dr. Huzang had planned and master-minded Colonel Omar al-Bashir's 1989 bloodless military coup. Considered the military government's *eminence grise,* the person who secretly wields great power and influence, Huzang prioritized political Islam and the imposition of *Sharia Law.* First it became legally binding on their fellow Moslems, *Muslims.* Now it ruled all the people of Sudan.

"Politics is my passion. It is always good to recall our roots," Huzang said.

"Yes. Speaking of the past, Osama bin Laden is due to return to Sudan next month to inspect our training camps for the Islamic Fundamentalist Front." The president paused, "Osama bin Laden sends his greetings to you as well."

"I look forward to meeting the leader of al-Qaida again."

The president smiled. Their friendship dated back to 1991 when Dr. Huzang co-founded the Popular Arab and

Islamic Congress and invited bin Laden to Sudan. President al-Bashir, who shared the same radical religious views, could not refuse Osama bin Laden's request to set up training camps for Islam's holy wars. The project commenced immediately to train elite *jihadist* troops, and still operated clandestinely.

"Our military camps have produced holy martyrs to advance the Islamic Movement internationally," the President said. "Most importantly, they've elevated our nation's stature in the Arab world." The President's head nodded slightly with self-approval.

"Yes, those were five good years for the Muslim Brotherhood," the Minister of Defense agreed.

"Now, we need to discuss an ongoing concern of mine, the incompetence of Major General Ahmed."

"Of, course," the Minister replied in an appeasing tone.

"I don't need to remind you that Major General Ahmed embarrassed my regime by allowing an American agent to cause havoc with our helicopter base and to inflict casualties among our troops. I wanted him purged three years ago!" the President stated, still obsessed with this affair.

"My advice remains the same. Major General Ahmed has married into an influential, patriarchal family with both religious and political ties. We must proceed with caution."

"Justice must happen before Osama bin Laden arrives!" President al-Bashir stated emphatically. He leaned forward and his fist pounded the desk with one swift blow.

"*Ma'aleesh*, put your mind at rest, the wheels of my plan turn as we speak. There may be a way for the Major General to exonerate himself. If all goes well, an important event will manifest itself within four weeks time. You will be pleasantly surprised."

"Good. It will be worth the wait. Now, we must discuss another important matter. It has also come to my attention that you disapproved of the Council's action to place Eli Mete under arrest."

"Yes. I've reviewed his articles in the Sudan News and View where he stated that in the 1996 election, by law, you were the only candidate allowed to run for the presidency. I didn't find his writing to be defamatory. Nor do I believe his imprisonment and torture is in Sudan's best interest."

"He's not yet signed the confession necessary to execute him."

"International pressure on Sudan from both the Arabic Nations and the West are calling for the release of Mr. Eli Mete."

Before President al-Bashir's rise to power, Khartoum published twenty-two daily newspapers and two monthly magazines, expressing a variety of political views. After his military coup, the president ordered his newly formed Council for National Salvation to purge more than one thousand journalists and disband the majority of these publications. Fifteen journalists, including the editors of <u>Sudan Vision</u> and <u>Sudan News and Review</u>, were sent to prison.

"When do we listen to the masses, and why should the internationals be concerned with Mr. Eli Mete?"

"As managing editor of Sudan's only English-language monthly magazine, his publication had a wide international circulation, and he's become increasingly popular."

"What would you propose?"

"I have arranged for Judge Zadat to expedite his trial. He'll appear before the court next Monday, and I'll provide legal council for his defense."

"Your power of persuasion and popularity with the religious courts are unmatched. Surely Mr. Eli Mete will be exonerated?"

"Yes, and I've already arranged for a journalist position for him in our newest venture, the Sudan government website. There his upcoming articles will be edited by official censors before being published. With your permission, I will proceed as planned."

The President's jaw dropped in disbelief that the pending actions might have commenced without consulting him first. His eyebrows knotted in disapproval but he said, "Proceed with the arrangements, but caution Eli Mete that we will be following his new career closely."

The President stood and bowed. Dr. Huzang did likewise and accompanied the President as he exited the office.

"There is no such thing as public

opinion.

There is only published opinion."

~ Winston Churchill

CHAPTER FOUR

Seattle, Washington
Summer, 1997

John Cafferty, Chief Editor of The Daily Times, worked with concentration at his computer in his prestigious third floor office at the Times Building. Even at his age, fifty-four, he retained a healthy full head of wavy brown hair which received weekly professional pampering. Mr. Cafferty repositioned his reading glasses on his prominent nose. His angular face focused on his monitor as his blue eyes scanned his work for spelling and grammatical errors. Satisfied, he clicked the print button and closed out the program. As he waited for his report, he glanced out through the glass wall to western skies where the Space

Needle, Seattle's highest structure, glistened as the sunlight bounced off its metal exterior.

Cafferty silenced the buzzing of his intercom by depressing the lit red button.

"Mr. Cafferty, there's a call for you on line one. It's Mr. Haile."

"Thank you, Ms. Wycoff, I'll take it now."

"Yes, Mr. Cafferty," she responded into the receiver.

Cafferty picked up the line.

"I'm glad you're back from San Francisco. What happened at the Newspaper Association of America Conference?" Haile asked.

"Well, Professor Seymour Toplin of Columbia University, the guest speaker, commemorated the 150th Anniversary of Joseph Pulitzer's birth."

The Pulitzer Prize honored excellence in journalism in twelve categories. Awarded every April, it is esteemed not as much for its monetary value as for its prestige.

"The Professor recounted the 1977 presentation of the Pulitzer Prizes. He recognized our Daily Times Investigative Reporting winner Eric Tyson and cited Marco Allende as a finalist in International Reporting. I'm sending you a full report with my comments."

"Good, I'm delighted our reporters got the recognition they deserve. But now I need you to clear your calendar." Mr. Haile paused on the other end of the line. "As you know, I'm involved with the World Press Freedom Committee. We serve as a 'watchdog' on issues of press freedom in the Third World. This year, we're focused on fighting censorship."

"I've read an editorial written by our competitor that the third world countries are clamoring to set up Internet news sites but lack technical expertise," Cafferty commented.

"That's correct. The United States is the world's leader in Internet sites, so we've received a special invitation from the Sudan News Agency, inviting our paper to cover the unveiling of their first web page, suna dot net, next Thursday. We'll provide some onsite technical support for maintaining their electronic news media if needed."

"I believe the latest online information services, especially those capable of providing streaming videos and audio to the consumer, are the wave of the future," Cafferty stated.

"Yes, that's why we're supporting Sudan's endeavors," Mr. Haile agreed.

"I have a current passport, but I thought the U.S. didn't have any formal relations with Sudan," Cafferty said.

"That's true, but I've already cleared it through legal. You'll leave this Friday for Nairobi, Kenya. You'll need to meet with Kenya's U.S. Ambassador for a visa to Sudan. Sudan has closed the U.S. embassy. On Monday you'll meet with Mr. el Aduda, the editor of <u>The Standard</u>. We assisted this Kenyan newspaper in developing their web-page, www newspaperboy dot com."

"I'd like for Marco Allende, my reporter on international affairs, to attend the ceremony," Cafferty said. "He has his passport and papers. He can write a professional news article regarding this event."

"Excellent idea," Haile said. "Both of you must arrive in Sudan by next Thursday, at the SUNA's office in the government building by 2:00 P.M."

"We'll be there."

"John, you're on the official guest list to attend the formal dinner at the President's Palace at 7:00 P.M. that evening," Haile said.

"Why are you sending me?"

"I need you to attend to a matter of utmost importance."

"Yes, what is it?" John Cafferty asked.

"It's in regard to my friend Mr. Eli Mete, the editor of the <u>Sudan News and Review</u>. He published the only monthly magazine written in both Arabic and English. I have it on good authority that the printing presses have been shut down. He's in Kobar."

"The prison for political dissidents?"

"Yes," Mr. Haile said. "The Minister of Defense, Dr. Mansoor Huzang, will be at the President's ceremonial dinner. He'll have an update on this situation."

"Of course, I'll talk to him."

"Please proceed with caution."

"Yes, Mr. Haile, I'll be discreet."

After replacing the receiver, Cafferty called Ms. Wycoff to reschedule his upcoming appointments and to book his airline tickets. Marco Allende, his international news reporter, answered the phone on the first ring. Cafferty omitted the formalities and informed Marco that he would be traveling to Sudan with him.

"My secretary will book your flight. Call my cell phone when your plane lands at the Khartoum Airport. A taxi will be waiting to drive you to the ceremony," Cafferty informed Marco.

After finalizing details, Cafferty hung up the phone and beamed from ear to ear.

I didn't really believe in fate until now. It's an unbelievable coincidence that Haile requested I cover the actual assignment that I intended to persuade him I should spearhead. Feature stories are usually not handled by editors. That up and coming reporter, Marco, may prove to be downright useful. This is kismet and it enhances my next career move.

In spite of the early hour, Cafferty didn't refrain from retrieving a bottle of expensive scotch from the wall safe behind his mahogany desk.

Reclining in his comfortable maroon leather chair, he

held a liquor glass in his hand and raised it into the air.

"This calls for a toast," he declared to no one in particular.

"Core values go beyond our behaviors and our wants.

Without being intentional about our values, we live back-

wards.

We often let our behaviors define our

values. Values should define our

behaviors."

~ John G. Blumberg

CHAPTER FIVE

Marco Allende stood six foot one with olive complexion, penetrating brown eyes and wavy dark brown hair. Handsome in appearance, he walked with the assurance of a determined young man who commanded authority. Ranking in the top ten of his graduating class, Marco had earned a master's degree in journalism from Columbia University in 1990. Currently employed by the Daily Times as a foreign journalist, his fluency in several languages had proved especially beneficial.

When on assignment in the Middle East or northern Africa, prominent dignitaries and local peasants often mistook him for a fellow *Muslim*. Although Marco publicly praised all religions, he privately despised them all. In reality, he professed no religion and prided himself in being a self-made man.

Marco's charisma and charm caused people to open up to him. His informative accounts of current events packed with interesting tidbits were featured in the <u>Nairobi Standard</u> and several international newspapers. His article, 'Trends in International Trade', earned him recognition as one of the three finalists in this years 1997 Pulitzer Prize for Literacy.

He realized, however, his achievements alone wouldn't merit him success, at least not the success he craved. He must position himself to rise to the top and to gain this status. Political patronage within the organization required that he become indispensable to those who influenced and determined public policy. It wasn't a matter of allowing someone to use you, but benefiting from the skills of each other.

The bottom line is that everyone looks out for himself, Marco thought as he retrieved his bags and walked out the parting glass doors of the Khartoum International Airport.

Khartoum, the capital of Sudan, is situated at the confluence of the White Nile and the Blue Nile. Founded in

1821 as an outpost for the Egyptian Army and as a regional trade center, it expanded into a thriving metropolis that over 70,000 people called home.

As Marco stepped out of the terminal and into the stifling heat, a man in a red cap held a white sign with his name written on it. Marco waved and briskly walked in the direction of the cab driver.

"I'm Allende. Take me to the Hilton Khartoum."

The driver nodded. He loaded Marco's luggage and drove into the oncoming traffic on Airport Boulevard.

When they arrived at the hotel, Marco directed the cab driver to wait while the bellman secured his luggage in a small room behind the hotel's granite counter.

Marco gave the taxi driver the address of the Sudan News Agency located in the government building in the downtown district.

After paying the fare, Marco glanced at his Rolex. The timepiece displayed 1:57 P.M. Second to his appearance, Marco considered punctuality a professional asset. Carrying a black leather case with implements of his trade – a Caran d'Ache gold pen, notepad and small tape recorder, he entered the building.

"Marco Allende. Right on time," Mr. John Cafferty shook Marco's hand. "Follow me."

They walked through the hallway and into an adjoining room. "The editor-in-chief has invited us on a tour of the facility before the presentation begins." Mr. Cafferty pointed to the left, turned, and proceeded to walk through the crowd, greeting several acquaintances on the way.

The purported ceremony, the unveiling of the new website - *suna.net*, lasted over an hour. At the conclusion, Mr. Cafferty thanked his host and offered the support of the Daily Times if the SUNA News Agency needed any future assistance in application or electronics implementations.

When they left, the men took a taxi to the Hilton Khartoum, located near the junction of the Blue Nile and White Nile.

"We're going back to the hotel. In my room, you'll have access to a computer with internet connection, an international telephone line, and a FAX machine. Write an informative article regarding this event."

"Yes, sir," Marco assured him. He intended to include its significance and impact on the modern world.

Cafferty is on his way to the top of the organization, and so are the men who are associated with him. I will make myself useful to him and leapfrog over all of those dumb workaholics who think they will reach the top by laboring long hours and keeping their noses to the grindstone. The secret is to work smarter, not harder, Marco thought.

When they arrived at the hotel, they passed the reception desk. It surprised him that no one stopped them and asked for their identification. Mr. Cafferty pressed the button for the fourth floor. After entering room 403, the men took off their jackets. Marco turned on the computer, referred to his notes and began pounding on the keyboard.

"I usually don't extend compliments, but this is a good piece of journalism," said Cafferty, after reading the results of Marco's writing.

"Thank you, Mr. Cafferty," Marco pasted an ingratiating smile on his face. He walked to the FAX machine to submit the story.

"Come with me," Cafferty called back, looking over his shoulder as he walked toward a writing desk in his large hotel suite. He sat down in a leather chair behind a desk of polished teak.

"Sit down," Cafferty pointed to the two chairs in front of his desk. He glanced curiously at Marco, who continued to wear a mask of inscrutability.

Marco complied and sat with his back rigid, his entire attention focused on Cafferty.

"I understand from my contacts that you may be a man I can depend upon," Cafferty stated.

Marco had done his research and decided to become indispensable to Mr. Cafferty. He made his choice and wouldn't even consider the possibility of switching horses. With determination, he'd work with diligence to earn the master's trust.

"Yes sir, I always deliver results to my superior,"

Marco replied.

With that response he conveyed both that he could get the job done, but that his loyalty belonged to his boss and not to the organization.

Perhaps we understand each other. Marco noticed a slight upward turn of the right corner of Cafferty's mouth.

"How far can you be trusted?" Cafferty questioned.

"My pen can easily extol the virtues of the worst liar or be converted into a lethal, sharp-edged tool. Who do you want to elevate or downsize? Maybe there is someone's closeted skeleton to expose?" Marco smiled sardonically.

"Your humor is in poor taste," Cafferty replied.

"Sorry, it won't happen again," Marco answered.

"Good, what I'm about to tell you cannot leave this room. There are people involved and events afoot of such magnitude, that the people involved would see stepping on a little piss ant like you a much smaller matter than worrying about whether you can be trusted. Do I make myself clear?"

"Yes sir, I understand," Marco nodded. He understood perfectly. Nothing of magnitude happens in this world by chance. Mysterious, powerful men changed the course of events or dealt with problems by defaming well known people. Words, wielded by the media, cut like a sharp knife to surgically remove officials from influential positions or to falsely shred the reputations of prominent people. Cafferty associated with influential people, some of whom were right here in Africa.

Is Cafferty a special envoy for the U.S. and involved in unofficial negotiations for a peace plan to stop the current civil war in Sudan? Or is he collaborating with a secret organization of Islamic terrorists? Marco wondered.

"But, first things first," Cafferty handed Marco a room key for room 307. He continued, "Get a shower and dinner. I recommend the Assaha Restaurant. Its international cuisine features exotic dishes and the waiters speak English. I suggest you try their appetizer, *'hubble bubble'.* I can't go with you. I've been invited to the Presidential Palace for dinner tonight."

"Yes, of course," Marco replied.

"Most importantly, I want you to catch the evening flight to Nairobi and pick up a package from this contact." Cafferty took out a piece of paper from the desk and placed it in front of him.

"Tomorrow, board the early morning flight back from Nairobi and bring the package here without opening or tampering with it," Cafferty continued.

This is a test of loyalty, Marco reasoned. "You can depend on me." He picked up the paper and put on his suit jacket.

Cafferty nodded. The look on Cafferty's face told Marco that he had been dismissed.

"Ambition is the immoderate desire

for power."

~ Baruch Spinoza

CHAPTER SIX

Khartoum, Sudan

John Cafferty, editor of the <u>Daily Times</u>, dressed in a pin-striped tuxedo for the ceremonial dinner at the Presidential Palace. The descending sun cast long shadows as he hailed a taxi.

The taxi moved along with the snail-paced traffic on *Shari'a Al-Nil*. Unlike the monotony of stone structures in the commercial district, Nile Street proved to be the most picturesque street in Khartoum. The flowing Blue Nile lapped the sandy riverbank as vessels propelled by egg-shaped sails traveled its waterways. Several people sat on top of the concrete wall, watching the activity below. On the opposite side, a walkway lined with trees and flowering shrubs nestled near former British colonial structures. Once the residences of the wealthy, they now served as private schools, chic boutiques and office buildings.

But John Cafferty registered none of this. He only took notice when the cab drove by the impressive old Palace Cathedral, located adjacent to his destination. Once an Anglican Church but now a Museum, it faced the Nile. It displayed many relics and pieces related to Sudan's administrative and modern political history, from paintings of Sir Gordon Pasha to the former presidential cars.

The taxi paused near an ornate, black iron gate. An official palace guard demanded identification. He waved the vehicle through after Mr. Cafferty showed his personal invitation. Pedestrians were not as fortunate. Another uniformed guard stopped them from walking in front of the property and redirected them.

The driver joined the procession of cars pausing briefly along the circular driveway to allow their passengers to exit. They proceeded toward the majestic, three-tiered, nineteenth century presidential palace. Reminiscent of a bygone era, the impressive white colonial residence, flanked by two wings, reflected the rays of the setting sun.

Cafferty joined other guests along the massive walkway, bordered by lush green lawns, palm trees and a variety of tropical shrubs. This procession of elegantly attired individuals approached the stairway to the main building. On either side were two sweeping staircases that led to the right and left wings of equal dimensions which extended north and south. At the top of each staircase rising to the mezzanine above the ground floor, stiff-lipped palace guards stood with weapons positioned in readiness.

As the guests proceeded and ascended the main stairway, several people stopped at the top step to read the Plaque. It commemorated General Charles Gordon's defense of Khartoum against the Sudanese Mahdists' onslaught in 1885. Disobeying orders and fighting for his principles, General Gordon died, speared through his side and beheaded. This unfortunate incident occurred two days before the British relief column broke through.

Cafferty accompanied the others and passed under the main arch, supported by stately columns. Two soldiers dressed in the official black and gold uniforms and white *turbans* with black plumes stood sentry at the double mahogany door. Upon their entering, a receptionist greeted them. In the enormous hallway, everyone passed under two giant elephant tusks protruding from above the arched partitions, and proceeded between two polished iron-wheeled machine-guns that had last seen service in 1898.

They strolled past a collection of tribal spears, shields, rifles and swords decorating one of the side walls. Turning right they entered the main saloon, a reception room where containers of burning bakhour wood chips emitted a blend of exotic spices that caressed the nasal passages.

President Omar Hassan Ahmad al-Bashir reclined on a

carved gold leather chair. Behind him, a six-foot gold leaf backdrop engraved with Islamic texts accentuated the presidential seat.

When Omar al-Bashir stood to greet his guests, his bodyguards and prominent officials in his administration joined him. Dressed in regal satin, a white *turban,* and matching gold trimmed *salwar kameez* Arabic suit, he bowed. With a guileless expression, he welcomed each guest.

Once they stepped into the adjoining room, everyone roamed freely. The chatter of voices could be heard above soft music. Tables decorated with fragrant fresh cut flowers and covered in fine linen were lavished with platters of hors d'oeuvres on ornate Melanine serving plates and an assortment of fine dining entrées.

On another table stood two huge chafes filled with coffee and a decanter of hot water for an assortment of exotic teas. Waiters also circulated, offering trays with goblets of mango juice.

As Cafferty, china platter in hand, contemplated which appetizers to choose, he heard his name and turned.

"Mr. John Cafferty, it is a pleasure to make your acquaintance. I am Dr. Mansoor Huzang."

Cafferty detected a slight British accent. Having done his research, he remembered that Dr. Huzang received an M.A. in Law from the University of London, England. He earned his Ph.D. in Law from the Sorbonne in Paris.

"Minister of Defense?" Cafferty asked.

"Yes, we hope you are enjoying your stay in Khartoum." With a wave of his hand he added, "The Jewel of Africa."

"Our mutual friend, Mr. Haile, sends his greetings," Cafferty said.

"Please, follow me." Dr. Huzang weaved among the guests, acknowledging many of them as he strode toward the double glass doors that opened onto the balcony. He stopped behind a potted plant in a nearby alcove.

"We can talk here. Please tell our mutual friend that final arrangements await his approval."

Mr. Cafferty, in a slight of hand motion, concealed a business card in his right hand and said, "Let's shake on that."

Cafferty discreetly transferred the card, which Dr. Huzang's promptly pocketed. On the card, a series of numbers depicted the secret account number of a Swiss bank account.

Apparently, these bribes go on all the time. This Minister of Defense seems quite at ease with this arrangement, Cafferty thought.

"Tomorrow, Abu will visit the prison and discuss our arrangement with the newspaper editor, Eli Mete. He'll also speak with the guard. Next Monday Abu will compensate the head warden as Eli Mete is being released into my custody. We're scheduled to appear before Judge Zadat on Tuesday."

"A trial?"

"Yes, but it's only a formality. Eli Mete won't be executed. He'll be exonerated but will have to pay a heavy fine. I expect everything to proceed as planned."

"I'll get to meet him?"

"Yes. He's been assigned to work with us on our special news story regarding the American terrorist."

Upon hearing the resounding dong of a bell, Dr. Huzang informed Cafferty, "We must go now. Dinner is about to be served in the Conference Hall. I've made arrangements for us to sit with Major General Ahmed, so that you can make his acquaintance."

Both men joined the other guests and entered the dining room where the ceremonies were about to resume. The affair proved interesting and entertaining. During dinner an electrical piano entertained them with soft classical music. The guests murmured favorably on the delectable gourmet cuisine.When the gala concluded Cafferty returned to his hotel. Upon arrival at his room, he e-mailed Mr. Haile regarding the portentous event. Due to the time change, he also sent a FAX to Mr. Haile's secretary because she'd still be working at her desk.

"The media's the most powerful entity on earth. They

have the power to make the innocent guilty and to make

the guilty innocent, and that's power."

~ Malcolm X

CHAPTER SEVEN

After leaving the Hilton Khartoum, Marco hailed a yellow taxi, tipping the driver in advance. The vehicle ventured in and out of traffic, making a mad dash to the Khartoum Airport. After obtaining a ticket to Nairobi, he dashed onto the plane as the door shut behind him. When he arrived at his destination, the customs process proceeded quickly because he carried no luggage. Next he took a cab to the Hilton. He obtained information he needed at the lobby desk and rode the elevator to the fifth floor.

"Well, handsome, what can I do for you?" Ms. Desmonica Houston asked after opening the door.

"My name is Marco Allende. I'm here to retrieve a package for Mr. Cafferty."

"Why wasn't I informed?" She questioned.

"I don't know," Marco answered, wiping the smile off his face.

"Why didn't he come himself?" Ms Houston demanded in a condescending voice.

"He had another engagement and sent me to pick it up."

"You look harried; stay a while for a drink. I know I need one," Desmonica said in a patronizing voice.

"No, thank you. I must deliver the package as soon as possible," he lied.

With reluctance displayed on her face, Ms. Houston hesitated before handing it over.

"Good-bye, Ms. Houston," Marco smiled and left the way he'd come.

Bewitching and attractive, she must be Cafferty's mistress. But she's definitely not my type, too sure of herself with no brains to back it up. You need both to succeed.

Marco preferred not to spend the night in Nairobi, so he decided to chance a return flight. After hailing the driver, he slid into the back seat of the taxi.

"Airport," Marco said.

At the registration desk, Marco booked a returning flight scheduled to leave in forty minutes. He upgraded his seat to first class. This calculated move insinuated that Marco regarded himself a first tier employee. He surmised that Cafferty wouldn't balk at the additional expense.

In Khartoum, the customs' line advanced at a snail's

pace. Marco didn't want to appear apprehensive while carrying the brown paper wrapped box with unknown and possibly illegal contents. Customs agents are trained to study people's faces. To distract his own attention and avoid any worry in his facial expression, he focused his thoughts on the difficulty of keeping his suit properly pressed and not sodden with perspiration in this stiflingly hot city. When he reached security, he projected an attitude of self-importance and experienced no problems with the custom agents. He hailed a taxi and proceeded back to the Hilton Khartoum.

What a grueling experience! It's only 10:30 P.M. This must be some kind of record, Marco thought as he entered the coffee bar in the foyer of the hotel. He sipped his coffee and ate half of a sandwich. Marco noticed that even at this late hour, this place seemed to be a favorite hangout of the local business class. When he finished, he phoned Mr. Cafferty from the lobby.

Cafferty answered on the third ring.

"This is Marco. I've just returned from Nairobi. I made the evening flight, and I'm back with the package."

"Bring it up," Cafferty said. The phone went dead.

When Marco knocked on door number 403, Cafferty answered.

"Come in, Marco, and put the package down on the coffee table," Cafferty announced in an expansive mood as he waved his hand toward the room.

Cafferty looks disheveled. He's drunk. Obviously he wasn't expecting me or any other visitor this evening, Marco thought.

"Did you enjoy the affair at the Presidential Palace?" Marco asked.

"The lavished affair featured prominent dignitaries and gourmet food. I even made several acquaintances. But disappointingly, the host served no alcoholic beverages." Cafferty paused and offered, "How about a drink, my boy?"

Marco raised an eyebrow in surprise. Sudan abided by the Islamic code and prohibited the selling of alcohol.

"I'll take a glass of bourbon," Marco relented. Just this one drink would suffice. He had no intention of becoming intoxicated.

"Well, sit down, while I educate you on a few things." Cafferty patted the top of a comfortable leather armed chair.

Cafferty poured whiskey in a glass and took a quick gulp. He placed the glass down with such force that its remaining contents splashed onto the counter.

"We are the power. Don't be fooled, the Media wields a mighty force. The most powerful man in the world is not the president or a king, but whoever rules our world of information."

Cafferty stood on unsteady feet and he approached

Marco.

"We don't just make the news, we make public opinion. We tell the gullible public what they should think. Did
you ever think about that?"

"Of course, sir." Marco raised his glass in affirmative
and took a sip.

"Of course, sir? You don't know the half of the truth.
Did you ever wonder why you never hear the term jungle
anymore? That's because now it's the bloody 'rainforest'.
How about swamps? Ever hear about those? No, because
now they're called 'wetlands'."

"But what good is that to us?" Marco asked.

"We've gotten 'Environmentalism' raised to the level
of a religion, a new system of beliefs," Cafferty laughed.

"When we kicked Christianity out of our public
schools, we had to replace it with something, didn't we?"

"How did we do that, kick Christianity out of the school
system?" Marco didn't follow this train of thought.

"Easy, we convinced the majority of the public that the
term 'Separation of Church and State' is in the Constitu-
tion, when it's not even there," Cafferty said.

"So now the masses need something to worship – some
higher power – so we give them Environmentalism. They
need some cause to crusade for – so we give them animal
rights and endangered species and their habitats. Did you
notice the featured article on the front page of the American

Edition of the <u>Times</u> on Tuesday?"

"No," Marco replied.

"Why not? We ran an exclusive story about saving those two worthless whales trapped in ice off the Alaskan coast. It only cost the taxpayers a few hundred thousand dollars apiece to rescue them. But a small article about thousands of human beings dying of starvation and disease along a road in Rwanda lay buried on page five. Did the public notice?"

Marco shrugged his shoulders and pretended to take another sip of his bourdon.

"No, and no one took issue or seemed concerned," Cafferty answered his own question.

"We have them believing that animals are more important then people – we did that."

Cafferty paused for another sip from his glass and saluted Marco with it before putting it down again. His face appeared noticeably flushed.

"Young man, have you ever heard of secular humanism?"

"Yes, but what has that got to do with it?"

"If you read the *Humanist Manifesto,* it states that one of the most basic tenets of secular humanism is that there are no moral or cultural absolutes. Think about it, how would we be able to convince an unsuspecting public of anything that we wanted them to believe if we kept bumping up against a crock of absolute values?"

Marco shrugged. He wanted Cafferty to keep going. With Cafferty's guard down perhaps he would reveal something Marco could use to his own advantage.

"I'll tell you – we couldn't. We embraced humanism because we had to, which put us on a collision course with religion, which is why we are slowly destroying it. Think about it, young man. Humanism conflicts with Judeo-Christian beliefs. They have the Ten Commandments – not the ten suggestions. We've gotten so-called courses in 'values clarification' right into their schools, right under their noses."

Cafferty swayed as he topped off his half-empty glass. Steadying himself, he continued.

"Did you know that if you repeat the same lie over and over the great unwashed masses will believe it? Even if it's contradicted by fact, they'll accept the lie.

"What if someone accused you of being judgmental?"

"I would tell them that I wasn't."

"Of course you are. If you hired a baby sitter would you screen the person to be certain you weren't entrusting your little darling to a convicted child molester?"

"Yes, I would."

"You evil, judgmental bastard," Cafferty sounded livid.

"Judgment is nothing but discernment, but we couldn't have the public applying absolute standards of right and wrong because that would have gotten in our way. So we made 'judgmental' into a bad word and now even so-called Christians apologize when they're accused of being 'judgmental'." Cafferty pronounced the word with a sneer.

He yawned and continued, "I don't believe in any God, but if I did I would tell you that the Ten Commandments states it's wrong to lie, cheat or sleep with your best friend's wife. If you accused me of being judgmental at least I would have the guts to look you in the eye and thank you for the compliment.

"Tell me young man, is profiling good or bad?"

"It's wrong," Marco said.

"Suppose you lived in a neighborhood where there were about a dozen teenage boys. Most were good kids who went to school and got good grades. But you know for a fact that the two brothers across the street have broken into and burglarized five houses in the neighborhood. Would you pay more attention if you saw those two hanging out near your house than if you saw two of the kids who are in a church group?"

"Of course I would."

"You evil, flaming hypocrite," Cafferty continued his ranting and raving. "You just profiled those two hoodlums. And just suppose you knew a shopkeeper in town who you caught short-changing you twice in the past. Would you be more likely to count your change in his store than in another?"

"Of course."

"You evil, hateful, religious right wing crackpot, narrow minded, mean spirited, bigot. You just profiled that shopkeeper."

"I see what you mean."

Cafferty refilled his glass and swallowed the contents in one gulp. He began to sway. He steadied himself by leaning on the arm of the chair and eased awkwardly into his seat.

"Profiling is good – it's nothing but common sense. People unconsciously do it every day in their own personal lives. But we've brainwashed them to believe that it's wrong on a higher governmental level. But when some terrorist attacks happen in the country, the statistical probability is over ninety-nine percent that it will be done by members of a certain extremist religious group. Airport security screeners are charged with profiling if they pay more attention to members of that group and don't strip search as many little old grandmothers."

"What about countries like Sudan where an authoritarian government controls the press?" Marco changed the subject.

"They only control their own irrelevant press. But we control who stays on top, and they kowtow to us, too."

Intrigued, Marco couldn't resist finding out more while Cafferty was both drunk and talkative. "How do they kowtow to us?"

"Sometimes they'll give us the stories that we want, even before they happen. If they feed me the story that builds my career, I'll make sure that they come out in it smelling like a rose."

Cafferty leaned back on the cushions. He yawned again, slurring some of the words.

"We specialize in feeding the public a steady diet of sensationalism. They love it, like the Circus mentality in the Roman Coliseum. Our articles feature the making and undoing of famous celebrities. We make it easy for our readers; they don't have to worry about real issues, like the steady intrusion of the government on individual liberties."

Cafferty emitted a loud yawn as his drooping eyelids fought a losing battle.

"The Media has an a..gen…da..aa, ya knooooow."

A shroud of sleep stealthily covered him.

"An agenda?"

But Cafferty, his neck bent at an awkward angle, had begun to snore. Where he lay on the couch, the smell of liquor lingered.

Cafferty is pompous, but he's no fool. He understands power, and how to use it. I can learn a lot from this man if I just manage my own usefulness correctly. I just hope his drinking is not going to be a problem.

After a quick glance back at Cafferty, Marco walked in

silence to the door.

Wonder if he'll wake up with a stiff neck, Marco thought as he left.

"Never be afraid to trust an unknown

future to a known God."

~ Corrie Ten Boom

CHAPTER EIGHT

Ensebbe Refuge Camp, Kenya

The Second Civil War had raged in Sudan for over fourteen years now. The *Janjaweed* had always raided the farmers south of the Sahara Desert with impunity, stealing cattle and people as needed. But the discovery of oil in Southern Sudan prompted the Khartoum's *Muslim* government to finance the *Janjaweed* bandits who devastated Christian villages in the South. Total destruction occurred when these assaults were accompanied by Sudanese Air Force bombing missions. Those who survived became destitute and homeless. They fled from places the United Nations identified as 'red no-go' areas and crossed the border into Kenya. While over two million people died in Southern Sudan, the western press had little to say regarding these atrocities, until the *Janjaweed* turned their weapons on Darfur and began to slaughter fellow *Muslims.*

To provide a safe place for the displaced people, Jim and Ellen Anderson, African American Missionaries, founded the Ensebbe Refuge Camp in Kenya. The camp received no government funds and depended upon charitable donations. The Andersons affiliated with an international evangelic relief agency to dispense medicine, mosquito nets, and food when available. Initially, the camp housed the Sudanese in thirty tents. As more innocent victims arrived, they constructed crude shelters of wood, plastic, tin and cardboard or whatever materials could be found. All the residents, particularly the numerous orphans, suffered not only from the elements but from the lack of basic necessities. Patasites in contaminated drinking water caused anemia, diseases and even death to the children.

Currently, the women collected water from a muddy stream about two hours walk away. When they returned to the camp, the women carried the water to stations equipped with BioSand filters. This water purification system used sand and gravel to filter polluted water. It decreased the incidence of cholera and diphtheria, major causes of deaths.

Lately sporadic laughter and increased activity filled the camp in anticipation of the new well to be drilled about twenty minutes walk from the main camp, near the Ensebbe Church. The deep aquifer system would provide adequate water, eliminating the dangerous daily trudge to the stream.

"It's a perfect place. The well will pump clean water, necessary for life, and the church will quench the spiritual thirst of the people," Pastor Rocco said.

Rocco Giovanni and his wife, Michelle, had taken a short leave of absence from their evangelistic ministry to help the Andersons to complete this vital project.

The sun, less than midway from the horizon to its overhead appointment with noon, glared with stifling heat as a tall slender blonde with a pony tail, carried a large gourd filled with water. Dressed in a straw hat, tie-dyed shirt, beige cargo shorts and leather sandals, Michelle approached the men working near the well.

"Rocco, I brought you some water to drink," Michelle called as she quickened her pace.

Rocco wiped the sweat from his brow as he looked up.

"What's this? Doesn't your lovin' husband deserve a glass of good Italian wine?" Rocco, built broad and solid with a Mediterranean complexion and brown hair, stood about an inch shorter than his wife. He wore a khaki shirt and dark green shorts with a brimmed straw hat covering his thinning hair and well-tanned face.

"Yes, my gallant knight," Michelle's eyes rolled up toward the sky and quickly back again, "but all I could find was this refreshing filtered water."

"Perfecto for quenchin' my raw throat. But please serve

the others first."

"Of course, there's plenty for everyone." Michelle filled the cups of two men and four boys at the site before returning to Rocco.

"Thanks, Michelle," Rocco smiled with sincere appreciation. He paused, cocking his head. "Listen, I hear a motor."

"I don't hear or see anything," Michelle said.

"Look at the dust on the southeastern horizon," Rocco's muscled arm stretched and his large hand pointed in that direction.

"Do you think it might be Jim?" Michelle asked.

"Wait just a tad to be sure."

Hand shielding his squinted brown eyes, Rocco's lips curved into a smile that revealed his upper front teeth.

"Yup, that's Jim's jeep."

"I need to tell Ellen the good news," Michelle said. She dropped the empty gourd on the ground and took off running in the direction of the Andersons' residence, about one half kilometer away. Rocco returned to his work.

About fifteen minutes later, the jeep stopped and Jim climbed out, with beads of sweat across his ebony brow. Rocco dropped his shovel and hurried toward him.

"Hey, Jim. Good to have ya back," Rocco gave Jim a gigantic bear hug and lifted the six foot man off the ground.

"Thanks, it's good to be home. How's the work on the

water system going?"

"Everythin's on schedule. Just got word they're comin' in with the big equipment on Thursday."

"Heh, that's good news."

"So, how'd your trip to the States go?" Rocco wanted to know. Before Jim could reply, he continued asking questions.

"I'll bet that Newspaper Association of America put on quite a shindig for their annual convention; and what about San Francisco? Did you get to ride on any cable cars or see any giant redwoods or anythin'?"

"I rode a trolley for the first time, and I treated myself to a sourdough sandwich at a local deli. But the convention didn't go as I expected. I need to share something important with you. Where's Michelle?"

"She ran like a cat with its tail on fire to tell Ellen that you're home."

"Good. Hop in the jeep."

"Now?"

"Yes, this is urgent," Jim stared into his eyes.

"Okay."

When they approached the small house, Rocco saw Ellen's coffee-colored face looking through the single glass window. Salvaged from a gutted office building in Nairobi, Jim had mounted the pane of glass to fill the hole in the wall.

Ellen reappeared behind the screen door. "They're here, Chele!"

"Well, let's go!" Michelle pushed the door open.

Ellen ran out the doorway, her black, kinky hair bouncing behind her.

"Jim, I'm so glad you're home." She cried out in excitement when she reached the stopped vehicle.

Jim jumped out of the jeep to embrace Ellen. He gave her a lingering kiss.

"I missed you and the children," Jim said.

"Let's all go inside, I can't wait to hear about your trip," Ellen suggested.

Rocco first noticed Jim's hesitation and lack of enthusiasm when they congregated at the small kitchen table. Apparently Ellen noticed it too.

"What's wrong? Are Dad and Mom alright?" Ellen's attractive dark-skinned face wore a frown.

"They're fine, and they send their love."

"Well, how'd the conference go?" Rocco asked.

Everyone stared at Jim, waiting for him to begin.

"Several thousand newspaper and media people attended the convention in San Francisco. About four hundred people sat in my lecture. Afterwards I talked with reporters from two national publications and one local paper. I also got an exclusive interview with Richard Wright from '*Freedom Fighters*' magazine. But the best events were unplanned. I received two speaking engagements to discuss our missionary work here in Africa. Tom Saunders, editor of *Christian Crusaders* magazine, invited me to his men's Bible Study, and I attended Sunday services with Ellen's parents. Because of their generosity, I just deposited $537.10 into our business account in Nairobi. God is good."

"Well, it don't sound so bad to me. Gettin' written up in one magazine and three articles in the press is good. Gettin' dough for the camp is even better. Right?"

"Well, here's the problem. It concerns our friends Travis and Karasa."

"They were at the conference?" Surprise registered in Michelle's voice.

"No, let me explain," Jim said.

Jim quickly recounted his conversation with a prominent Daily Times newspaper executive, John Cafferty, and a pending dilemma regarding the Martins.

"First, Mr. Cafferty expressed interest in flying to Khartoum to locate a slave market to determine if human trafficking really exists in Sudan.

"I told him it was both real and risky. And that it's against the law to buy back slaves, but I'd make the necessary arrangements.

"But, he only wanted Travis Martin, claiming it would be a human interest story about a hero going back under the gun to meet with Karasa's lost son Twangi. He promised his agency would also guarantee safe passage from Sudan in return for a feature story."

"They know where her son, Twangi is?" Rocco asked.

"They say they do, and they'll give him to Travis if he goes to Khartoum to give them a story."

"I smell a fish, a rotten fish," Rocco cut in. "I ain't sure they're really after a story. If they know where Twangi is and they can buy him, then they already know that there's slavery goin' on. What did you tell them, Jim?"

"I told them 'No Way' and showed them the door."

"That probably wasn't the best thing to do," Rocco said.

"What do you mean?"

"Cafferty doesn't come across as an upfront guy. If you'd pretended to play along with them you might've bought some time to warn Travis."

"I'm leaving tomorrow to warn Travis."

"It's over two on his shoulder boards and a half hours away, give or take a bit if some lioness isn't interested in eatin' you for dinner," Rocco said.

"Yeh, but if I'm up at first light, I can go there and come back before night fall."

"You may be too late already," Rocco pondered the situation.

"It's a chance I'll have to take."

"I don't know what these people are up to but it sounds like it's pretty well planned. They'd hoped to use you for some reason. But now that they can't, they'll move on without you. My guess is that someone else will approach Travis or Karasa," Rocco reasoned.

"Perhaps it really is a human interest story," Ellen said.

Jim didn't answer, or even meet Ellen's eyes.

"Maybe – and just maybe these melons will grow wings and fly," Rocco smirked, picking up a cantaloupe from a bowl in the center of the table.

Rocco sensed the invisible arrows that Michelle's narrowed eyes shot at him as she patted Ellen's slender hand.

"Sorry, Ellen," Rocco paused before speaking in a hushed voice. "What we really need to do right now is to pray."

And they did.

"You can accept yourself as a new person. You truly are in Him; just as the Father accepts you - perfectly."

~ Billy Graham

CHAPTER NINE

Usually Ellen taught in the mission school where Jimmy and Lisa and the other children received their daily instruction. But today her assistant took charge as she walked past the church, deep in thought.

Jim should be back late tonight. The plumbing engineers and special equipment used to install the well will arrive tomorrow. I need to finalize plans for the dedication and the distribution of the water to our people.

At the roar of the flat-back truck, Ellen looked up.

Rocco must be on his way to check the final preparations for the well site.

"Hey Rocco," she waved.

That's strange, he didn't even wave back.

Continuing toward her small house, she noticed Michelle standing about thirty meters away in front of her tent. She stood rigidly, staring into emptiness as if unaware of her surroundings.

Something's terribly wrong with Michelle.

Ellen ran up to Michelle and gave her a hug. Michelle's eyes looked red, her cheeks were moist with tears and her brow furrowed as if in pain.

"Michelle, what's wrong?"

Michelle faced down toward her feet, shook her head but made no reply.

"Let's go to my place. I'll make some coffee," Ellen suggested.

An uncomfortable silence lingered even as they sat at the table sipping coffee.

"Ell, I can't talk about it," Michelle whispered, without taking her eyes off her mug.

"Is it about Rocco?"

"Yes, he just left."

"He left the camp?"

"Yes."

"What? Did you have an argument?"

"No, our relationship is fine. But Rocco and I share a dark secret. We agreed we'd never talk to anyone about it."

"You can tell me, and I won't tell a soul. Not even Jim."

"I'm really a-scared, Ell."

"You're afraid for Rocco?"

"Yes, I may never see him again," Michelle wept. "And I'm so afraid that if you knew the truth, you wouldn't want to be friends anymore," she continued through her sobs.

Placing her arm around Michelle, Ellen handed her a clean dishcloth to dry her tears.

"You're my friend, Chelle. Nothing will ever change that."

Michelle straightened up, sniffed once, and looked Ellen in the eye.

"I can't tell you what's wrong without telling you about our past."

Ellen had a retort ready regarding Michelle's New Joyzee accent, but decided against it.

No, not the time for humor, Ellen thought as she sat down again on her chair.

"The Bible records that the Apostle Paul persecuted the early church. He put Christians to death until God called him to be one. God can change any life – he can use anyone. His strength is shown in our weakness," Ellen said.

"Well, when I was young, I made some bad choices." Ellen waited. She knew that Michelle's confession would be difficult for her.

"When I met Rocco he belonged to the Mafia. He hurt people for a living – an enforcer. I worked for them too, but my job was pleasing men."

She raised her gaze a little, but she could not quite meet

Ellen's eyes.

"The girls at the brothel were making fun of one mafia tough guy who had found Jesus. The Capo and his crew had a habit of coming by after work at the end of the week and winding down. This guy was one of the crew. He would just want to sit, talk about Jesus and read his Bible to his broad for the night. Once he chose me, and I didn't laugh. I had such an empty hole in my life that I craved more. When the time came for him to go, I felt sad. He visited me twice more, and on his third visit I got on my knees in the middle of that place and prayed for Jesus to forgive me and to come into my life."

Michelle paused and smiled.

"That night Rocco told me I became a new creation in Christ. He said that I needed a new home because I didn't belong there any more. Taking my hand, he led me out, right past everyone."

Michelle paused again, but Ellen knew that Michelle had to finish her story.

"Rocco brought me to his house. I thought for a minute that he was just like all the others. But he showed me my own bedroom, and he told me I could stay there as long as I needed until I found a job and got on my feet. He didn't try to touch me."

"That's beautiful," Ellen said.

Michelle looked at Ellen, believing she mocked her.

"I know you think less of me now . . ."

"No way. God put you two together, and he called you both for a purpose. Look what you're doing now. Look who you are. I'm proud to have you for my friend."

"At first it seemed like there was this wall between me and Rocco; a wall of my own making."

Michelle recounted her abusive childhood experiences. Being a sensitive and timid child, she had difficulty coping with her parents' constant scolding, ridicule and neglect. Her self-esteem took a dramatic turn for the worse when she was sexually violated as an adolescent. Discarded as a young adult, prostitution provided an income and place to stay. But after her conversion, Michelle felt ashamed of her past and unworthy of Rocco's affections.

"Would you believe that Rocco thought I was too pretty and wouldn't pop the question," she giggled.

"Didn't he ask you to marry him?" Ellen asked.

"Not at first. But God worked in each of our hearts. So when he finally suggested we tie the knot, I was so happy that I cried. Then he kissed me." Michelle involuntarily fingered her wedding ring.

Ellen understood. "You looked into Rocco's heart and not on his outward appearance.

"Yeah, I still love him so much."

"But I don't see what you're scared about." Ellen didn't understand.

"You've heard stories that once you are in the Mafia there's no way out. They don't let you quit – ever."

Michelle explained that if a member of the Mafia ever tried to quit, he'd likely end up in the East River. So it became a problem because they both felt called to be missionaries. Rocco decided to take a chance, and he and his boss, Mick – The Muscle, went to see the Don. Rocco asked permission to leave. The Don became amused when he'd heard about Rocco preaching to the floozies in the whore house. Surprisingly, he granted Rocco's request to 'go straight' and to live in Africa with the promise that he'd never return.

Ellen had this 'Oh No' look in her eyes.

"Where did he go?"

"He's on his way back to New York to ask the Don a favor, for the Mafia to put pressure on the press to call off the dogs on Travis."

"Isn't the Mafia a group of gangsters who just rule local territories."

"Sure, that and more. The New York Mafia is an Italian-American organized crime network with national and even international connections, too. The Mafia also does legit business with their Associates, and some have influence in high places."

"So Rocco believes that the Don may have connections or even influence with the national media?"

"Yeah, and he's willing to risk his life for it." Tears began to well up in Michelle's eyes.

"Rocco has courage to follow his convictions," Ellen said.

"Rocco sure is brave, but I don't want him to die," Michelle sobbed.

Ellen grabbed her Bible, searched the scriptures and found Jeremiah.

"Listen, Chelle, to God's promise for you," Ellen continued to read. "I know the plans I have for you . . . to give you hope and a future."

Ellen glanced up at Michelle, who breathed a sigh of relief.

"Once you make a decision, the universe

conspires to make it happen."

~ Ralph Waldo Emerson

CHAPTER TEN

"So you're still in the import and export business?" Travis asked.

"Yes. But right now business is slow, and I'm doing odd jobs," Kookie returned.

"I appreciate the detour to Lapaki."

"No worries, besides this reminds me of my home, The Lucky Country." With one hand on the wheel, Kookie waved the other toward the endless grassland of the Savannah.

"Are you saying Kikuyu grass grows in Australia too?" Travis knew that Kikuyu grass was native to this region of Africa. It provided good pasture for the livestock.

"Sure does, we use it for garden lawns because it's cheap and drought-tolerant. We call it 'the weed'. But it's bloody aggressive and chokes out the native species."

They heard the trumpeting of a bull elephant in the distance and caught sight of a family of three feeding off an acacia tree. As they continued in silence, the rover bounced along the rutted dirt lane to Lapaki. They passed the open markets on the outskirts of the small town before arriving at the *Simba Safari Adventures, Ltd.'s* headquarters.

Safari means journey in Swahili, and Travis had naturally eased into his current occupation as a tour guide. He transported his clients, mostly from Germany and the United Kingdom, to camps in Kenya's National Parks. Game viewing tours were conducted on foot and in dugout canoes, land cruisers, minibuses, hot air balloons or twin-engine bi-planes. Old-time, isolated tented camping could be combined with the comforts of first class hotels such as the Ark. Travis helped his guests locate and photograph Africa's Big Five: lion, leopard, buffalo, elephant, and rhinoceros.

"You know, Kookie, I always look forward to going on a *safari.* I'll miss the excitement. But the worse thing is my boss will be furious."

"It can't be helped."

"Yeah, it's time to face the music."

"What music? Oh no, not another one of those Americanisms," Kookie groaned.

When Travis and Kookie entered, Moran stood behind the counter dressed in traditional Maasai warrior attire - a colorful red and blue toga *Shúkà* wrapped around his body.

His elaborate upper body adornments, including leather, beaded jewelry, and fancy head gear accentuated his deep black, chiseled physique. Moran probably spent hours weaving his thinly braided hair strands into an ornate design. Warriors are the only members of the Maasai community allowed to wear long hair.

At fifteen years of age, Moran had participated in the Maasai custom mandating that each male youth kill a lion with a spear, a ritual for the rights of passage ceremony into manhood. When he accomplished this feat, the whole village honored his bravery and celebrated his successful return with the traditional ceremony that included an adornment of a personal ceremonial mask. Now, the authorities discouraged lion hunting in East Africa, except when a lion mauled Maasai livestock.

"*Jambo,* Moran. Wow! You're dressed for the occasion. The migration of the Blue Wildebeest must be close at hand."

"Yes, the boss is talking on the phone in the back room. He'll be glad you've arrived earlier than expected."

"Moran, this is Kookie. This Aussie is my new client." Travis felt a brief nudging twinge of guilt prick his conscience. But he convinced himself that without deception, he wouldn't be able to protect Karasa.

"*Jambo.*"

"We need to talk to Brett now. It's urgent."

"Sure," Moran raised his eyebrows. "Just knock and go in," his voice expressed curiosity.

Travis entered unannounced and broke the news to his unsuspecting boss.

"Spit the dummy! This is the worst news I could get on such short notice," Brett Blair shouted.

"Boss, look I . . ."

"You know this is our busiest season. It'll take some fancy foot-work to replace you without notice," Brett Blair cut in.

Twenty minutes of serious discussion and brainstorming elapsed before Brett calmed down and dealt with the crisis to his satisfaction. Afterwards, he even relented and expressed concern.

"Look Travis, I don't like it, but I do understand. Your secret stays right here."

Travis thanked Brett and went back out through the doorway to the reception area.

"I won't be working with you on this trek, I'm doing another charter," He informed Moran. Travis leaned his head back over his left shoulder toward Kookie.

I still don't like telling a lie to a friend. Travis turned quickly to avoid any further conversation.

"Well, happy camping . . . and good luck," Moran called after him. He stared at Travis suspiciously from the corner of his eyes as if he suspected Travis might need the luck he bade him.

Heading toward Nairobi, Kookie veered off the solid packed dirt road to take a shortcut over some rugged terrain. In an attempt to pamper his vehicle, he slowed down about ten miles-per-hour to avoid wear and tear on the shocks and suspension. Still jostling its occupants, the reduced speed spared one's backside with less bouncing, but it allowed a hovering dust cloud to overtake and engulf them. The palpable particles of dirt left a gritty film on theirs lips, stung their eyes and entered their air passages. Covering his face with a bandana didn't prevent Travis from coughing.

"Look," Travis jabbed Kookie on the shoulder and pointed to the northeast. Squinting, in the distance they caught sight of a herd of impalas and roan antelopes prancing past a spattering of acacia trees.

Distinguished by black markings on their faces and spear-shaped horns that bend back and upward, the roan antelopes are easily excitable and aggressive. Their only natural enemy, besides man, is the lion.

Kookie turned the wheel sharply to avoid a meter high termite mound. After thirty minutes of jarring through the Savannah, they both breathed easier when the rover finally clambered out onto a firm dirt road. Eventually it widened and funneled into a paved road leading to Nairobi. Even at the distance of five kilometers they could see the towering gold and bronze Kenyatta Conference Center. Circular in structure, it loomed over the other modern government buildings in Center Square.

A cosmopolitan city, the capital of Kenya stands in stark contrast to the primitive villages surrounding it. Also called the 'Green City in the Sun', its wildlife parks are the most famous in the world, making Nairobi a favorite photo-*safari* destination.

Arriving in Nairobi, the rover turned onto Jogoo Road. Lined with blossoming tropical trees, the street hummed with the heavy traffic. Minibuses called *matatus,* bicycles with baskets, four-wheel drive trucks, motor bikes and a variety of automobiles sped past scurrying pedestrians.

"What's the plan, Mate, you wanna go straight to this hotel? It'll be about four in the arvo," Kookie asked when they stopped at a crossroad.

"Not today. I have some things I must do this afternoon."

"Good, we'll head for my digs."

Kookie navigated the busy streets of Nairobi with ease as the rover approached an older section of the city. The quaint homes showed some disrepair with overgrown foliage in places, but this appeared to be a friendly neighborhood. Several people waved as they slowly passed by.

"You can stay at my place tonight, Mate."

Kookie pulled up in front of a small, attractive bungalow with a large porch wrapping around two sides. The house featured large windows that could be left open for a breeze. Trimmed tropical bushes and a vibrant bougainvillea bush gave the property curb appeal.

Travis asked, "You married?"

"No, Mate, no complications."

"You like gardening?"

"No. One of the luxuries I afford myself is hiring good help. A family across the street has a couple of teens. I pay the girl to clean inside and the boy to take care of the landscape."

"Your place looks real nice," Travis said.

"Thank you, Mate. Come on inside, and I'll pull you a cool one."

Kookie pushed hard and opened the front door. Travis followed.

"Don't you lock your doors when you're away?" Travis asked.

"I live in a safe place. The neighbors all look out for each other," Kookie assured him.

His home, constructed like one big room, was designed to maximize the cooling breeze flowing through it. Kookie switched on the large ceiling fan in the center of the room as he entered. The kitchen nestled in an alcove in the corner. A partion sectioned off the bedroom for privacy.

"I can't get Fosters here. You want one of these native

brews?" Kookie asked as he opened the refrigerator door.

"No, I'll take one of your Cokes." There had been a time when Travis drank more beer than he cared to remember, but now he had given it up.

"Suit yourself." Kookie handed him the Coke. "You want more, Mate, you help yourself. Anything here is yours."

"Thanks, Kookie."

Kookie sat on a chair besides a small table and Travis joined him.

"Mate, you're packed for a *safari* and your clothes look like you slept in them. If I were you, I'd 'show pony' and dress to impress. Why not get a set of new clothes before tomorrow's meeting. There's still time to shop."

Strange advice coming from a nattily dressed oddity, Travis thought.

"Well, you're probably right, but in a couple of hours I'll need to make an important phone call to my lawyer in the States."

"That's not a problem. A family down the street has a phone; we just have to reimburse them for the call."

"While we're out, supper's my treat. Afterwards, I'd like to brainstorm possible problems and solutions back here at your place."

"Reckon!" Kookie nodded his head in agreement.

"We are not the same persons this year as last; nor are those we love. It is a happy chance if we, changing, continue to love a changed person."

~ W. Somerset Maugham

CHAPTER ELEVEN

Karasa entered her hut after completing several morning chores. Built of local materials with a dirt floor; the interior featured a single circular room measuring five meters in diameter. An adult could only stand upright within three meters of the center, the highest point where the roof pitched sharply upward.

A decorative object caught the light of the morning sun. The Maasai ceremonial wedding mask, their most prized possession, hung on the wall where it would be visible upon entry. Restricted to essentials, other items in the home included one low wooden table with eating utensils scattered upon it, four stools, and a wooden chest. A multicolored cloth separated the space for the bed mats, bedding, a baby's cradle, and an open crate.

She put the bowl of goat's milk down and attended to her irritable toddler. Karasa handed Tamara a toy that Travis made out of a small gourd and dried beans. Enthralled, Tamara cooed at the sound of the shaking rattle while Karasa changed her diaper.

I only go to the river twice weekly to do the family wash. That is often enough to hear about what is happening in the village, Karasa thought.

Before the rainy season last year Travis brought home a fifty-five gallon metal drum. He mounted it on top of a tree stump and installed a real faucet near the bottom. When the dry season approached, Travis crept down to the river under the cover of darkness, making several trips to fill the drum to capacity. He wanted to avoid the taunts of his friends who considered carrying water to be women's work. Now Karasa walked just several steps to retrieve water for their daily needs. She appreciated the convenience of the ingenious device

Karasa thought about her conversation with her sister regarding the community's reaction to the water barrel.

Ayella tells me that most of the villagers are amazed, but some of the women are jealous and others regard me with suspicion.

Holding Tamara, Karasa stepped outdoors and walked toward her garden. The morning birds, singing a melodious chorus, quietly hushed in deference to the roar of an approaching jeep. Shielding her eyes from the sun and turning toward the noise, Karasa recognized the vehicle. When Jim Anderson stepped out of the jeep, she hurried to greet him.

Jim and Ellen are good friends, but they do not visit often. I wonder why Jim has come, Karasa thought.

"*Jambo*, Jamala." Jim called Karasa by her given name as he closed the gap between them.

"*Jambo.* How are you, Ellen, and the children?"

"Everyone's fine. This must be Tamara. How she's grown."

"Yes," Karasa replied as Tamara shyly turned away.

"I was heading this way, and I wanted talk with Travis. Is he about?"

"No, he's out on a charter. He won't be back for thirty days. Can I help?"

"No, it's not important."

He looks disappointed.

"Would you like some water to drink or food to eat?" Karasa asked.

"No thank you," Jim paused. "I would like to speak with your father."

"Look, father and mother walk toward the banana tree," Karasa pointed.

"*Kwaheri,*" Jim hurried away.

"Tamara, wave good-bye," Karasa coaxed.

Retracing her steps, Karasa stopped to ponder by a fragrant oleander tree. She turned back in time to watch as the men turned toward the cattle kraals. Karasa knew her father's habits; he walked to that secluded area for privacy.

Could something be wrong?

But she soon dismissed the thought and began working the garden. About thirty minutes later she heard a motor start. She stopped and stepped toward the road in time to see a dust trail. It didn't travel up the left fork in the road that led to a nearby mission village. Instead the decreasing dirt cloud headed north toward the refugee camp.

If Jim is going back home, he came all of the way here just to talk with my husband, Karasa reasoned.

Karasa rinsed some of the vegetables she'd gathered and walked toward her parents' dwellings. Her mother expressed thanks for the beans and sweet potatoes. After a brief visit with her mother, she received permission to enter her father's thingira.

"Greetings daughter and granddaughter."

He kissed them.

"We are happy to be here. I have a question," Karasa told him. "I wondered what you and Jim Anderson spoke of. Does it concern my husband?"

"Yes, we spoke of Travis."

"What was said?"

"It is not a woman's concern what men discuss."

"Is my husband alright?"

"Even now, your husband cares for you and provides for you. Do not be afraid. You have nothing to fear."

"Father . . ."

"I have spoken, and you must take your leave."

"Thank you, Father."

Putting his hand on her head, Bahrundi prayed, "Go with my blessings daughter."

Karasa left but not with the reassurance she'd hoped for.

I will feel better when Travis returns.

"You can't live a perfect day without doing something for someone who will never be able to repay you."

~ John Wooden

CHAPTER TWELVE

Kookie prepared a delicious brekkie of fresh fruit and garnished omelets.

Travis wore his new button-down collar, khaki shirt and a comfortable pair of beige trousers. He followed Kookie down the street to the rover and threw his new Nike backpack onto the rear seat.

"You're certain that's a good idea, to head to the U.S. Embassy?" Kookie asked. "I wouldn't pull the bureaucrats into this if it was my affair."

"Yes, I trust this man," Travis affirmed.

"Take 109, exit at the traffic circle to Langata Road, and turn right onto Magadi Road," Travis gave directions.

"I know the way. I live here," Kookie said.

They drove toward Central Square where the KICC building towered over the Amphitheater like a mammoth representation of the traditional African hut. Here heritage met modernity. Like other tourist destinations, men dressed in business suits and the women wore trendy apparel. But most city dwellers sported a combination of western garb and colorful African prints.

The sight of the uniformed marines at the U.S. Embassy gates brought back nostalgic feelings to Travis. After passing the sentries, Kookie parked under the shade of a palm tree near the side of a Kenyan government building. Travis leapt out.

"You go ahead, Mate, I'll wait here. Courtrooms and government buildings give me the shivers," Kookie said.

"Surely you jest." Travis' eyebrows raised in surprise.

"No, Mate."

"Okay. This should take about fifteen minutes." He hurried toward the entrance.

Travis climbed the stone steps in front of Kenya's Nyako House, swung wide the double doors and passed a guard. The guard carried a semi-automatic and his facial expressions confirmed he was ready to use it. Travis had no problem with the 'good guys' using weapons in their own defense. The lobby walls appeared freshly painted and the bamboo floors were polished. A small royal palm, standing sentry in a row of potted plants, graced one corner of the room and lent a tropical decor.

Travis greeted the main receptionist and stated his request. After checking his I.D. and calling on the phone, she motioned him toward the spiral staircase.

"Mr. Nogamo's office is on the second floor."

Having visited here several times, Travis knew the way. At the top of the stairs Travis turned right toward the door marked 210 and walked in.

"I would like to speak with Mr. Nogamo," Travis addressed the secretary in Swahili.

"*Jambo*, Mr. Martin, please take a seat." After conferring on the phone, she said, "Mr. Nogamo will see you now. Please go right in."

Travis entered Thomas Nogamo's immaculate office. The Assistant Director of Immigration loved his country and cared about its citizens. He regarded his office and the people he served with respect. He came around his desk to shake hands.

"Have a seat, Travis. What can I do for you?"

"I have a problem."

Travis withdrew the letter from his pocket. Thomas Nogamo took the letter and sat down at his desk to read it.

"Travis, you realize relations with Sudan are strained. Your U.S. Government is especially concerned about Sudan's state-sponsored terrorism and has suspended U.S. Embassy operations in Khartoum. Ambassador Tim Carney departed in 1996. It's almost a year now and no new ambassador has been designated. There's some tension with Kenya as well."

Holding up the letter, Thomas Nogamo continued. "In regard to your situation, you would need a current visa to legally visit Sudan; but that could take months, even if you were not a wanted criminal there."

"You were so much help to Karasa and me when we settled here in Kenya. But I don't think there's anything you can do now. I expect to walk into their trap."

Thomas waved his hand in the air as if to tell Travis to slow down. "Be careful what you tell me. Once I know something, my friend, I cannot un-know it."

Travis nodded.

"Other than finding some reason to arrest this woman in the hotel and try to make her talk, I can't think of any other options," the government official stated.

"No, Ms. Houston is just an underling. If she's picked up, they would have someone else contact my wife."

"But, there's one thing I must caution you on. The last time I was able to shield you because you arrived with two American missionary children whom you had rescued from slavery. Khartoum did not want you badly enough to risk a public spectacle. But if you return there based upon nothing more than this unsigned note and commit a crime, I don't have the political capital to refuse their request for extradition. Do you understand?"

"Yes, if I kill anyone; I shouldn't come back here."

"You could hide out of sight, but I would prefer not to

know. I can't violate my oath and lie about your location. It would be best if you flee to another country. Otherwise, you might be picked up by our police and sent back to Khartoum. That's the political reality here. Islamic forces assert their grievances and make more and more demands."

"Understood."

"There's one thing I can do for you. I'll expedite the paperwork for emigration to the United States if your wife and her family wish to leave Kenya."

"I'd appreciate that. Can you could start the wheels turning now?"

"Of course, I have all the necessary information on file."

Travis gave him George Mitchell's name, address and telephone number. Between George Mitchell and Thomas Nogamo, if it could be done, they would no doubt find a way to get his family to America.

"Please wait at least a month before contacting Karasa," Travis cautioned.

"I will."

"Thank you."

"Goodbye, Travis. I hope we meet again," Thomas Nogamo grasped Travis' hand and shook it firmly.

The hands on the wall clock read 9:30 A.M. as it dinged once for the half hour. Travis left the building and climbed into the Land Rover. He acknowledged Kookie with a quick nod.

"Go okay?" Kookie asked as he pulled into traffic.

"Yes, he's going to start the wheels turning to get my wife and her family out if things go to hell."

"I'll bet that's a relief. Where to now, Mate?"

"The Chase Manhattan on Murang'a Road," Travis answered.

"Yup, you'll need moolah," Kookie nodded.

When they arrived, Travis entered the bank, filled out a withdrawal slip and positioned himself in front of the teller's window. When the cashier mentioned the exchange rate, Travis shrugged his shoulders even though the rate on the black market was at least fifty percent better. Travis withdrew the equivalent of two thousand U.S. dollars from his account with one half of the money in Kenyan currency, one half in Sudanese dinars. He tucked the money into his blue Nike shoulder bag and walked back to where Kookie stood waiting.

"I need to fetch something from the safe deposit box," Travis told him.

"No worries."

Ten minutes later they walked out of the bank, ready to ride.

"Get what you needed?" Kookie asked.

My intuition tells me that I can trust him, Travis thought.

"Sure did. Here, take a look inside." Travis handed over the large manila envelope.

It contained Travis' authentic passport plus another forged passport and a driver's license with Travis' picture; but they bore the name of a Mr. Jervis Tingle, a resident of Kingston, Jamaica. A third passport with Travis' photo identified Dr. Wellington Bacon, a resident of New York City. The driver's license for Dr. Bacon had expired a few months ago.

"Passports look official." Kookie shoved the contents back into the envelope and handed it back to Travis. "Where to now, Mate?"

"You know of a drug store around here?"

"They don't sell drugs in stores, and you don't want to mess with that stuff. It'll mess up your life!" The Aussie looked concerned.

"No," Travis punched him lightly on his shoulder. "A pharmacy, you daffy oaf."

"Oh, well, why didn't you say so? You had me worried there for a moment."

Kookie turned the rover left on Mici Avenue and traveled two kilometers. At the store, Travis bought a shaving kit, tooth brush, tooth paste, razor blades, deodorant and epoxy glue. He placed all of his purchases into his backpack.

This section of the city could be compared to an urban

planner's nightmare. Here, single-family shacks with wood-burning stoves and smoke emitting from chimneys were nestled among store front businesses.

Heading back, they passed a smiling but toothless, wrinkle-faced elderly woman bending over a crude side-walk stand. Travis paused and bought a piece of fruit that he didn't want. He offered it to Kookie, who wasn't hungry either. So he stuffed it into his bag. Somehow it felt right to do a good deed before walking into the lion's den.

"I would have liked to go to mass one more time, or at least stop at a church and let a priest hear my confession," Travis shared.

"You don't strike me as a religious man," Kookie said.

"There are no atheists in foxholes."

"I know what you mean. I was in the O.S.S. myself."

Travis glanced at Kookie with new respect. The Australian O.S.S. was on a par with the American Green Berets.

"I was raised a Baptist myself. I still believe in the Big Guy, although I don't make it to church too often," Kookie continued.

"My wife is a Baptist, too," Travis replied.

"No kidding. I'm glad that someone in the family has some sense," Kookie smiled teasingly.

"Ha, ha," Travis pretended to chuckle.

That moment Kookie turned down Nyeri Road and swung the rover to the curb, singing lines from 'California

Dreamin', "Stopped into a church – I passed along the way-y-y. Well I got down on my knee-e-e-s, and I began to pray-y-y."

"You'll never hold a candle to Mama Cass," Travis told Kookie as he swung himself to the sidewalk and advanced toward a sign that read 'Holy Trinity Catholic Church'.

"Baptists don't light candles," Kookie called after him.

"That's okay, Kookie; I'll say a prayer for you anyway."

The corners of Travis' mouth turned slightly upward.

"A pessimist sees the difficulty in every opportunity; an

optimist sees the opportunity in every difficulty."

~ Winston Churchill

CHAPTER THIRTEEN

"We did well, and it's almost lunch time," Kookie said.

Travis' stomach growled.

"First, I have a personal errand I need to run," Kookie stated matter-of-factly.

"Lead on," Travis said.

Kookie drove in silence with a focused intensity to reach his destination.

"So, where are we going?" Travis asked.

Kookie pulled over to the side of the road and turned a serious face to Travis.

"Look, Mate, I'm going to need to show you something that could get my arse shot off. I'll be breaking some rules and getting some dangerous people as mad as a Tasmanian devil. I just have to hope that they can trust you the way that I do."

Kookie paused for emphasis.

"Go on," Travis expressed curiosity.

"What I told you was basically true. I run errands for a living. But some of my clients like to stay in the shadows."

"Criminals?"

"No, they're the good guys, but not from this country. Do you know what I'm saying?"

"Yes, I've got a good idea," Travis affirmed.

Kookie might work freelance for the Brits' MI6 or the Australian ASIS. Indeed, powerful people in high govern-ment positions react with intense rage when an agent's cover becomes compromised. I wonder?

"Do I have your solemn word, on your honor as a man, that you will never tell anyone what you are about to see? Not your wife, not your priest, not even God?"

Kookie's gaze fixed Travis' brown eyes.

"I think that God probably knows already, but you have my word that I'll never tell anyone else," Travis assured him.

"Good onya."

Satisfied, Kookie restarted the engine. Pulling back into traffic in this commercial section of the city, he turned right at the corner. Five minutes later he parked across the street from a single-story building displaying a large sign: 'Elec-tronics'. Although metal bars covered the windows, indicating a concern for security, the black wrought iron grid didn't look out of place.

"Okay, just let me do the talking. Say nothing unless you're asked to." His usual cocky smile had disappeared.

Travis nodded. He realized there was more to this crazy Aussie than met the eye.

Kookie wore a poker face with his hazel eyes darting both ways as he led the way across the street.

As they entered the store, a slightly built, balding man with a sparse mustache looked a bit warily at Kookie.

"What can I do for you?" the man forced a smile.

"I need help choosing some capacitors," Kookie replied.

Apparently Kookie spoke in code. The clerk went around the counter, locked the front door, and put an 'Out to Lunch' sign in the window.

He tilted his head toward Travis saying, "Who is this sep-po?"

"This is my American friend, Travis Martin. He's the bloke who went into Sudan three years ago and brought out those slave kids. He's okay."

"What's this all about? Why did you bring him here?"

Kookie turned to Travis and said, "Show him the letter."

Travis took out the folded letter in his pocket and handed it to the man who posed as a clerk. The man read it quickly without comment.

"What does this have to do with us, or our interests?"

He shoved the letter back to Travis.

"I'm tagging along with him. I want to borrow three items I've used before."

"Such as?"

"I need a quirk, one item for research, and one for defense."

The man frowned and stared at Kookie in disbelief.

"Well?"

"Mr. Smith is going to be extremely angry with you."

This aliased Mr. Smith must be their superior, Travis surmised.

"Tell Mr. Smith that I would trust this man with my life," Kookie assured him.

"You are," the clerk informed him. He let that sink in before adding, "Come back at 2:00 P.M. this afternoon, and I'll have an answer for you."

Kookie turned and left without another word. Travis followed him out.

"Well, that went far better than I had hoped," Kookie let out a sigh of relief.

I'd hate to think what would have happened if it had gone badly, Travis thought.

They got into the rover, but Kookie didn't start the engine right off. He opened his glove compartment, took out a pair of sunglasses.

"What are we waiting for?" Travis asked.

"Professional courtesy," Kookie answered. "Just polishing my sunnies on my shirt. We'll be followed until we return, so I'm giving our shadows time to get into position."

This guy is a spook.

Travis sat dumbfounded.

Kookie slipped the sun glasses into his shirt pocket before starting the engine. He pulled away from the curb and entered the light traffic. He turned onto Museum Hill Road and stopped at a popular restaurant.

"Let's cut lunch," Kookie suggested.

After sandwiches and fries they walked a short distance to the National Museum of Kenya. They viewed several antiquities including the prehistoric artifacts discovered by the Leakey family, and fossils from Lake Turkana. Stopping amidst various exhibits of over nine hundred stuffed animals and birds, they discussed possible scenarios in hushed whispers.

"It's the little things that make the big things possible.

Only close attention to the fine details of any operations

makes the operation first class."

~ J. Willard Marriott

CHAPTER FOURTEEN

At precisely 1:55 P.M. they approached the entrance to the electronics store.

Before entering Kookie turned to Travis and revealed, "I'll be talking ala mode again. You know, the code."

"That's what I suspected," Travis replied.

After receiving the code, the clerk locked the door and walked behind the counter.

He retrieved a bag with a jacket and wristwatch, a large box containing a computer and monitor, and a smaller rectangular box. Kookie gathered the items without comment, motioning to Travis for assistance.

The clerk squared his shoulders and stared down on them.

"Considering your imprudence, Mr. Smith advises you to proceed with caution, and he reminds you that the borrowed items must be accounted for and returned."

"Understood," Kookie replied.

"He said to remind you that you are responsible for the actions of this man," he nodded at Travis. "If he causes problems for us, it's just as if you did." He wore a serious expression.

Kookie nodded his head.

The clerk, wearing a serious expression, walked back around the counter to unlock the door. They left without further conversation.

And this guy is on our side, Travis thought, as he followed Kookie out the door.

Starting the engine, Kookie pulled back out into traffic. "We're off to my unit."

Neither he nor Travis spoke a word as they drove away.

"How do these gizmos work?" Travis asked when they arrived at Kookie's place.

"I'm going to give you instructions. But remember, it's strictly spy gear, and I trust you to forget you ever saw it."

"You got it," Travis replied.

"This wristwatch was meant for eavesdropping, and not to duplicate the function of a radio. It houses a built-in transmitter. By necessity the face is two inches in diameter; the width is large enough to conceal an extra battery to power the transmitter."

"How do you hear what I'm saying through this watch?"

"This jacket conceals a built-in receiver with a wire that goes from the collar to an ear piece. The range is only a few dozen meters. When you meet with your contact at the hotel, I'll stand out in the hall. If you turn up the gain, I'll overhear anyone standing close to you, too."

Travis tried on the jacket while Kookie strolled a few hundred feet down the street while singing Waltzing Matilda. The volume changed as Kookie swung his arm.

"How's the transmission?" Kookie asked when he returned.

"Good, I could hear you all the way."

"You'll need to know how the transmitter works."

Kookie pointed at the base of the watch, "Press that little spot right there. Push this hidden button once to turn it on, and then push it again to turn it off."

Kookie turned Travis' wrist so that he could see the watch's face, "See that little dot there at the bottom?"

"Yes," Travis saw the tiny yellow point of light.

"That tells you if it's transmitting," Kookie continued. "Remember, don't turn it on while you're flying to Khartoum because it can mess with the airplane's electronics, and they'll know something is up."

"How long is the battery good for?"

"About a dozen hours, give or take a couple. When you get to Sudan, turn on the transmitter when it's safe. That way I'll be able to find you and help if I can."

"I'll do my best to safeguard this equipment, but what if it falls into enemy hands?"

"They have fail safes. If it isn't turned on just right, all info will get scrambled."

While they talked, Travis hid the extra passports, yellow fever certificate and most of his money in the bottom of his blue Nike backpack. A stiff bottom panel lifted on three sides making it easy to slide something underneath. He mixed the epoxy glue to fasten the bottom down.

After hiding his real passport, he placed one that identified him as Mr. Jervis Tingle, a citizen of Jamaica in the top zippered side compartment for easy access. If necessary he could slip a small padlock through the top zipper.

"Mate, you'd need a visa to get into Sudan if those newspaper blokes weren't toting you around and skirting security. That's a pretty good sign those mongrels have some plan up their filthy sleeves."

"For sure. What about the computer?" Travis asked.

"We'll use it to do some research."

"I know almost nothing about the city of Khartoum."

Kookie tapped the computer.

"This computer is innovative. It'll provide the most up-to-date information available, and I can get on the Internet without needing a phone, or a modem." Kookie paused. "For security reasons, you'll have to turn around while I turn it on and key in the necessary code."

Kookie set the monitor on top of the computer, connecting it with a cable. He plugged them both into the wall using a special power cord. After he hooked up a keyboard and a mouse, he pressed the start button.

Behind him, Travis heard the soft hum of the motor, the music of the monitor and Kookie pounding keys.

"Wow," Travis exclaimed when he turned around.

The computer screen displayed an aerial view of the ground from a high altitude.

"This computer has a special internet connection built into it. One of the programs includes maps that will orient you to the city so we can plan your best escape."

"What is this on the screen?

"Okay, we're looking down at Sudan from one of your American satellites in orbit."

"But how?"

"I don't really know, Mate, and I don't want to know, if you get my drift."

"Yeah, sure. But why is it so secret if I already know you can do it?"

"I don't know if our lads found a way to sneak into your computers, or if someone in America told us how to do it, but it's really secret on our side that we can. Can I trust you with this?"

"Of course, I'll never tell anyone."

"That's a load off. They'd probably whack someone if they needed to in order to keep this secret, and my neck's on the line with yours. Anyway, we have to get off in twenty-five minutes.

"Thanks, Kookie. I owe you for this."

"Nah, maybe made up a bit for that shonky package I brought yuh, that's all."

Kookie grabbed a couple of books from a shelf along the wall and opened them to a section on Sudan.

"Here, Mate, if you look at these maps of Africa you can put what you're seeing in better context. It helps me get oriented if I find the Nile, and follow it. The Blue Nile and the White Nile meet near Khartoum. Its name is derived from the Arabic word meaning the 'end of an elephant's trunk', referring to the narrow strip of land extending between the Blue and White Niles."

"Thanks Kookie."

"I have a feeling this will take awhile, I'll start us some supper," Kookie said.

"How current is what's on this screen?"

"It's what's going on right now."

"Can this be right, it looks like there are deserts all around it?" Travis asked.

"Certainly is, Mate. Natural dangers in this area include

snakes, scorpions and dust storms. If you try to walk across the dessert, you'll be easily spotted from the air. I've been to Khartoum, and I can confirm that it's a nasty place to get out of if there's some heat on you.

"Sudan's largest airport, Khartoum International, is located at the southern edge of the city. There are sixty-three airports in the whole bloody country, but only the twelve largest have paved runways."

"Should I try to sneak out on a charter plane from a smaller airport on the outskirts of Khartoum?"

"Are you a pilot?"

"No, just ride in them."

"Well it's a possibility, but let's explore all the other alternatives first," Kookie suggested. "There are some unreliable buses and one train line connecting cities in some parts of Sudan, Port Sudan, El Obeid and Egypt.

"Could you steal a boat?"

"It wouldn't work. The travel on the river is pretty sparse, and no one who could take you anyplace speaks English. The few motor boats belong to the rich and they're guarded. The locals have these little sailboats called *felucca* with strange triangle sails. Unless you've sailed one before, you'll stand out like a tourist in a Canberra corn field."

"Aren't there some Nile steamers?"

"Ace, it's the only commercial transportation on the Nile, and there's absolutely none that can take you south, back home toward Kenya. You could book a passage in advance at the Nile River Transport to Wadi Halfi, a small city near the Egyptian border. It leaves from Bahri just outside of Khartoum and travels north. But you must show your Sudanese visa or a letter of recommendation from your embassy. I'd leave the river alone and go by land if I needed to leave the city in a hurry."

Kookie walked back toward the computer.

"Now we need to get off the system," Kookie told Travis.

"How come we can only get internet connection at certain times?"

"Don't know, Mate. All I know is they told me that the bloody Yanks, no offense, won't know we were on their system as long as we get on and off at certain times, and follow secret rituals to get in and out. Turn around now, I'm going to disconnect."

Travis faced away while Kookie disconnected.

"Something smells good," Travis sniffed.

"Dinner's ready. I cooked Nile perch smothered in coconut sauce with fufu. That's a dish made from the cassava plant. Let's bog in while it's hot," Kookie suggested.

"Imperfect action is better than

perfect inaction."

~ Harry Truman

CHAPTER FIFTEEN

Kookie put the last of the dishes in the cupboard.

"Well, it's back to the computer. The camera will wander about randomly and zoom tighter on Khartoum, close enough to see cars on the street. There's no way to control it."

"Sounds good," Travis answered.

This may be a one-way trip, unless we can figure out a plan that will work, Travis thought.

"Listen, here's something you should know." Kookie opened a hard-covered book to a section labeled, 'General Information,' and read verbatim.

"Khartoum is perhaps the hottest major city in the world. June is hot and arid with temperatures as high as 127 degrees. During the dry season, there's little relief at night with temperatures averaging about 80 degrees."

Kookie looked up. "It's important you don't get dehydrated, but don't drink untreated water. The open market called *Souq Arabi* is several blocks from the center of Khartoum proper, just south of the Great Mosque, *Mesjid al-Kabir.* You can buy bottled water or iced juices at reasonable prices."

Travis gazed in fascination at the computer, barely attending to Kookie's advice. The image on the monitor zoomed in tight, and Travis lost his sense of direction.

"Kookie, what's on the screen now?" Travis asked.

Kookie identified a location in the city and used a pencil to point out corresponding places on the maps in his books.

"Most of the city is residential with over ninety percent of this area in small single-family homes on dirt roads. You shouldn't have any cause to go into these areas."

His fingers glided to another part near the river where there were a lot of paved streets and some big buildings.

"Government buildings and the big hotels are located in this section. The three main tourist hotels - Al Salam Rotana, the Grand Holiday Villa and the Hilton Khartoum are situated about one click apart. I would recommend the Hilton, where English is still widely spoken. The government is pushing a new 'Arabization' program to suppress English and promote Arabic speaking only. They aim to wipe away the last vestiges of the old English rule. Do you speak any Arabic?"

"No."

"Right, I only have a bit myself. You want the Hilton."

"Has the political situation changed since the country's last election?" Travis asked.

"No, it's still an authoritarian republic. The current president is Omar al-Bashir, who took power in 1989 in a military coup. He, along with his representatives in the National Congress Party, has complete power.

Kookie continued. "If the police or military pick you up you can't depend on any due process whatsoever. The courts combine civil and *Sharia Law*. The legal system will convict you for murder and probably skin you alive because you're an infidel."

"That's a given," Travis said. "But if I escape, I can't be tried or convicted. So let's look at transportation in and out of the city."

"A paved highway leads to Port Sudan on the Red Sea where there's international shipping. As a last resort if you can slip over the border into Egypt, you could sign on a foreign ship as a deck hand if you're by yourself. They won't allow a deck hand to bring along a dependent. If you have your boy, it's a no-go."

Kookie thumbed through a book and read, "A bus line and train travel to Port Sudan, too.

"I know a bloke who took a train once. So many passengers crowded the bloody thing that many people had no choice but to ride on the roof. The trip took fifty hours, and the train didn't even break down. It only runs twice a week on Sunday and Wednesday morning. I'd consider it a second resort to the bus."

"Were you that bloke on the train?" Travis asked.

"Couldn't say, Mate."

"Look, Kookie, I know that you've been to Khartoum before. Why don't you just tell me what you know?"

"You're getting deeper in my business than I should allow you to be, and I gotta be able to tell Mr. Smith I didn't tell you anything. As long as I tell you that some guy told me something, then I didn't tell you what I knew about it. You get my drift?"

"Okay, what about buses?" Travis sighed.

"There are both buses and trucks that provide passenger transportation between Khartoum and Port Sudan. Either way you have to go through either Sennar or Kassala."

Forgetting his former pretense of searching for information, Kookie continued. "I would recommend Kassala if you have to make a dash. The trip to Kassala takes eight or nine hours, the bus spends the night there, and it takes a few more hours the following morning to finish the trip into Port Sudan."

"How would I find a bus ride?" Travis asked.

"The downtown touristy section of the city is full of canary yellow cabs. Find a driver who speaks enough English to get you to the bus station. Or just draw a picture of a bus and show it to him.

"If the guy behind the counter at the bus station doesn't speak English, point to Port Sudan on a map. Every bus that comes in, you show the driver your ticket until one motions you to get onto his bus."

Travis asked, "What about the trucks?"

"The trucks get stuck in the sand less, but the drivers are not a trustworthy lot."

"Okay, it seems the bus is my first choice. The trucks are second. The train is my third option, and anything else comes after that."

"Remember that Friday is the day of worship for Moslems, and all banks, stores, and government offices are closed. Also, Khartoum has a curfew from midnight until four in the morning. But this time of year it gets dark around 6:00 P.M. So you'll have a six hour window to travel in the dark without raising undue suspicion."

"Thank you for all your help,"

"No worries, it's time to call it a night."

"The purpose of our lives is to give birth to the best

which is within us."

~ Marianne Williamson

CHAPTER SIXTEEN

After breakfast, they reviewed and finalized plans.

"Kookie, what's in the other box?" Travis asked.

"It's a Glock," Kookie replied with pride.

The Glock, a polymer handgun, could pass through most airport metal screening. It cost more than most men in the U.S. earned in three months.

Kookie handed the gun to Travis, who inspected it with interest.

"This Glock is one of a kind and has a combination of three automatic safety features – trigger, firing pin, and drop safety, which systematically disengages when the trigger is pulled. The central pivot of the trigger is the most important and the first to disengage. This Glock's trigger pull is lighter; and the better balance increases accuracy. It has a smoother, shorter design that promotes a fast trigger speed. Double taps come very rapid," Kookie revealed.

This Glock may prove more valuable than its weight in gold, Travis thought.

Travis returned the Glock. "That's something that I may need."

Kookie put in a clip, loaded the gun, engaged the safety and put it in a holster.

"Here, Mate, clip the holster over your belt, slip it inside your pants and hide it in the small of your back. Leave your shirt out to hide it. It won't be comfortable to sit down anywhere without it poking you in the back, but even airport screening shouldn't find it. The ammunition won't show up on x-ray either, but you've only got ten rounds, so make them count."

Kookie adjusted the gun so it appeared less noticeable.

* * *

Travis and Kookie arrived at the Nairobi Hilton at 3:00 P.M. They entered a spacious, luxuriant lobby with marble floors and ornate walls. Expensive leather, straight back chairs and tables were arranged around an elaborately designed Turkish rug. The opulent décor contrasted the stark living conditions of most local inhabitants.

Kookie looked about suspiciously.

"Dunno, Mate, maybe we should wait until tomorrow."

"The last flight for today on Sudan Airways, the main carrier to Khartoum, has already left and will arrive there at about 6:00 P.M., just before it gets dark. Also, the charter we checked out doesn't schedule their flights to land at night," Travis reminded him. "Nothing is going to happen tonight."

A young man dressed in hotel uniform addressed them in Swahili.

"No, I don't need any help," Travis replied in English.

The man bowed respectfully and walked back to his station, careful not to show annoyance.

"Do ya think we're dressed Ritzy enough for this place?"

"Can't say, this is a Hilton, not a Ritz," Travis replied.

They both laughed.

"I'll have to check at the counter for a room number," Travis said.

Kookie sat down in a lobby chair to wait, nonchalantly observing the six hotel guests who milled about the lobby.

"Hello. May I help you, sir?" the gentleman behind the counter asked in a heavy English accent.

"Yes, I have an appointment with Ms. Desmonica Houston. May I have the room number, please?" The clerk spoke into the phone and handed it to Travis.

"Hello."

"Who is this?" an abrasive female voice inquired.

"This is Travis Martin, who is this?"

"Who did you call? Come upstairs to room five-twenty-seven," Ms. Houston instructed.

Click.

She had slammed the phone.

She's obnoxious, and I dislike her already. Travis shook his head in distaste.

Kookie followed Travis to the elevator. Two people exited the elevator before Travis and Kookie entered. Travis pushed the number five button.

"Wait," Kookie pushed the pause button when the elevator reached the fifth floor. He checked the transmitting device on Travis' wrist watch. Lifting Travis' jacket, he adjusted the Glock pistol.

"Okay, Mate, I'll be loitering about in the hall."

When Travis left the elevator he turned right and walked until he stood in front of the correct door. He knocked and waited.

"Come in and have a seat." An attractive woman in her thirties with straight black hair motioned for him to enter the room and sit down.

Going right to the heart of the matter, she continued.

"I'm Ms. Houston, Agent at Large. I'll need your signature on this release form. Please read and sign by the x. It's only a formality."

"Before I do this, I've got several questions."

"Sorry, I've been directed not to answer any questions. When you complete this small matter at hand, I'll deliver you to your final destination."

"You're a real Princess," Travis said sarcastically as he took the paper and pen.

Scanning the document confirmed what he suspected, a typical disclaimer. But he felt as if he'd just relinquished his right to life. Considering the options, Travis had no choice, so he signed and dated the document.

"Here, it's signed." Travis handed it back to Miss Houston who put it into a legal size envelope.

Travis' eyes searched the room. The upscale suite featured a large entertainment center on the right of the couch and a wet bar beside a large picture window. A slightly ajar double door revealed a separate bedroom.

This woman is just a minor underling with delusions of grandeur, unless her boss is someone important. Travis decided to find out.

Travis stood up and walked slowly to the wet bar and took out a glass.

"Sit down. I have something important to tell to you." Her tone sounded imperious.

Travis shifted his eyes up to her before he dropped cubes of ice into a glass. He opened the small refrigerator and grabbed a can of coke. Drink in hand, he walked leisurely back and sat on the sofa. He studied Ms. Houston, trying to hold back his desire to take her by her throat and to shake the truth out of her. But she probably didn't know enough to solve his problem, anyway.

If she is the decision maker, she'll take time to evaluate the situation. She'll ask me questions in order to figure me out and call backup if necessary. But if she reacts emotionally my hunch is right – she's nothing more than a lackey.

She rounded in front of him, hands on hips, and blustered.

"I'm here to move you from point 'A' to point 'B' and to ensure that you are not going to get someone killed. Do you think that you can play along?"

"I'm here because you people are pulling my strings and manipulating me. You have something I want, and I need to give you something in return."

"I have the authority to tell my client that it's a go, or to call it off and send you packing," she bristled.

"Well, if you do that," Travis said. "You'd better have a good reason, better than just accusing me of being rude."

She glared at him.

"Where are we supposed to go next?" Travis softened his stance in hopes of gaining information.

"I'll ask the questions first." She regained some composure. "I hardly think that you are going to walk out on me if I fail to cooperate with you, either."

Travis didn't take her bait. He said, "Proceed."

"What's in your bag?" She asked, indicating Travis' shoulder bag.

"Change of clothing, money, shaving kit, and the letter and picture you sent me."

"Are there any weapons?"

"No, they wouldn't get through the airport anyway."

"I'll have to check your pack."

"Have at it." Travis picked it up and tossed it at her feet.

"Later." Ms. Houston stepped around it and proceeded to the bar for an iced drink. She returned savoring an expensive scotch.

She checked his bag and kicked it back over to him.

"Okay, smart guy. We'll leave here in about fifteen minutes. I'll accompany you as far as the airport. You'll fly directly to Khartoum. There you'll meet an executive from the company."

Hairs stood up on the back of Travis' neck.

"What are you talking about? The last commercial plane to Khartoum has already left."

"You're going by chartered plane."

Travis' face registered surprise. She smiled wickedly and continued.

"In less than four hours you'll be on the ground in Khartoum."

She walked over to the telephone and dialed.

"Bring it around to the front. I'll meet you downstairs."

She walked toward the door. Travis fetched his pack and fell in behind her. Exiting the room, they headed toward the elevator.

He passed Kookie in the lobby and studiously avoided meeting his eyes. Circumstances prevented Kookie from getting a flight to Khartoum tonight, and he'd be even less likely to locate Travis tomorrow. Travis had to do this solo.

Lord, I can't do this on my own. I need your miracle working power to see me through, Travis prayed.

"A lie can travel halfway around the world while the truth

is still putting on its shoes"

~ Mark Twain

CHAPTER SEVENTEEN

Andre Jones, a nationally accredited correspondent with Asbury Park Journal, walked with a skip in his step. John Cafferty, the editor of one of America's most influential newspapers, the Daily Times, selected him as part of his team to cover an international event.

Unknown to Cafferty, Andre flew to Nairobi, Kenya, early to meet with the editor of Panapress, which provided news coverage in both English and Arabic. Having worked with these associates previously, he ventured to the fourth floor headquarters on Lenana Road to prepare for the story. After the meeting, the editor introduced him to Simri. Strikingly beautiful but shy, she worked behind the scenes in circulation and advertisement.

"*al Salamu Alaykum*, Peace be with you. I'm new in town. May I take you out to dinner at your favorite restaurant tonight?" Andre asked.

"I am sorry. But that is not possible. *Muslim* women are not permitted to be seen in public with a man who is not related to them."

"May I visit you at your home?"

"I will inquire and let you know."

"When?"

"Tomorrow."

"Yes, that will work. I must return here tomorrow afternoon for a follow-up meeting."

When Andre met with Simri again, he grinned from ear to ear when she told him of her family's invitation to her home that evening.

I have been blessed by Allah. It is my hope that Simri and I can become more than just friends. Andre felt ecstatic.

Of African-American heritage, he blended in with the local people of Nairobi.

However, at five feet eleven inches in height, Andre appeared taller than most of the people he passed. He wore *halal* aftershave, spicy scented oil, for this special occasion. Strict *Muslims* neither consumed alcohol nor wore it on their skin.

I'm tall, handsome and intelligent. I should make a good impression on the family of such an attractive woman, Andre thought with confidence.

Andre found the address. The plain house, poor by

American standards, appeared about average in this community. When he knocked on the door a mustachioed man
in a blue T-shirt opened it. The man measured within a half
inch of Andre's height but with larger biceps, broader
shoulders, and meatier build.

"*al Salamu Alaykum*, you must be this Andre?"

"I am. Peace be with you, too"

"Come in. I am Jaafar," He bowed.

Andre bowed and entered the residence. Once inside he
noticed another man standing by the side of a low table.

"Welcome, I am Simri's brother, Hassan. Please join
us." He bowed slightly from his waist and pointed to the
pillows on the floor near the table.

As he walked toward the table laden with food, he saw
the beautiful Simri at the rear of the room, eyes cast down.
Neither of her brothers acknowledged her presence.

Andre positioned himself on a pillow. Jaafar and Hassan sat along side of two other pillows. Andre slid off his
pillow and imitated his hosts, only leaning on it. Jaafar
leaned sidewise and with one elbow on his pillow he motioned to Simri. She brought them each a steaming cup of
hot coffee. Andre looked up at her, but she avoided eye
contact with him. She did not join the men at the table.

"Please help yourself to the refreshments on the table,"
Jaafar insisted.

Andre watched his hosts. Emulating them, he consumed

the same portions of food. The exotic aromas that promised his palate the taste of tangy spices proved true.

"My sister says she met you yesterday at the Panapress headquarters," Hassan said.

"Yes, I am covering a story for my newspaper, and I met with some senior people at Panapress. Throughout my career, I've specialized in foreign affairs, particularly in the Middle East. Recently, my articles have been focused on Africa, particularly Sudan."

"Simri has told us that you have recently converted to Islam. Is that true?" Jaafar asked.

"Yes, I studied the *Qur'an*, the authentic words of Al-lah. I have also read the *Hadith,* the report of the sayings, deeds and approvals of the Prophet *Muhammad,* Mohammed.

"After my conversion, I began to view the world differently. I adhere to the Five Pillars of Islam: faith, prayer, concern for the needy, self-purification, and *Hajj,* the pilgrimage to Mecca when possible. I also understand the importance of *Jihad* in ushering the coming of the *Twelfth Madi.* I believe this last and greatest *Madi* will come soon and will bring world peace under Islamic rule."

"But you still go by your birth name. Why is that?" Hassan asked.

"For right now I prefer that my conversion would remain a secret. My true name is Abdul Karim Amun."

"But why do you not go by your true name?" Jaafar asked.

"Today it is more fashionable to be a Moslem in America than a Christian, but that could all change with an attack on American soil. I bide my time in order to be in a position to help my new people at the right moment."

I don't need to justify myself to these guys, Andre thought. *But if I want to date the sister I need to have their approval.*

"How does it assist you in helping your people for no one to know you are *Muslim*?" Hassan looked up from sipping his coffee.

"John Cafferty chose me to join his team and to cover an exclusive story. He's the number two man for the largest newspaper in America."

"What will you write about?" Jaafar asked.

"I don't know the full details. However, Mr. Caffery is taking a personal interest, so it's important."

"Is this a good career move for you?" Jaafar asked.

"Yes, now I'm in a position to report stories with the slants I choose when hard times come."

"What hard times do you speak of?"

"I look at the world and see the big picture. As an expert on Middle Eastern affairs, I foresee turmoil in the future and attacks on American embassies and western business interests. When these events occur, I'll report it and spin the news for the Muslim Brotherhood."

"*Jihad* is what some wish for," Jaafar inserted.

"A year ago I interviewed a leader of Hammas. Even today I can contact the man if the need arises."

"*Jihad* can also be unsuspected, for the gullible. Enforcing *Sharia* Law and *Sharia* Finance on all western nations is our purpose. This will be the downfall from within of our enemies, especially the Great Satan – America," Jaafar hissed.

"But we'll discuss this topic another time." Hassan spoke calmly but gave Jaafar a look of warning.

Andre didn't notice the exchange between the two men; he thought only about Simri.

"Thank you for the delicious supper," Andre wiped his mouth and stood up.

"It was our pleasure," Jaafar said. Both men also stood and bowed.

Andre decided to push the question that he had come here to ask. "Do I have your permission to invite your sister out to dinner?"

"*Inshallah.* If Allah wills it, it will happen," Jaafar replied.

Simri stood, head bowed and eyes cast downward as Andre turned to leave. Jaafar walked him to the door.

Andre looked back one more time to see Simri clearing the plates from the table, and he left the house.

After Andre departed, Simri draped her arm across Jaafar's shoulder, and she kissed him. But she did not kiss him the way that a woman kisses her brother.

"A man's life is what his thoughts make of it."

~ Marcus Aurelius

CHAPTER EIGHTEEN

Cafferty awoke with a splitting headache and an upset stomach. One hand cupped his head; the other wrapped his queasy stomach. A greenish tinge suggesting nauseousness spread across his face.

Must have had one drink too many last night. All I remember is Marco bringing the package, and me talking up a storm. He paused and thought about what he remembered saying. *My blabbering didn't do any real damage, but I need to take control of my drinking.*

"OHHH, I feel lousy," Cafferty spoke out loud to no other living soul.

The clock beside the bed read eight-thirty.

I need a couple of aspirins. But I'd better put some food in my stomach first, even if I'm not hungry.

He swung his legs to the floor. Unsteady in his balance, he stopped short as a momentary surge of pain raced to his forehead. He quickly reached for the phone and dialed. His administrative assistance picked up on the second ring.

"Hank, bring me breakfast," Cafferty hung up with no further conversation.

His administrative assistance, Hank Douglas, stayed in a room two doors away. Hank knew Cafferty's dietary likes and dislikes. He didn't always agree with his employer's choices, but he could be counted on to be consistently dependable, efficient, and conscientious.

Hank's honest streak sometimes gets in the way of serious business, Cafferty thought. *I can't completely trust Hank with my most ingenious plans. The idiot stinks of moral principals. He might even feel justified in betraying me if he acquired evidence that I'm masterminding a devious, dangerous plan for my own profit.*

Within twenty minutes Hank Douglas knocked and entered with a breakfast tray. He set it down and began to tidy the room, ridding it of evidence of last night's binge.

"You've secured the rest of the liquor we hid from customs?" Cafferty asked.

"Yes, it's stashed away safely in my room as you requested."

Cafferty knew Hank always spoke the truth because he adhered to his ridiculous absolute moral standards. This bothered Cafferty who believed that only the uninformed masses embraced morality. The real world, the world of power, ran on enlightened self interest.

"Later, I might have need of a bottle. But for now you're dismissed," Cafferty said.

After breakfast Cafferty showered and dressed for his scheduled 10:00 A.M. meeting. When Cafferty left the Hilton Khartoum, a uniformed attendant hailed a cab for him.

Leaving the cab at a public park, Cafferty paid the driver and walked into the park through a sidewalk entrance. He followed a path that curved left toward a side street. When he arrived at his destination, Cafferty turned back, checking to see if he'd been followed. People strolled by but no one looked suspicious. He wasn't aware that from a distance someone watched his every move. About four minutes later a white van pulled to the curb. The side door opened.

"Get in," a heavily accented voice commanded.

Cafferty climbed into the back of van and sat on a bench beside the windowless side door. Three men sitting around him were dressed in *chechai* garments and *djbellah* head pieces, the typical dress of the Arabs in this desert region. They rode in silence. Cafferty couldn't see over the front seats to look out through the front windows, but it seemed as if the van traveled at least twenty kilometers and circled several times before stopping. When the side door opened, Cafferty stood on the grounds of a historical estate. Several hundred years ago it may have been the residence of a wealthy sheik.

Cafferty followed the leader on a stone path and up worn stone steps which had been opulent before centuries of traffic. The man opened an immense wooden door and indicated that Cafferty should enter. An old butler inside bowed, turned and led Cafferty through a richly carpeted room with tasseled, velvet tapestry to another heavy wooden door. When the butler knocked, a voice answered in Arabic. After opening the door and standing aside, the old man made a respectful motion for Cafferty to enter.

"Welcome, Mr. Cafferty, it's good to see you again." Mansoor Huzang bowed and Cafferty returned the greeting.

"You've already met Abu al Sadir," Mansoor Huzang's hand swept sideways.

Abu al Sadir, the man who contacted him in the United States and arranged this meeting, stood beside Mansoor Huzang and bowed slightly.

Cafferty inclined his head and watched as al Sadir exited the room.

"Sit down, Mr. Cafferty." Huzang took a seat at one end of the long rectangular wooden table and indicated Cafferty should sit at the other end.

Dr. Mansoor Huzang wore a stylish, three-piece business suit and a *djbellah* on his head. As Minister of Defense, his position placed him one heartbeat away from the becoming the next leader of the country.

"Please help yourself to the refreshments," Huzang said

and sipped his coffee.

Cafferty noticed the empty cup and plate set in front of him. A carafe and pastry tray stood in the center between them.

"Thank you." Cafferty poured himself a cup of coffee. Sipping the black coffee, he glanced about the room. Heavy draperies framed a large window that looked out onto the grounds. The border, hand painted in gold leaf around the ceiling, represented an intricate Arabic scroll. Cafferty decided it must be real gold. However, he thought the room required repainting and refurnishing. The furniture belonged in some museum, including the long table and eight chairs that occupied the center of the room.

"What is your relationship with the present leader of our country?" Huzang asked.

"I have never met the man. But in my profession we do craft an image for the masses that we want them to see," Cafferty answered.

Cafferty wanted to convey his ability to control public opinion without disavowing loyalty to the man in the seat of power.

Could Huzang be assessing if I can be trusted with some important information? He took another sip of his coffee while he studied the other man over his cup.

"You are number two man at the Daily Times. Your boss' name is Walter Haile. What's he like to work for?"

Huzang asked.

The question took Cafferty by surprise. Obviously Huzang would have already considered approaching Haile with his offer, and rejected this option in favor of contacting Cafferty. If this were not the case, Haile would be here instead.

This man understands the nuances of power, Cafferty thought.

"I believe that he is being prepared for retirement, but it would certainly not be my place to repeat any rumors that would be disloyal to my employer. However, I would like to offer my services if the situation arises, whereby we can be of mutual advantage," Cafferty offered.

"What if you were forced to choose between your own interest and that of your newspaper?" Huzang inquired.

"There are two sides to every story. This is what we call a 'slant' in our industry. My company's goal is to sell more papers and thereby earn more money through advertising. The side that we take in a story only has meaning as to which side will generate more circulation, so to take a slant in exchange for inside information would always be in my paper's interest as well as my own. So you see, the two will always agree," Cafferty explained. He had assessed the man in front of him as intellectual. *However,* Cafferty thought, *his people's civilization peaked a thousand years ago and has only gone downhill from there. They can still be useful. A desert lion might be feared by the jackals, but cunning men still capture them and place the kings of the beasts in iron cages in zoos, to be fed chicken guts while they amuse their betters.*

Now Cafferty asserted himself, letting his voice turn slightly acerbic. "Surely you did not bring me across the Atlantic just to play 'what if' games with me."

"He who sacrifices his conscience to ambition burns a

picture to obtain

the ashes."

~ Chinese Proverb

CHAPTER NINETEEN

Mansoor Huzang sampled a pastry and looked patronizingly at Cafferty, even as he silently weighed both options.

If we write this article as planned all will be well. But if Cafferty puts a slant on this that favors the United States, our nation's deteriorating relationships will only get worse. That may cause other nations to align with the Americans' desire to expand existing sanctions on us.

Huzang decided to collaborate with Cafferty.

"You've been commissioned to write the story of Travis Martin's reunion with his stepson, whom he claims was captured and sold into slavery. But my country is interested in bringing this man to trial for the crimes he committed against Sudan. So your article will include an unusual twist - justice will be served and our president and people will celebrate."

"Of course, I will deliver the spin that exonerates your actions," said Mr. Cafferty.

"In exchange we'll be providing you with crucial, factual information on two other top secret rumors that you can verify – Osama bin Laden's training camps and al-Qaeda's affiliation with our pharmaceutical factory in Khartoum North. Two of the four buildings on the complex manufacture medicines for the cure of malaria and tuberculosis. One building produces veterinary drugs to kill parasites which pass from herds to herder. It's especially beneficial in Sudan which is mostly a pastoral country. But the fourth building generates a deadly Nerve Agent, VX. This site will be marked on the photos you receive."

"Why would you risk your government position or your own life revealing these military secrets?"

"These chemical weapons will not only be used against your country but my people as well. Moderate Moslems and Black Arabs in the North, as well as the Christians and animists in the South,will experience the deadly assault of these chemicals as early as next year if something is not done to prevent their manufacture."

"But, why share this secret information with me?"

"First, no one will suspect that the editor of a liberal newspaper will have an interest in this information. Second, we have no official ties with your nation. Since 1995 the U.S. placed economic sanctions on Sudan for our government's involvement in Egyptian President Hosni Mubarak's assassination attempt. But with your help, your government can know about this pending threat. Most important, the U.S. has the capability to strike a single target. The packet will list the dates when the complex is closed, such as *Ramadan* and other national holidays, thereby avoiding unnecessary bloodshed. Architectural and aerial photos will also be included."

"Why should I risk my life?"

"You've already taken the risk when you put a foot on our soil. You've also accepted the monetary rewards. Now you can gain prestige in your profession. It may prove the ultimate wedge needed to pry open and grasp control of your newspaper agency."

"It's tempting. How do you propose I get this information out of the country and past your security?"

"You have a FAX machine in your hotel room. Isn't that correct?"

"Yes."

"Abu will meet you at the designated time and will supply you with all this information. When the task is completed, he'll leave without delay to destroy the evidence in a most discreet manner."

"It sounds like a plan that might work."

"It will. Of course, you'll receive an advance now." Huzang pulled out a card with the number of a Swiss bank account and a dollar amount beside it. "The amount of your initial advance is indicated on this card as well as your account number in UBS AG, one of Switzerland's leading banks. A final deposit will be made upon completion of this whole affair."

Cafferty accepted the card and placed it in his pants pocket.

"We are both men of the world. You will understand that several important details will be discussed in their entirety later. My man, Abu, will make arrangements to contact you when the time is right," Huzang informed him. "Of course, we invite you to join our president and prominent dignitaries at this significant event. Your presence is highly favored."

Cafferty fidgeted and his eyebrows furrowed over his darting eyes.

"I am bringing you the American rebel as a sign of good faith," Cafferty reminded Huzang.

"Yes, that is a good symbolic gesture. Because this event will trigger international repercussions, you will acquire an exclusive story for your western newspaper. Our local newspaper, the SUNA, will confirm your account," Huzang informed him.

"Yes, I'll be there," Cafferty affirmed, careful not to reveal the reluctance that he felt.

Cafferty stood to leave.

"We have an understanding." Huzang gripped Cafferty's hand and shook it. "Abu will show you to the door. A vehicle is waiting to take you back to your hotel."

Cafferty bowed slightly to the Minister of Defense and left the premise.

"Create the highest, grandest vision for your life be-

cause you become what you believe."

~ Oprah Winfrey

CHAPTER TWENTY

Khartoum, Sudan

The sun, descending from its zenith in the western sky, cast rays of heat upon Major General Ahmed. Facing east for the Azaan, the Islamic call to prayer, he lay prostrate on his prayer rug. It blanketed the hot sand of this semi-arid desert on the outskirts of Khartoum. His personal aide and his other officers dealt with the hot sand clinging to their outstretched palms and uniform the best that they could. All of the worshipers strained to hear the *muezzin's* melodic last lines.

The final phrase '*Is ilaha illa Liah*', meaning 'there is no God except *Allah*', signified the end of the ritual. When possible, worshipers went into a *Mosque,* but a good Moslem prayed wherever he happened to be.

May it be Allah's will to favor me at this meeting,

General Ahmed prayed.

He returned to his personal vehicle, an armored personnel carrier with a plush interior. The middle vehicle in the motorized procession, it followed a van with his entourage aboard.

The Minister of Defense's aide spoke to me personally. But the orders were not written, and this in itself is worrisome, Major General Ahmed recalled.

The Minister of Defense, the second most prominent man in the country after the president, prefers to seek power and wage wars with his tongue. He's the right hand man of the president, who's a ruthless dictator.

The Major General's convoy pulled to a stop in front of the private home of Mansoor Huzang. His entourage stood in proper order, in absolutely straight lines. Chosen for their personal appearance rather than their fighting ability, the Major General promoted each to top rank and paid them well. In return, Major General Ahmed demanded their complete loyalty.

The General's buttons glinted brightly in the sun. With so many medals, his tailor sewed a special lining of a stiff material into the chest of his jacket to support them without his uniform sagging. He displayed a significant array of awards for one who had never fought in combat. Indeed, rank had its privileges.

When the Major General approached, the men snapped

to attention in his honor. Surveying his squad, the General saluted and proceeded to the residence of Dr. Huzang.

Good, the Minister of Defense should be impressed. General Ahmed waved to his personal aide, Colonel Asmath, to accompany him as he strode toward the front entrance.

"A reputation for a thousand years may depend upon

the conduct of a single

moment."

~ Ernest Bramah

CHAPTER TWENTY-ONE

The Minister of Defense looked up from his paper work as Abu slipped into the room.

"Major General Ahmed has arrived with more than twenty soldiers. I told him your instructions to come alone," Abu al Sadir looked worried.

"It's alright Abu, the man is a fool, but fools can also be useful. Is he coming in alone?"

"No, he approaches here with one of his personal aides."

Huzang thought about this for a moment.

"I must talk to the Major General alone. Wait here, Abu. I will use you to detach his man," Huzang com- manded.

"Yes, sir."

An elderly butler ushered in the guests.

"Good afternoon, Major General Ahmed," the Minister of Defense said and bowed.

The Major General saluted and made the introduction. "This is my aide, Colonel Asmath."

The Colonel saluted.

Huzang nodded his head. "*al Salamu Alaykum*, Peace be with you, Colonel. Please enjoy some refreshments while the Major General and I converse. Just follow Abu al Sadir." Huzang made a sweeping motion with his hand.

The Colonel hesitated and looked at the Major General before proceeding.

The Major General looked slightly concerned.

"*Ma'aleesh*. There is no need to worry. Abu will take good care of your officer," Huzang assured him.

The Major General nodded his approval, and the two men left the room.

Dr. Huzang pointed to an empty chair. "Now, why don't you have a seat and take some refreshment with me."

"Thank you." The General wore a plastered-on smile as he sat down before an empty place setting. A large bowl of fresh fruit and a plate with a variety of pastries appealing to the palate occupied the center of the table. A carafe of coffee and Arabian demitasse cups with saucers also graced the ornate hardwood table.

"I had requested that you come alone. I can't image

how you would've arrived had I suggested that you should bring a small party." Huzang smiled as if he found the matter humorous. He needed to establish rules for the future, but not at the cost of making this fool feel insecure.

If a stupid oaf such as this becomes paranoid, his usefulness will be ended.

"I'd wanted you to view the caliber of my most trusted officers, and I brought only my personal guard inside," General Ahmed explained.

"Today we meet to discuss personal matters. Your elite guards are not needed now but will be called in the future for service to our president.

"Of course, sir," General Ahmed shifted his eyes back and forth, feeling uneasy.

Huzang had made his point. He decided to diffuse the General's tension and to move on. Huzang held up his hand and motioned as if flicking a fly.

"Let's not waste time on trivialities; did you have a pleasant drive getting here?"

The General relaxed slightly at this shift in conversation.

"Yes, Defense Minister."

"Please call me Mansoor when we are alone."

"Yes, sir, I mean, Mansoor. It is quite agreeable to spend time with you. I have always wished that we could become better acquainted."

"Sometime *Allah* wishes it to be so," said Huzang. For several minutes longer they chatted about pleasantries.

Major General Ahmed, the fifth most powerful general officer in the nation's service, held his rank only because of political patronage based on his wife's family. His chance of being promoted higher was as likely as a Tsunami engulfing the Sahara Desert.

General Ahmed is ambitious, despite his lack of ability, and I suspect that he despises General Araak and the other four generals over him as much as they ridicule him, Huzang thought.

"I would prefer to chat all afternoon, but we should probably get down to business," Huzang said.

"Certainly, Mansoor, duty must come first."

"This concerns the matter that occurred three years ago at your military base. The president is still disturbed regarding the incident. Do you recall it?"

"Yes, I do. Three years ago an American terrorist and an SPLA rebel attacked our base, killed several soldiers, blew up ammunition, and destroyed nearly a third of our helicopters. Deplorably, they escaped on a nearby security river boat that wasn't properly guarded and later destroyed it."

"Yes, that is correct. This unfortunate incident, disappointed and embarrassed our president greatly, but he is offering you an opportunity to exonerate yourself. Would you be interested in hearing his proposition?"

"Of course."

"You and ten of your elite guard will participate in the capture and return of the American terrorist, Travis Martin. You and your men must be ready on a moment's notice. The mission will include transporting ten soldiers in helicopters to a designated location. You and your personal guard will arrive separately in an army vehicle, but prior to your soldiers' arrival.

"I require the complete loyalty of you and your officers. If for any reason you are not available to command, your officers will take their orders directly from me."

"We are at your service. When will this operation initiate?"

"Soon. Information will be sent by a trusted courier or Abu al Sadir. When possible, I will personally confirm this by a telephone call. If you have something to report to me, think of al Sadir as my own eyes and ears."

"Yes sir. I will be your loyal servant until the day that I die."

Huzang invited the General to stay for dinner and had the kitchen staff feed the General's men outdoors.

He covered a few more points of their futuristic political plans between personal talk about the glorious histories of their two regal families. At 7:00 P.M. the Major General and his men left.

Huzang invited Abu to join him in the sitting room.

"Abu, my trusted friend, the meeting went as expected. Tomorrow I will need your services. You will carry a message to our loyal supporter Colonel Arok Mekki and give him a personal update of our current plans. Already he has provided me with the most current information regarding internal affairs. Colonel Mohammed Isam will also receive an update by courier."

"The newly appointed commander of the National Islamic Front?"

"Yes."

"But his loyalties are to the president only," Abu noted.

"Yet his presence will be necessary for this military operation to succeed."

"Values are not just words; values are what we live by.

They're about the causes that we champion and the

people we fight for."

~ John Kerry

CHAPTER TWENTY-TWO

Khartoum, Sudan

Sudan's newest flag hung in a prominent place, behind the podium in the parliament, *the Majlis Welayat.* The flag featured horizontal red, white and black stripes, with a green triangle at the hoist. This combination of colors has been linked to the Arab people and Islamic religion for centuries. The red stripe represents Sudan's struggle for independence and the sacrifices of the country's martyrs. The white stripe stands for peace, light, and optimism. The black stripe names the country. 'Sudan' means black in Arabic. Green refers to Islam, agriculture and the prosperity of the land.

Dr. Mansoor Huzang stood and walked to the podium.

He glanced around the Chamber where the assembled representatives were dressed in a kaleidoscope of colorful traditional garb and stylish western apparel. This legislative body clearly reflected a true cultural melting pot where Arabia met native Africa, representing over 590 tribes and speaking more than 130 languages.

Dr. Huzang bowed before the newly elected parliament and gave a short speech of acceptance as Speaker of the National Assembly.

"I am honored to be your Speaker and pledge to work with you to solve our problems and propose solutions that are in our country's best interest. The president has asked me to extend his congratulations to each one of you. He's also asked me to inform you that Sudan has proposed the opening of a trade center in Dubai in the United Arab Emirates. This proposal will help our farmers and shipping companies on the Red Sea. In the future, I will be sharing current updates. Now it's time to hear from each of you about the status of your prospective states."

The Federalism Decree of 1991 divided Sudan into nine states. These states had borders and names that were similar to the historical nine provinces of Sudan during the colonial period and early years of independence. The people of each state elected their representative to the National Assembly to voice the concerns of their constituents. The recent elections increased these administrative divisions. The new

1997 Parliament now hosted representatives from twenty-six states. But the states remain economically dependent on the central government and have limited control of government affairs.

Dr. Huzang called on a member who raised his hand.

"Mr. Speaker, I am Bior Majok and I represent the State of Kordofan. My district is concerned about the new oil project with the Chinese government run by the Greater Nile Petroleum Company. Armed militia has forcibly displaced thousands of Southern Sudanese who lived along the projected fifteen-hundred mile pipeline to the Red Sea. Entire villages in the Abyei Region were razed to the ground. Those who resisted were slaughtered. The majority of the survivors remain homeless today."

"I will make note of this and discuss this with the Committee for Economic Expansion," Dr. Huzang replied.

When the representative took his seat, Dr. Miheisi spoke into the microphone.

"Mr. Speaker, I am Dr. Omar Miheisi, and I represent the State of Jebel, in Southern Sudan. My constituents question the government's refusal to renew permission for Operation Lifeline Sudan to bring in needed food and water.

"Normally relief agencies sponsored by the OLS make about thirty flights during June and July. But since the Sudanese People's Liberation Army is gaining popularity with some of the people in this region, the Khartoum government has put a stop to OLS flights to punish the people by eliminating these deliveries of food and medicines. As you are aware, both the Northern nomadic regions and the Southern regions face serious drought and a looming danger of famine."

"Internal Affairs will investigate this matter," Dr. Huzang said.

"Thank you."

"I am Deng Khalil and I represent the Dinka people in the State of Kangen. We strongly disagree with the imposed *Sharia Laws*. In the past, the Khartoum government has sent militia to annihilate our people. Over ten thousand of my fellow tribesmen and their families have been tortured and lost their lives. Our children have been taken into captivity by the Janjaweed. Still villages burn and wells are made useless. Survivors cannot return to their homes and must reside in make-shift camps along the borders. We request that the government stop funding these bandits."

"I believe you are in error to state that the Khartoum government supplies the Janjaweed with weapons," stated Dr. Huzang.

"Not only does the Khartoum government supply the Janjaweed with weapons made in China, it also pays the raiders a salary," Deng Khalil replied.

"The homeland security committee will investigate

your claims," Dr. Huzang assured him.

The Assembly continued discussing matters on the agenda until 5:00 P.M. when they adjourned for the day.

When the first session ended, a man dressed in native attire approached the Speaker.

Dr. Omar Miheisi handed Dr. Huzang a written invitation. "According to the Congressional Calendar, you will visit our district next week. I would like to invite you for lunch when you travel to Juba."

"Dr. Miheisi, I am going to Juba to assess the damage done to the city by the SPLA."

"Although the SPLA are gaining strength in numbers, their artillery hasn't damaged our buildings," corrected Dr. Miheisi. "But they've managed to cut off the supply lines to the government garrison located just outside of Juba."

"Thank you. I'll inform you if time will allow me to accept this gracious offer." Huzang bowed and turned to exit the building.

* * *

The following week, Minister of Defense Huzang booked an early morning flight on the feeder airline to Juba. After his plane flew over the Juba Kujor Mountains, he glanced down at the city of over 55, 000 people.

When the plane landed at the Juba Airport, Colonel

Atem Jungroor, the garrison commander, greeted Dr. Huzang. Next they traveled by jeep on one of two paved roads in Juba toward army headquarters. On the way, their vehicle slowed and detoured around soldiers repairing the road. Upon their arrival at the base, a formal inspection of the troops transpired. Next Huzang and Col. Jungroor traveled by jeep to assess the damage caused by the SPLA. Structural damage to the port on the Nile River would take months to repair.

"Have the rebels returned since the initial attack?" Dr. Huzang asked.

"Yes, until two weeks ago skirmishes continued. Three days ago they fought our troops in Yirol. The battle lasted five and a half hours and over 700 of our soldiers stationed there were killed. The others fled here to Juba. The SPLA captured large quantities of arms and ammunition. Our sources claim that the rebels are advancing northwest to join forces with the Justice and Equality Movement," stated the Colonel.

"These Justice and Equality people. Who are they?" Huzang asked.

"They are black Moslem dissidents from the Darfur region."

"They are followers of Islam?"

"Yes sir."

"Indeed? Fax me a report and keep me informed," the

Minister of Defense commanded.

Dr. Huzang proceeded to his next scheduled stop, Governor Roussus' residence. The first floor of his home served as a government office where the men conducted official business. Upon completion, he left for his next appointment. Before the chauffeur could pull into traffic, a procession of two bicycles, three motorized vehicles and a herd of fifty cattle passed by. Their car followed and ventured out into the slow moving traffic.

As prearranged, Dr. Huzang and Dr. Miheisi met for lunch at a secluded family-owned café. Dr. Huzang dismissed his driver with instructions to return in an hour.

The proprietor of the café greeted Dr. Miheisi with a kiss on both cheeks and bowed respectfully to the Minister of Defense. He escorted them both to a table at the far corner of the small restaurant.

Sudanese cuisine reflected the diverse nature of the country. Southern Sudanese cookery had much in common with Ethiopian cuisine. However the dishes served in northern and western Sudan reflect an Arabic influence.

The proprietor served the house specialty. First, a plate of *garaasa,* Sudanese flatbread topped with sesame seeds, and small bowls of jams were placed on the rough wooden table. Next his wife brought their guests each a Sudanese *Aubergine Salad,* made with purple eggplant and a touch of peanut butter. Carrying the dish with flare, the proprietor brought the main course, *Maschi* - an aromas spicy dish of minced beef and tomatoes.

"The house special for dessert is a surprise."

Dr. Miheisi nodded and a soldier came from the back room and sat down at their table. "Dr. Huzang, I'd like you to meet Dr. John Garang, leader of the SPLA."

For a brief moment time stood still as the Minister of Defense quickly assessed his predicament. From the corner of his eye he saw Abu sitting at a table near the door and waiting for a signal to interfere. But Dr. Huzang regained his composure, blinked his eyes once and shook his head slightly back and forth.

"Dr. Garang, what an unexpected encounter. You risk you life being in my presence knowing that I would be shadowed, and I risk being accused of conspiracy against my government." Dr. Huzang stated. "Nevertheless I admire your boldness. So what brings the leader of the resistance here?"

"You're a prominent politician in our country and a lawyer by profession. I've come to plea our people's cause before you." He paused. "We both have something in common: you and I were born in Sudan but graduated from Western universities. Most important we're both familiar with western democratic governments where every citizen enjoys certain liberties."

"Yes, it's true that I hold a Ph.D. degree in Law from

the University of Paris, but how is this important to our discussion?"

"We are rebels with a cause. We fight for our right to exist, for *uhura* - freedom from slavery, freedom from torture, and freedom from genocide," John Garang stated with a controlled, firm voice.

"Our government presses for unity of our country over racial, ethnic and tribal identity. But your people and the tribes of the South have disobeyed the laws of Sudan," Dr. Huzang countered.

"Sudan's dictatorial government brutally imposes Islamic fundamentalism on Christians and animists. *Sharia Law* denies us the right to practice our own religious beliefs. Referring to us as infidels, you justify your practice of Jihad on the innocent, denying us the right to live." Dr. Garang made a decision not to dwell on the horror of the truth he spoke but on the purpose of this discourse.

"Our government has used the military to advance the Moslem cause at home and abroad," Dr. Huzang explained.

"Due to our different ideologies, our nation has engaged in our nation's Second Civil War for twenty-one years," Dr. Garang reminded him.

"It's a war that our present government will win. Our army officers are disciplined, and our soldiers outnumber your rebels. Our modern weapons and equipment outperform your antiquated guns. The Chinese government will supply us with an inexhaustible supply of artillery to meet our needs. So why do you continue to fight a battle you can't win?" Dr. Huzang's face looked perplexed.

"What we lack in machinery, we make up for in purpose, heart and sacrifice."

"You must know that our military superiority can't be surpassed," Dr. Huzang stated emphatically.

"I respectfully disagree. Your eyes are blinded to the source of our strength. Our God in Heaven and one soldier fighting for a righteous cause is ultimately an unbeatable combination." The assurance in John Garang's voice was unmistakable.

Huzang decided to return to his favorite discourse and reiterated.

"Politically, I am a progressive and seek the cooperation of all of our citizens to promote economic growth and prosperity to our nation. Unfortunately this has not yet occurred. Instead our freedom from colonial rule has brought greater bloodshed, poverty and division. It concerns me that a nation divided against itself cannot stand."

"This division will eventually destroy our nation as we know it," Colonel Garang agreed. "So what do you propose to do to bring peace into this situation?"

"Reform begins with our Parliament. It provides a voice for all the people of Sudan. I believe democracy for all people is possible within an Islamic State. The writings of our great Prophet *Muhammad* may provide the answers we seek. During the days of the prophet, the Jews of Medina were not subjected to *Sharia law.* So why should we *Muslims* today force *Sharia law* on Christian subjects?"

"Perhaps, for the same reasons that Hammas wishes to annihilate the Jews living in Israel. Neither the Moslem radicals nor President al-Bashir, who uses the military power to violate human rights, tolerate anyone who disagrees with *Sharia law.*"

"It is my vision that we would continue *Sharia Law*, but that it would only apply to *Muslims.* Both *Muslims* and Christians would share power in a federal system of government."

"For that to happen, we'll need the influence of the United States and the United Nations to force our government to a cease fire and allow the people of Southern Sudan the right to vote. We would choose either to unite as one nation or secede and form an independent state."

"That's an interesting concept." Dr. Huzang felt as is he'd just finished dessert as one of his favorite activities included the discussion and interchange of political ideas.

"Perhaps if you and I work together for peace, we may find a way. Now I must leave, but I hope we'll talk again."

"I look forward to another exchange," Huzang said.

"Until that time comes, my people will continue to fight for freedom." Colonel John Garang rose from his seat.

Immediately, two soldiers with rifles ready joined him. Sandwiched between his men, Colonel John Garang proceeded to the back of the building. Abu, hand on his weapon, watched as the enemy exited.

"The current state of the news media is partially to blame for the public's general lack of information vital for responsible citizenship in a democracy. The news media has become an aspect of show business, offering merely infotainment. It has evolved into an entity that tends to function as a public relations agency for wealthy and powerful multinational corporations…."

~ Teresa Stover

CHAPTER TWENTY-THREE

Walter Haile, publisher of one of the largest international newspapers, the Daily Times, flew from Denver, Colorado, to Switzerland in response to an invitation from Mr. Rufus Spurlock. Rufus Spurlock, widely reputed to be the richest man in the world, possessed tremendous influence. Walter Haile, dressed in a three piece suit and carrying a leather attaché case, paused in the lobby of the

Central Plaza Hotel to consult with his Rolex. The time-piece's face showed 9:30 A.M.

"Walter?"

Haile turned at the sound of his name and saw an old friend. "Sir Richard, what brings you to Zurich?"

"Probably the same as you, a request from the Great One, Rufus Spurlock."

"Indeed? And how is everything at the <u>London Times</u>?"

"I can't complain," Sir Richard said. "But we aren't the only ones with invitations. When I first arrived, I chatted with Yoshiro Nagasumi and Jose Gonzales. I also met a newcomer, Robert Stone, the publisher of Spurlock's latest acquisition, <u>Modern Media</u>. They've already gone into the hotel restaurant for coffee. Now I'm certain that it's no co-incidence that we, the publishers of some of the largest in-ternational newspapers, have converged here."

"Whose economy is he planning on destroying this time?" Haile's face registered alarm.

"Well, The Great One is already making strides toward breaking the bank of England and destroying the pound sterling."

"No way!" Haile shook his head in disbelief.

"Yes, inflation is at a new high in England. But watch out, after the U.K. your United States economy could be his next domino."

"I don't think so," Haile said. "He has a lot of investments in the United States that would be affected. Even Bill Gates wouldn't like it."

"Spurlock wouldn't care," Sir Robert said. "He has major investments in the United Kingdom, and he'll leverage most of them so that he'd make more money if the pound sterling fails. And his nibs wouldn't care about Bill Gates or Microsoft. They're minor players; Gates only has one billion dollars. Spurlock's balance sheet shows over twenty billion dollars on his ledger, or so I'm told."

"What's this meeting all about?" Haile asked.

"I haven't the foggiest notion. We'll have to just wait and see."

"Rufus Spurlock didn't become rich spending money on airline tickets when telephone calls would suffice. This meeting must be important," Haile reasoned.

"He's a mover and a shaker. Surely he's planning the future, but without our consent," Sir Richard stated.

"What's more frightening, if you peak behind his mask you'll see a narcissist. His disguise as a philanthropist makes him treacherous because his only true concern is promoting his own self-interests and power grabs." Changing the subject Haile suggested. "We have less than a half-hour before the scheduled meeting, let's join the others."

"Cheerio," Sir Robert said, leading the way.

"Whoever controls the media, the images, controls the

culture."

~ Allen Ginsberg (American poet)

CHAPTER TWENTY-FOUR

"Gentlemen, thank you for coming." A confident Rufus Spurlock addressed the audience of ten chief executives of major international newspapers as well as two special guests who entered the small but elegant meeting room.

"Please help yourselves to the drinks at the bar and to the refreshments."

The uniformed waiters filled orders for the finest wine and assorted alcoholic drinks. Drink in hand, the gentlemen descended on decorative covered tables with a variety of specialty appetizers. Some chose seafood cocktails or hors d'oeuvres while others preferred the caviar and canapé.

Rufus Spurlock turned and whispered to the commander of his specialized security squad. "After everyone is seated, dismiss the servants. Is everything in place?"

"Yes sir, the room is clean. There are no listening or recording devices, and our localized EMF shield surrounds the room."

"Good, Charles, continue to monitor."

The six foot one, stern faced man with military cut hair nodded with a quick motion of his head.

Rufus observed those assembled. These publishers, the top men in major newspapers he owned, required a small dose of reality. Occasionally, they got delusions of grandeur and had to be taken down a peg and reminded to whom they owed their true allegiance. He had made them, and he could break them.

"Gentlemen, we hope you're enjoying the refreshments. I've called you together to share privileged information concerning an upcoming event. After you receive this brief overview, you'll be aware of my personal concerns when the time for action arrives. As usual, this meeting never took place, and I never made any statement regarding this topic. Furthermore, if anyone reports a story against my interests he had better have his retirement planned. Is that understood?" The haughtiness in his demeanor spoke louder than his words.

Heads nodded around the room and everyone murmured in agreement.

Rufus sensed an air of apprehension in the room. Some of the members appeared physically tense. Marvin Turner used a white handkerchief to dab the beads of perspiration on his forehead even though the room's thermometer read 75 degrees.

Fear can be an effective tool. But right now, I require the loyalty of my employees. Furthermore, I will assure these gentlemen that their commitment will be rewarded.

He addressed the assembly again.

"Please take your seats." Rufus paused allowing his guests to comply. "Now let's commence our meeting. You're here because you will be part of imminent changes in our world for the good of all mankind. You will all be key players on my team in this transformation."

Everyone nodded and murmured agreement.

"Good, any questions so far?"

The Brit, Sir Robert, lifted his right hand about half way up over his head. "Sir, when we write our editorials regarding current events and concerns, isn't it our responsibility to report the facts; specifically to present both sides of the issues?"

Rufus thought about putting this man in his place.

"Sir Robert, as you know, we abide by all regulations of the FCC and strive to serve the public interest. My organization purchased your newspaper and other media outlets for a variety of reasons. The meager profits your newspapers have been earning is not the major one. You are. You've all proven that you're the top in your profession, and I pay you the salaries you deserve because I can count on you to print information designed to enlighten the masses. Look around you, we are an elite group. It is our duty to convince the people of our great planet that a united government is their source of security, and this goal deserves our complete loyalty. We are birthing a better idea and this process is rather intense, even painful as delivery approaches. Of course, there are always some misguided thinkers who may need convincing or monetary enticements. Gentlemen, let me illustrate. Notice the black vase on the cloth covered table beside me. I'll pay one thousand dollars to anyone who can convince me that it is really red," challenged Rufus.

He held up a crisp one thousand dollar bill.

"You may come up and inspect closer, but you may not touch it. Would anyone like to take my wager?" The room became silent as if in a void.

"No one?"

Rufus pulled one portion of the covered cloth to reveal a hidden small, round button. When he pressed it, the black vase instantly changed to crimson red.

"Wow."

Audible exclamations and other spontaneous utterances filled the room.

Mr. Spurlock grinned. "Gentleman, YOU control the button. You have the power. Remember that.

"Now I will share vital information that must not leave

this room."

Sir Robert is leaning forward and displaying signs of subservience Rufus thought. *However, Haile's body language reveals nothing and his facial expressions are masked. That's intriguing.*

He finished his brief scan around the room.

"One of our organization's other interests includes the control of natural resources. We are here today to discuss the acquisition of oil. Oil drives our world's economy. Specifically we want the rights to drill for oil in Southern Sudan. This location is the most recent site of major discovery, but most of the contracts to build and extract oil from the wells are going to China. The Chinese have also proposed to build an infrastructure of roads to transport the oil from the wells to the Nile. They'll export this black gold to their own country."

Rufus Spurlock paused; a serious look crossed his face. He raised his voice and commanded, "Our organization desires those contracts!"

Pausing again, he smiled genuinely and waved one arm at the two guests dressed in black business suits, wearing white chechias on their heads.

"Fortunately Sudan's Minister of Defense and the leader of the National Islamic Front are more closely aligned with our interests than the current Sudanese president is. Does everyone grasp the significance of this?"

Heads bobbed up and down as the entire room filled with murmurs of approval.

"Good," Rufus continued. "If there is ever cause to report on this subject, remember whose side you are on, and be certain your stories are on page one, and not buried on page five."

Rufus made eye contact with every publisher in the room, seeking affirmation.

"Good, my friends. I'm heartened we are all on the same page. Together we'll make positive changes, thereby changing the world as we now know it.

"I must leave for another appointment, but Colonel Mohammed el Isam and Mr. Abu al Sadir will answer your questions regarding the slant we deem essential. Gentleman, I give you Mr. al Sadir and Colonel Isam, the leader of the National Islamic Front."

When Colonel Isam approached the microphone, Rufus bowed. When he stood upright, Rufus introduced his primary speakers. Everyone applauded.

"Please give Colonel Isam and Mr. al Sadir your undivided attention."

Rufus bowed again and exited discreetly. He'd previously assigned his security crew to record the remainder of the meeting. He would review it later at his convenience.

"The best thing about the future is that it comes one day

at a time."

~ Anonymouos

CHAPTER TWENTY-FIVE

Kenya, Africa

The morning sunlight shone down on the Savannah as Karasa walked the familiar path to her sister's hut. Secured in a cloth carry-all on her back, eighteen month-old Tamara slept as she gently rocked to the gait of her mother's strides. In the distance Karasa watched several small groups of children entering the village Mission School. Passing the banyan tree, she turned down the path to Ayella's hut.

"*Jambo,* Jamala. The children have left for school and I'm ready to go," Karasa's younger sister Ayella said, exiting her home. A young widow, Ayella had two children, fourteen year old Myonne and ten year old Wema.

Adjusting her shopping bag over her right shoulder,

Ayella grinned and bubbled with enthusiasm.

"Good, we will go now," Karasa said.

Karasa's family and friends called Karasa by her birth name, Jamala. Only Travis used her warrior name, which meant mongoose in Swahili. She earned it in combat fighting with the Sudanese People's Liberation Army because she had killed snakes, both animal and human.

Their weekly trek to market would take about thirty-five minutes. Strolling north about thirty meters on another dirt path, they approached their mother's hut.

"There's no need for us to stop," Karasa spoke abruptly.

"What?" Ayella glanced at her sister in surprise.

"Yesterday, mother told me what she needed."

"But you know how much she enjoys seeing Tamara."

Following tradition, as the eldest daughter, Jamala named her first daughter after her mother's mother. However, she didn't believe, as common practice among other African tribes, that the spirit of her grandmother dwelled in Tamara. She believed that God created each baby with his own unique personality and attributes. More importantly, Tamara could invite the powerful Holy Spirit to reside in her once she chose Jesus Christ as her Lord and Savior.

"We'll visit later." Karasa's firm tone indicated this conversation had ended.

Walking in silence, they passed their parent's small

garden and orchard.

"Look, the Cranberry Hibiscus still blooms." Karasa pointed to two pink flowers with scarlet centers on a crimson bush on the edge of their parents' plot. As she stepped closer, she plucked a maroon leaf and began to munch on the tangy tasting leaf. Ayella did likewise.

The Cranberry Hibiscus, domesticated in Sudan, grows wild in tropical Africa and adds a distinctive flavor to salads or cooked rice. The leaves and young shoots were edible and the stem provided a good quality fiber source.

A slight breeze from the west swirled the red dust as it rose with each footfall, as if the dirt road had transformed into a living thing that sought to prevent their departure from home. On the outer edge of the pastoral community, they waved to Jacob as they passed the family's herd of goats, grazing on the thick mat of kikuyu grass near the kraals.

Trailing the other villagers at a distance far enough to avoid being heard, Ayella renewed their conversation.

"Jamala, is there anything wrong? Anything you want to talk about?"

How do I share with Ayella my deepest burden? I will just speak it out, Karasa thought.

"Ayella, I think something has happened to Travis, maybe something bad. I believe that Father and Mother have information they are not sharing with me."

"I would not worry. If it were important, you would have been told."

"Maybe you are right, but I want to visit the *Simba Safari*, the place my husband works. It is in town, not far from the market place."

"Well, if it is important to you, we can go there after we get our supplies."

"That is a good plan," Karasa agreed.

"The doors we open and close each day

decide the lives we live."

~ Flora Whittemore

CHAPTER TWENTY-SIX

Lapaki, Kenya

Karasa and Ayella continued on their journey to the open markets on the outskirts of Lapaki. Starlings flew overhead and java sparrows feasted on the insects concealed in the grasses. Low scrub boxwood bushes and palm trees increased as the path neared the stream that wandered past their village. The waters had begun to recede.

"Isn't this where you and Travis killed that big crocodile last year?" Ayella asked.

"Yes, but it happened later in the dry season when the low water levels turned the river to a stream of mud," Karasa said.

"I would have been frightened," Ayella confessed. "That beast was enormous."

"That croc traveled overland looking for water. When it

charged, we had no choice but to shoot it."

Karasa carried a heavy .44 magnum revolver while Travis favored a lighter Walther P-38 9 mm automatic. Travis favored accuracy over knock-down power. However, he refused to admit that she had killed the twenty-one foot croc. Firing simultaneously, the bullets penetrated its skull and smashed the croc's brain, stopping it in its tracks.

"That ugly croc was not afraid of his little bullets," Karasa boasted. "My shot brought it down."

"Your husband said you were wrong, that his shot hit it between the eyes and killed the croc instantly."

"No, my bullets are bigger and went deeper into its skull," Karasa contradicted.

"I'm just saying what Travis told me," Ayella countered.

Karasa sighed and rolled her eyes. She lifted her loose fitting blouse to adjust the heavy revolver on her right hip. She transferred her canvas shoulder bag over her left side to hide the slight bulge.

"I have not needed it since that day, but I am prepared."

The Kenyan officials levied fines to poachers for killing crocodiles, but if a crocodile left the water and ventured close to a village, it becomes fair game. It was too dangerous for it to be otherwise.

"Well, Mother's tasty crocodile stew could have won a cooking contest," Ayella said.

"Best of all, the meal fed everyone in our family and our friends, too."

Tamara woke up.

"May I carry her?" Ayella asked.

"Of course."

"Hoppie," Tamara pointed. A big, weirdly colored grasshopper jumped up from the road ahead of them.

"Grasshopper," Karasa affirmed.

Ayella put Tamara down on the path as it flew by making a strange, clicking, *nack, nack, nack* sound as if warning them not to follow.

Tamara chased after the grasshopper. The insect hid in the foliage, now camouflaged. She searched without success to locate it.

"Look, Tamara. I see a bird." Karasa pointed at a ruby-cheeked sunbird in a tree. Her attempt to distract Tamara succeeded.

"Come, we will look for more animals." Karasa and Ayella each grabbed Tamara's hand, as they walked leisurely on the path with the child between them. They reached the outskirts of the marketplace.

When the path widened, they glimpsed a big baobab tree that offered little shade as the dry season approached. Its leaves fluttered softly to the ground. Spread out near the baobab tree, the nearby villagers assembled a community market of wooden booths with poles to support the palm thatch ceilings. Merchants displayed their wares on stands or in containers made of woven baskets, large gourds or hemp bags. Items also hung from cords attached to the roof. Most shops were collapsible, carried off at night and stored away along with the vendors' goods.

Here local residents, most living at subsistence level, purchased household items and seasonal produce. Besides the common staples, several vendors sold locally made items like woven cloth and home-made jewelry.

"*Jambo,*" the merchants waved and shouted at prospective buyers who began to converge on the area.

"Mother needs some rice, and I want to buy cornmeal to make ugali porridge," Karasa said

"Jamala, I am going to shop at Roroa's stand. Roroa is like her name, she is always talking."

"Roroa feels important when she shares the local news, but her words sound more like gossip. I try to avoid her," Karasa said.

"That's why I'm going there. To find out what I can. Besides, I need some black beans." Ayella dashed off.

Karasa stopped by the nearby stall of Mama Phoebe, a friend of hers.

"*Jambo*, do you want a drink?" Mama Phoebe touched a faded blue cooler. Having neither ice nor electricity the drinks cooled in a few inches of water. Mama Phoebe drank none of the contents she offered because she couldn't afford to consume her merchandise.

"Yes, I will take a bottle of juice. Tamara is thirsty." She chose a juice and gave Tamara small sips to quench her thirst.

"I would also like a small bag of rice at the usual price," Karasa said.

Using a gourd with a handle, Mama Phoebe scooped out the rice from the large burlap bag and began to measure it out.

After the sale, Karasa headed to the center compound to purchase cornmeal. She noticed that Ayella still lingered near Roroa's stall inspecting other food items. Two other women chatted with Roroa.

By the time Karasa had made her purchase, Ayella rushed up to her panting.

"Guess what I just overheard," Ayella paused to catch her breath. "Itikada's husband has just been hired by *Simba Safari.* They needed to replace someone right away. Itikada is so happy about her husband's new job and can't stop talking about his good luck."

"What does this have to do with Travis?"

"Maybe Travis is the one who left."

"But why would he leave the job that he really enjoys? We must find out."

Fifteen minutes later they had entered the town of Laikipia, and walked to the *Simba Safari Adventure, Ltd,* headquarters on First Street.

I'll wait out here with Tamara," Ayella offered.

"I won't be long."

"*Jambo,* Moran." Karasa greeted the man behind the counter, dressed in traditional Maasai attire. "I want to check if Travis will be back on schedule?"

"I don't know," Moran looked discomfited. "He came in and cancelled his scheduled *safari.* Instead, he booked a private tour with an Australian."

"What did Kiambu say?" Karasa asked.

"Kiambu exploded with anger at the news on such short notice. He calmed down only after Travis helped him to locate a replacement."

"Thanks, I want to speak to Kiambu."

"He's busy right now."

"I will wait!"

Moran reconsidered and entered the back office, shutting the door behind him. When he reappeared, Moran wore a serious expression.

"You may go in."

As Karasa went through the door, the portly owner of the company greeted her warmly.

"*Jambo,* Kiambu. What is going on with my husband?" Karasa asked.

Kiambu avoided Karasa's stare. "Travis had his own charter. It cut me short, but I understand that helping to make a Hollywood movie was too good an offer to pass up. I just wish they had offered it to my company instead of going straight to him."

"A movie company? Is that what this is all about?" Puzzled, Karasa clenched her fists and crossed her arms in front of her.

Kiambu began to fidget, seemingly at a loss for words.

Kiambu is not a man who lies well. But Travis trusts this man, and Kiambu will not betray my husband's secret. I will get no further information from him. With turmoil within, she remained outwardly calm.

"If you see him would you ask him to contact me?" Karasa asked.

"I certainly will," Kiambu nodded with a sigh of relief.

Ayella met Karasa as she exited the front door and couldn't contain her curiosity. "What happened?"

"Travis quit the scheduled twenty-three day *safari*. He went on his own charter with Kookie. Kiambu said the Australian is from a movie company. But I do not believe him. Travis did not mention making a movie." Karasa frowned, still upset that she couldn't extract the truth from Kiambu.

"I must learn the truth. I must know *kweli.*"

Karasa held out her arms to Tamara. "Come."

Tamara embraced her mom.

"What are you going to do, Jamala?" Ayella asked as

they walked back toward the marketplace.

"I will go to the Ensebbe Refugee Camp. If Jim knows something, then Ellen knows it also. One thing I am certain of, Ellen will never lie to me."

"What about Tamara?" Ayella's face conveyed concern.

"Will you take her home with you?" Karasa's eyes were moist with sorrow.

"Of course," Ayella replied.

"Father will burst in anger like boiling porridge."

"Yes, I know. But that is what sisters are for, to help each other in times of need. Besides, Father also understands that Tamara must be cared for until you return. I will do it, even if I am reprimanded and restricted to the village."

"I am sad that my disobedience will fall on your shoulders," Karasa said.

"If it must be, then let it be so."

"My home is your home. You must make use of the supplies, water tank and garden to help provide for our two families. Promise me."

"Yes. All will be well. Myonne will help and Wema will play with Tamara."

"I knew I could depend on you." Karasa reached over to give Ayella a hug.

"You will need supplies for the journey. Here, take the

fresh fruit and nuts that I have purchased."

"You must take this bag of rice to mother."

They made the exchange and hugged again.

"Thank you." Karasa's lips parted slightly in an attempt to smile. She kissed Tamara and returned her to Ayella.

"Go with God. He will bring you home again," Ayella said.

Karasa waved, turned, and didn't look back. Only a tiny tear that trickled down her cheek betrayed her true emotion - fear. The fear of what she did not know and fear of what she might find out. Both haunted her as she departed.

"Do what you feel in your heart to be right- for you'll be

criticized anyway. You'll be damned if you do, and

damned if you don't."

~ Eleanor Roosevelt

CHAPTER TWENTY-SEVEN

On the midmorning of the third day of Karasa's trek she veered from the dirt road and approached the Ensebbe Refuge Camp. For the protection and safety of the inhabitants, a wall of acacia branches covered by a multiplicity of thorns surrounded the camp. The acacia tree grew thorns the size of large sewing needles and just as sharp.

"Halt," commanded the gate guard. The young man, dressed in a mismatched green uniform, held up his right hand. Tall and lanky with a complexion as dark as coal, the Dinka warrior bore a series of bold scars on his forehead that identified his clan. If necessary he'd enforce the request with an automatic rifle slung on his shoulder. For good measure a basket of pineapple grenades with their pins in place lay on the ground just inside the gate.

"*Jambo*, Micah. It is me, Karasa," Karasa paused. "It has been over three years since we fought together with the SPLA."

"I didn't recognize you at first. Now I remember. You fought beside Captain Jeshi to defend our people against the slavers. Today we've gained even more support for our cause. I will be reporting back to active duty in two weeks now that I have recovered from a gunshot wound. Colonel Garang believes that in the near future we will win. We will be free, *Uhuru*! "Micah shouted.

"Yes, we will because of you and the brave men who still fight," Karasa said. She changed the subject, "You look well. How is Jeshi?"

"He fights with his men. I have not seen him for two months now. What brings you here to the camp?"

"I am here to see Pastor Ellen Anderson," Karasa said.

"Come with me," the man smiled.

Karasa followed him into the tented community. He stopped beside a young man stoking a fire in an open pit.

"Kip, please take our guest to the pastor's residence," he said.

"Of course."

"*Kwaheri*," the soldier turned on his heels and strode back to his post.

They walked through a pandemonium of chatter. The people in this tented community busied themselves with morning chores and cooking their meals over small open fires.

Hearing the splashing water, Karasa turned her head toward the sound where a glimmer of light reflected from a shiny new pump that stood on a flat surface. Laughter from the crowd surrounding the pump could be heard above the cranking of the squeaking handle that moved up and down with each spurt of water. About twenty people waited patiently in the shade of a large wooden structure, secured on six solid wooden posts. Each person held an empty, jerry-rigged container that would soon be filled with pure mineral water from the deep, subterranean well.

"We are happy because we no longer thirst. Pastor Ellen has ordered seeds, and soon we will plant a community garden," the young man grinned from ear to ear.

"Clean water is good," Karasa agreed.

Kip greeted several acquaintances along the way. Soon they arrived at a wood frame house, raised up off of the ground on concrete blocks. This allowed cooling breezes to circulate underneath.

Ellen came out to greet them. "Jamala, what a surprise! It's so good to see you."

Several seconds later the front door slammed open and the cries of children filled the air.

"Aunt Jamala, Aunt Jamala!" Jimmy and Lisa rushed out the door, erupting past their mom to give Karasa a hug.

But gladness quickly soured when Karasa felt through his cotton shirt the raised scars on Jimmy's back. These had resulted from the beatings he had endured at the hand of the overseer's whip. It had been three years since she and Travis had rescued them.

She hugged the children warmly as Ellen approached.

A slender thirty-six year old woman, Ellen measured one inch shorter than the athletic Karasa. Ellen's dark brown complexion still reflected her African heritage.

"*Asante,* for bringing our guest to our home," Ellen smiled at the young man.

"*Kwaheri,*" Kip waved and left.

"Jamala, please come inside for some coffee." Ellen embraced Karasa.

As they walked into the Anderson's home, Ellen motioned to the table and chairs illuminated by a shaft of sunlight shining through a small, single glass window.

"Come and sit down." Ellen poured Karasa a cup of coffee.

"Where's baby Tamara?" Lisa asked.

"Tamara is not a baby anymore. She's walking now, and she's at home with her Aunt Ayella," Karasa smiled at Lisa.

"How did you get here?" Jimmy asked.

"I rode a small *matatu* bus to the Samburu National Reserve. There I waited about an hour and a half for another *matatu* to take me to Kargi. Instead a young British couple invited me ride with them to North Horr. By this time, it was almost evening and not safe to be out alone. I met a kind, old widow coming from the local market, and she invited me to spend the night in her hut. The following day I repaid her kindness by helping her with some heavy chores. On the third day, I left before the morning light and walked here."

"That's a long way," Jimmy observed.

"Weren't you afraid?" Lisa asked.

"Only once when . . ."

Ellen's face registered surprise and she quickly interrupted.

"Children, children, your Aunt Jamala and I have some things to talk about. Later you will have time to spend with her. Now it's time to complete your chores before school begins."

The children looked disappointed as they waved goodbye and left the house.

Karasa sipped her coffee, "How are Jimmy and Lisa coming along?"

"Better every day. Jimmy occasionally wakes up with nightmares and Lisa mentions her invisible friend, Mercy, less frequently. Yet, they both seem to be overcoming their ordeal. Time is a great healer," Ellen said.

Ellen served Karasa a bowl of sorghum which she ate

with gusto.

"Thank you; I didn't realize how hungry I was," Karasa said.

"You traveled over four hundred kilometers. Is everything okay?" Ellen asked.

"I have come to ask you about my husband. Jim visited our village recently looking for Travis. What is going on?" Karasa demanded.

"I can't tell you." Ellen faced her squarely.

"What do you mean you cannot tell me? You owe me something," Karasa's voice rose.

"Yes, I do. I will always be grateful to you and Travis for saving the lives of my children. But I can't tell you this."

Now Karasa no longer suspected but knew for certain something was wrong. Ellen's refusal to reveal what she knew felt like a slap in her face. What was Travis hiding from her – another woman?

"Who is she?"

Ellen looked confused for a moment.

"No, it's nothing like that. You don't have to worry about Travis, he's a one-woman man. Even Jim has told me that Travis always talks about how happy you have made him."

"What has happened to Travis?"

"I can't say."

Karasa puffed herself up with temper and leaned a bit closer to Ellen.

"I thought you were my friend," Karasa spoke with exasperation.

Ellen responded to the implied threat in Karasa's body language.

"You can hit me if you want. It wouldn't make me feel any worse. I don't like to be put in this position, but believe me, there is nothing that you can do but make matters worse. It's better for you if you don't know right now."

Infuriated with vexation, Karasa stomped out. The weariness from her recent trek prevented her from leaving at the faster pace she desired.

I'll go back later after I calm down.

Karasa hadn't walked far when she caught sight of Michelle approaching from the opposite direction.

Michelle too knows. Perhaps I can trick her into telling me, Karasa thought, and she made a quick plan of action.

As she approached, Michelle's face first showed surprise. Her facial expression, however, quickly turned to worry, as if anticipating that Karasa would ask her to reveal the secret she could not tell.

Before Michelle could say anything, Karasa held up her hand and told a lie.

"It is okay, Ellen already told me what is going on."

"I didn't think that she would," Michelle eyed her sus-

206 ~ Kweli – the Truth Unmasked

piciously.

"I reminded her of what she owed me, and I promised that I would not do anything stupid," Karasa said.

"Oh, Sweetie, this must be tearing you apart." Lowering her guard, Michelle's expression changed. She put one arm around Karasa's shoulder.

"It is, Chelle," Karasa switched to her short name that Ellen often used. "But there must be something that I can do?" Karasa felt lousy about lying.

"Sweetie, all you could do is to make matters worse. You know the terrain of your country but you don't know your way around big cities."

"Of course," Karasa agreed. She wanted as much information from Michelle as she could glean.

"Besides, he might fit in wearing one of those Arab garbs if he keeps his mouth shut. But women dressed in *burqa*s have less freedom to move around on their own."

Khartoum?

Karasa felt an ice cube pass through her body, right through her heart.

But he has a death sentence there! So do I.

"He should have told me," Karasa thought out loud.

"He couldn't, Sweetie. Don't you see, he has a much better chance of bringing back your boy if you stay here?"

Surely Michelle speaks of Twangi! Karasa gasped. She could barely contain herself from asking a myriad of questions. But she had to keep Michelle talking.

Michelle looked up and Karasa turned and followed her gaze. Both watched as Ellen quickly approached.

"Ellen, I know that Travis has gone into Sudan to bring back my son."

Ellen glared at Michelle with a 'what have you done' look.

"She told me you had already told her," Michelle raised her hands, palms up.

"I lied," Karasa answered, as if to settle an irrelevancy.

Ellen stood speechless.

Michelle stepped back from Karasa. Her face expressed her feeling of betrayal.

The balance of power had shifted. Now Karasa pressed her advantage. "How did he find out where Twangi is?" she demanded.

"If we tell you the whole story you have to promise that you won't do something irrational or something you will surely regret," Ellen said.

"I can not promise you that. The only thing I can promise you is that I will leave for Khartoum right this minute if you do not tell me everything I need to know."

Michelle and Ellen exchanged apprehensive glances.

Michelle relented and motioned for them to follow her. They walked silently to the shaded area under a piece of canvas suspended on posts. She indicated some mats and positioned a little red flag in a holder.

"Why did you put up a red flag?" Karasa wondered aloud.

"It tells the people in our community that we're talking about official mission business and not to interrupt us," Michelle answered.

Over the next several minutes they told Karasa what they knew about the newspaper executive named Mr. Cafferty contacting Travis and wanting a newspaper story in return for turning over her son and allowing Travis to bring him home. He had first approached Jim in America. They did not tell her that no one really trusted the newspaper people, and everyone suspected some ulterior motive.

"So you let him walk into the hyena's feast?" She could anticipate the outcome.

"He had no choice. He knew that you would go if he didn't, and he has a better chance of finding his way about in a city than you."

Changing tactics, Ellen said, "Chelle's husband has laid his life on the line along side of your husband's."

"He went with Travis?" Karasa's eyes widened in surprise and her face registered confusion.

"No," Ellen said. "He knows some powerful people in America who are criminals."

"Criminals? How could a missionary know such people?" Karasa asked.

"They are people that Rocco knew before he became a missionary.

"Why does he talk with such men as criminals?"

"These criminals deal with well known, legitimate business men world wide. Rocco will ask the most dangerous of them all to threaten the men who run the newspaper. If they are willing to help, they can tell the men who run the newspaper that they will be angry if anything happens to Travis. Even newspaper executives are afraid of men such as these."

"Do you think they might help?" Karasa looked at Michelle, trying to comprehend how this all worked.

"They may be willing to help. But they could just as easily murder my husband and just make him disappear," Michelle said.

Karasa noticed tears escaping from Michelle's eyes and empathized with her. But she didn't know how to comfort her.

Ellen reached for both of their hands and prayed for God's intervention.

Surely God's mercy is the one thing that would stand between their husbands and death. Karasa believed this.

"Nothing gives one person so much advantage over an-

other as to remain always cool and unruffled under all

circumstances."

~ Thomas Jefferson

CHAPTER TWENTY-EIGHT

Two brawny men, the kind of muscle who could be re-cruited in pool halls or bars across the world, flanked Travis. They climbed into a white SUV parked just outside the Nairobi Hilton and drove away with Travis sandwiched between them.

The driver sped into traffic, bypassed the main airport terminals and pulled into the parking lot of one of the many small air charter companies. The van pulled directly up to a private jet, a glossy red and white twin engine airplane. As Travis got out he noticed another man standing near the plane.

He'll want to search me, Travis thought.

Travis studied this stranger with a ready stance. He still had the Glock pistol tucked under his belt at the small of his back.

I'm not giving up my Glock, Travis decided.

A plan formed in his mind as Travis strode ahead of the two guards and marched straight up to the man.

"Raise your arms, I want to search you for weapons," Travis said.

The hard man looked at him incredulously.

"Get out of my way."

Travis shouldered past him and raced up the four stairs of the drop down ramp and into the airplane. The sentry, caught off guard, made no attempt to stop him.

Worked like a charm. Travis' mouth curved slightly upwards.

Inside the plane Travis stooped in the narrow cabin and moved forward, ignoring the command from behind and selecting a seat closest to the pilot. He sat down, bracing himself with his legs to keep his back firmly pressed to the seat. He also turned off the tracking device, hoping that Kookie had already picked up the signal.

"Hey buster, get back out here," one of his two escorts yelled as he dashed up through the open door.

The two other men followed and sat behind Travis, but the leader confronted him.

"Get your hands up!" The brute grabbed hold of Travis' upper arms, forcing them up. His hands felt like vice grips as he inched his way down Travis' arms, torso, and legs in rapid succession, searching for the suspected weapon.

"Hey, hands off!" Travis shouted. Shaking his shoulders and pulling away, he struggled to be free of the muscle's vice like grip.

Hearing the commotion the pilot turned and spoke with authority.

"We're scheduled for take-off. Everyone must sit down and fasten your seat belts." The pilot stared at both men.

"Now!"

"Be warned, we're going to body search you when we land," the muscle sneered as he released his hold.

"Whoever puts a hand in my pocket won't get it back," Travis said.

"You think so?" the muscle snickered as he sat down behind Travis and buckled up.

Undoubtedly, there'll be some physical confrontation when we land. I'll have to convince these men that their boss will be upset if they rough me up, Travis thought.

The plane taxied down the runway. Except for when the pilot talked on his radio, they flew about thirty minutes in silence.

"Did you get the special instructions?" Travis asked the pilot's back. He wanted to start a conversation and gain information.

"What special instructions? I'm following standard procedures and will land this aircraft at the normal place," the pilot replied with a European accent Travis couldn't identify.

"Who actually booked this charter?"

The pilot looked like he thought this to be a strange question, but he answered.

"Charters are booked by the front office. I'm only told where to fly. Someone else does the accounting."

The leader, the one who previously accosted him, asserted himself again.

"All you need to worry about is doing what you're told," he leaned into Travis' face. Travis could smell the beer on his breath.

"All that I agreed to is giving your boss an interview. The agenda will be between the newspaper pukes and me."

"I'm keeping my eye on ya," the leader relented and returned to his seat.

"That fellow could use some Listerine," the pilot glanced over his shoulder.

"What is the terrain down there like?" Travis asked, changing the subject.

"We're over desert for the rest of the way. Why don't you come up here to the copilot seat so you can look out through the window?"

"Thanks," Travis moved up and sat next to the pilot. As the darkness pursued the sun over the horizon, Travis saw only miles and miles of sand. *Kookie was right, leaving*

Khartoum on foot is not an option.

Darkness shrouded the small plane on its descent to the airport in Khartoum with only a dim light to guide its taxi to a hanger.

Two of the men got out quickly. The third lingered, allowing Travis to exit next.

About ten feet from the plane the two men twirled around and blocked his way. Travis heard the stomps of boots dismounting the stairs behind him.

"Raise your arms," a voice yelled into his ears.

Travis had no intention of giving up his Glock if he could help it, but he had no illusions that he would be able to physically oppose all three of these goons.

"The first one who touches me is going down." Travis turned sideways and dropped his pack. He stood alert, hands ready and his feet spread apart for emphasis.

The two men in front moved forward in unison, wearing the same smile that anyone who has ever confronted a school yard bully would recognize. The younger man advanced, grabbed Travis by the shirt, and easily lifted him up into the air.

It might be better to give up my weapon to avoid a beating, Travis thought.

The approaching roar of a motor and the screeching of tires distracted his would-be assailants. The rear door of the limo opened. Wearing an expensive suit, a tall immaculately dressed man stepped out and approached them.

"Put him down," the newcomer commanded.

Looking disappointed, the burly man complied.

Travis retrieved his bag and walked toward the limo in the shadows. He couldn't help but notice the obvious differences between the two men. The brawn, with the muscular build wore tight fitting pants and pull-over shirt. This contrasted sharply with the man from the limo who could have passed for a male model for some expensive line of clothing.

"I'm Marco Allende, and you're Travis Martin?" he asked.

"That's right."

"Get in."

The leader of the goon squad sat in the passenger area opposite Travis and Marco.

"He hasn't been searched," the brawn informed Marco.

Marco seemed to turn this over for a split second before shrugging it away. "Don't worry about it, Lars," he said to the goon.

The limo pulled out and sped away.

What happened to the other two goons? Travis wondered.

"Travis, we're going to the hotel," Marco said. "It's imperative you stay in your room and not leave it for any reason. If someone recognizes you, there is nothing we can do to help you.

"Tomorrow you'll meet your stepson. Any questions?" Marco asked, as he turned slightly to face Travis.

"What's on the agenda for tomorrow besides meeting my stepson?"

"I honestly don't know. Two reporters will be setting the agenda regarding their stories. You'll meet them tomorrow. One is from a newspaper in New Jersey, and the other is from a tabloid, The Liberal Enquirer."

The limo pulled up in front of the Hilton Khartoum. Marco handed Travis a floppy-brim straw hat and dark glasses. During the day they'd block the sun, but tonight they'd conceal his face. He hoped no one would question his wearing sunglasses after dark.

"Your suite is booked under the name of John Smith. Just follow me past the desk. No passport problems that way. Understand?" Marco asked.

"Yes, I do," Travis said.

As Travis hastened through the luxurious lobby, he scanned the people he passed for any sign of interest but saw none. Marco stopped and pushed the elevator button for the third floor. When they arrived, they walked down the hall and Marco unlocked the door to one of the rooms.

Travis followed him into the room. Lars closed the door and stood as if guarding it.

The accommodations included a spacious entrance, two

bedrooms and a bathroom. Larger than Travis had expected, a writing desk with stationery, sofa and a television filled the front living room.

Marco opened a door into a bedroom with a single bed and Travis placed his backpack on top of a small dresser. Another door led into a spacious bathroom.

"My guards will bring you something to eat from room service if you're hungry," Marco said.

"No, I'm not hungry."

"Lars will sleep out here on the sofa for your protection."

Travis eyed Lars with disapproval.

"Anything else?" Marco inquired.

"No, nothing. Good night." Travis just wanted to be rid of him.

"Okay, I'll see you tomorrow."

When Marco left, Travis ambled into the bedroom and locked the door. The bed's thick mattress comforted his tired body, but sleep proved as elusive as these newspaper people's plot.

"Not everything that is faced can be changed.

But nothing can be changed until it is faced."

~ James Arthur Baldwin

CHAPTER TWENTY-NINE

Long Island, New York

Towering over Rocco, a pair of six-foot, hard-faced sentinels pressed against each of his shoulders with their muscular arms as they escorted him down a narrow hall into Don Giuseppe Garibaldi's private chambers.

Bam!

Rocco blinked his eyes and jumped slightly when the double wooden doors slammed behind him. He knew without turning that another sentry stood guarding the entrance. Without moving his head, Rocco's eyes glanced about the room. The decor hadn't changed. Looking as if furnished from a nineteen-fifties catalog, it cast a touch of nostalgia with its claw-footed coffee table, overstuffed furniture, solid oak desk, and an ornate floor lamp positioned near the Don's padded leather chair.

The Don's bodyguards left Rocco standing in the center of the room and hustled to their assigned posts. Alert to any sudden movements and braced to protect the Don with their lives, the men stood straight as statues. The Don's consigliere referred to a notebook, leaned over the Don's right shoulder and whispered into the Don's ear.

Theoretically, the Mafia doesn't exist. Nevertheless, Rocco stood before the most powerful man in organized crime's northeastern region. He remembered when the Don had complained, in jest, that the director of a recently broadcast Sci-Fi television series should have asked his permission to use his name for one of the show's characters. When the Hollywood director got word, he became scared to death that he had offended the Don. The esteemed director booked the first direct flight to New York to offer a personal apology. Even though they had already filmed a dozen shows, the director gave his assurance he'd change the name and re-film the scenes. The Don had assured him that no offense occurred. He gave permission for the use of his last name, as long as the character's first name differed from his own. The Hollywood geek wobbled away with his knees knocking. The cop named Garibaldi stayed in the show. Now, that's power. Within the next few minutes Don Guiseppe would wield that same power again.

The Don will be decidin' if I live or die. I'm ready, Rocco thought. He had set his spiritual house in order.

The consigliere finished his agenda and took a seat behind the Don. Rocco waited, resigned to his fate, for the Don's final judgment.

"Rocco, I don't understand you. I grant you a favor that no one has ever been given before. I allow you to leave and become a missionary in Africa with the single condition that you stay there and don't ever come back. Now here you are, back in my office. What am I to make of this disrespect?"

"No disrespectin' intended, sir."

"Why are you here?"

"Somethin' downright unfair is happenin' to a good man. I think that God would want you to help. You are the only person alive with the power. Just a . . ."

The Don lifted his hand as a signal to be quiet.

"You talk about God, but you're not even a Catholic missionary. You know that my families are all Catholics."

"Yes sir. The man who I speak of is a Catholic. And he's a good man. If you knew him I know that you'd like him and want to help him."

"I remember reading about him. He's the one who attacked an entire African Army base all by himself and blew up a bunch of helicopters and half of their base. The guy's got style, I've got to give him credit."

"His wife was with him."

"Yeah, some native girl, right?"

"Yes sir, she's Sudanese."

"But what is he to me that I should involve my business?"

Rocco knew that this question would come. This would be the acid test of whether he would live or die.

"Don Giuseppe, one day we will all stand before the throne of God. On that day when God asks us about the good deeds we did, you can say, 'Look, I helped that guy who saved all those little slave kids'," Rocco replied.

The Don uttered not a word but his facial expression read, 'Are you for real?'

Rocco quickly explained the situation of the newspaper guy named Cafferty who had Karasa's son and was blackmailing Travis to come back to Khartoum where he had a death sentence.

The Don looked annoyed. Rocco couldn't determine if the Don became angry because of Travis' predicament or his own audacity.

"What do you propose that I do about this problem?"

"Sir, just a word from you to the publisher of the newspaper that you would prefer that this man was not harmed…"

"You still have not explained why this man is my personal problem." The Don appeared deep in concentration, as he mulled this matter over in his mind.

The Don turned to one of his men and ordered, "Put

him on ice." The Don had made his decision.

Effectively dismissed, Rocco complied with the silent instruction of the bodyguard who motioned for Rocco to walk ahead of him. Bruno, a senior enforcer for the Garibaldi organization, met them at the door.

"The Don says put him on ice."

Rocco breathed a small sigh of relief. At least they were not going to kill him immediately. They had no intentions of letting him go, but they weren't killing him right this minute, either.

Bruno looked disappointed. He had kept one hand in his jacket pocket where Rocco knew he carried a gun. He directed Rocco to exit the backdoor behind the building. Even though Rocco carried no weapon, the Don's men frisked him again for the fourth time. Satisfied, they pushed Rocco into the backseat of a car and drove to an old dilapidated house in the country. Once inside, Rocco remained immobile and handcuffed to a heavy chair bolted to the floor. Bruno and another man guarded him. The room's scuffed floors exposed missing linoleum tiles, and yellowed peeling paint covered sections of the undecorated walls. A small aged television helped the men to pass the time. Bruno moved the TV to the edge of the counter so Rocco could watch the show.

"Thanks."

Rocco appreciated this consideration even though he

knew that they would kill him just as quickly if the Don sent word.

Both men pretended they didn't hear him. That wasn't a good sign.

Again, Bruno ignored him and walked to a side room, leaving the door ajar. Rocco eavesdropped on Bruno's end of a telephone conversation.

"Hey, Bert, can't deliver the laundry tonight. Can you hold the project until Monday?

"Yeah, the project in Jersey, where the forms are already built and concrete is being poured in the morning.

"Oh. Well, see if you can hold it up one day." Bruno sounded disappointed. "I'll call you back later."

"Tough luck, Bruno?" The other guard asked.

"Yeah, but there's more than one way to skin a cat," Bruno stared at Rocco.

"If curiosity killed the cat, hope he's the cat that satisfaction brought back," Rocco chuckled.

Bruno shook his head in disbelief.

"A can-do attitude makes the

impossible, possible."

~ Scott Beare

CHAPTER THIRTY

Karasa considered her options. She had no way of contacting her brother Jeshi and even less a chance of locating his unit.

The journey to Khartoum, the capital of Moslem dominated northern Sudan, was far too dangerous to venture into alone, even if she had a jeep to make the four-day trek. However, her biggest obstacle was the language barrier. She understood a few words of Arabic but could neither read, write nor speak it effectively.

I will think about this later. I only have enough shillings to take the matatu back to Nairobi. I will find my way to Khartoum from there.

She knew Ellen and Michelle would be upset, but she planned to leave without telling them of her intentions. Karasa waited until an opportunity arose and walked back toward the front gate.

"*Kwaheri*," Karasa called back to the guard as she left the camp. After a two-hour hike down a rugged dirt path, she arrived at a bus stop. She had no idea how often the buses passed here. She sat down to wait and twenty minutes later an ancient orange bus pulled up and stopped. Karasa got on and paid the fare to Nairobi.

It cost less than I thought. That is a good sign.

Seven passengers had already boarded the bus. Karasa chose a seat near an open window anticipating a slight breeze once the bus started to move again. Instead, dirt blew through the window as the bus bounced along the uneven road. But she preferred the sting of the sandy particles over the unbearable heat that would overcome her if the windows remained closed.

The dirt road gave way to pavement when they approached the city. As the ride got smoother, Karasa dozed off. The clank of the door opening and the noise of the exiting passengers woke her up when the bus pulled to a stop at the terminal.

She shouldered her bag and climbed down the steps. Standing there alone in a strange place, anxiety began to nibble at the corner of her mind. But her decisiveness soon dispelled it. Karasa entered the bus station and asked directions to the Barclays Bank.

"You'll need to take bus number thirty-three to get downtown," the man at the ticket window told her. Karasa paid for a ticket and boarded the bus, informing the driver of her destination. She watched the activity in the busy city during the short trip.

"Madam," the driver pointed to her. "This is your stop."

As she exited the bus, he directed her in the general direction of the bank.

This place looks familiar, Karasa thought as she walked down a major street amidst fancy buildings. She kept searching. Two blocks later she found Barclays Bank. Before she entered she realized she wore the same clothes she'd slept in. Being embarrassed by her appearance, this did not prevent her from going in. The air-conditioned, opulent lobby felt refreshing, just wonderful.

When Karasa approached the counter to withdraw money from their account, the bank teller asked for her identification papers.

"I don't have any," Karasa replied. It had never occurred to her that she would need any.

The bank teller called her manager, Mr. Smythe. The middle-aged Caucasian man courteously invited Karasa to come with him.

Looking up from the computer on his desk, he pointed to the monitor. "This is a statement of your account. It is active, and I can vouch for your identity. How can I help you?"

"Thank you. I need both Kenyan shillings and Sudanese

dinars."

"Your husband made the same request three days ago," Mr. Smythe informed her.

"How much did my husband take out?" Karasa's face remained impassive, but she felt a churning inside.

Mr. Smythe checked his computer screen again and replied, "He took out one hundred and twenty-five thousand shillings."

"I need the same amount of Kenyan shillings and the same amount of Sudanese dinars," Karasa said. She felt slightly overwhelmed requesting an amount equivalent to over two thousand United States dollars.

Mr. Smythe presented the paper work for her to sign and excused himself. He unlocked a heavy metal door of the vault and entered.

Returning with the requested amount, he counted the money out to her. Mr. Smythe put the cash into a large bank envelope and handed it to her.

"Thank you." Karasa placed envelope in the bottom of her shoulder bag.

"Is there anything else I can do for you?"

"Yes, I have a friend who operates a company called the Outback Flying Service. Can you help me to call her on your telephone?"

"Do you know her number?"

"No, I do not," Karasa shook her head and gave him her

best smile. "Could you please help me to find it?" she implored.

He seemed a bit taken aback for a few seconds before answering, "I would be happy to."

Mr. Smythe obtained the necessary information and dialed the number he had just written down. Handing the telephone to Karasa, he walked away to afford her privacy.

Karasa held the phone tight to her ear, hoping Maude would answer. A friend of her brother's, an elderly entrepreneur, she excelled in aviation. More important she sympathized with the plight of the people in southern Sudan. So Karasa felt a flood of relief when Maude answered on the fifth ring.

"Maude, this is Karasa," she said. "I need your help."

"What do you need? Is everything safe with Jeshi?"

"Yes, Jeshi is fine. I'm in Nairobi and I need to talk to you."

"Where are you now?"

"I'm at the Barclays Bank."

"Which branch?"

"Downtown."

"Just wait there. I'll be right there to pick you up." Maude hung up the phone.

This is working out far better than I could have ever hoped for.

Karasa walked to a leather chair beside a large bay

window in the front lobby and sat down to wait for Maude in the luxurious air conditioning.

"It is not what you give your friend, but what you are willing to give . . . that determine the quality of friendship."

~ Mary Dixon

CHAPTER THIRTY-ONE

When Maude's jeep pulled up in front of the bank, Karasa went out to greet her. The gray-haired woman motioned for Karasa to get in as a thin-lipped smile creased her weathered and wrinkled face. She had emigrated from New Zealand with her husband, now deceased, almost twenty years ago and started their flying service. They had risked their lives to rescue over one hundred Southern Sudanese refugees fleeing from deadly raids. She still delivered food and medicine to the starving, remote villages during droughts. Once a thriving business, she now piloted the only airplane the company owned, an old converted military cargo plane.

"*Jambo*, Karasa. Are you here in Nairobi all by yourself?" Maude asked.

"Yes, I am. I have a problem and need your advice."

During the drive back to Maude's office near the edge

of the airport, Karasa explained her predicament. When they arrived, they entered a metal building that displayed Maude's company logo. They walked into a partitioned office where Maude motioned for Karasa to sit down. The double doors opened onto the back storage area and Karasa saw spare airplane parts, motors, tools and other odds and ends neatly stacked.

"Here, have a cup of *Rooibos* red tea and some refreshments." Maude placed a cup and saucer and a plate of honey-covered biscuits in front of Karasa.

"Thank you, I will," Karasa said.

"I don't trust these people, Karasa. There's something more to this," Maude said.

"I don't trust them either, but they won't know that I'm coming."

"You'll need to be in disguise so no one will recognize you. If you wore a Moslem *burqa* and veil, it would cover you completely. Only your eyes would show."

"I want to find this Mr. Cafferty newspaper man. A man like him will stay in one of the most expensive hotels in Khartoum. I will go to the counter and ask for him in each hotel."

"Perhaps you could call on the telephone and ask to speak to him. After locating the right hotel and they put your call through, simply hang up before he answers the phone. He'll think someone dialed the wrong number."

"How can I get his room number?

"Go to the reception desk and hand them an envelope addressed to Mr. Cafferty. Turn, walk away and sneak into the ladies room. Change your scarf; wear a different color. No one will know that you're the same woman. Choose a seat in the lobby and wait. When Mr. Cafferty arrives, the receptionist will hand him your envelope. You can follow him into the elevator and right to his door," Maude suggested.

"Although the outfit will be hot, I will blend in. This plan might work," Karasa agreed. Her face clouded over. "My one worry is that someone will talk to me while I'm sitting in the lobby."

"Just ignore them. In their culture it wouldn't be unusual for a woman to refuse to speak to a strange male, and women are second-class citizens. No man would trouble himself if one woman annoyed another."

Maude continued, "Still it would be best if you had a companion who spoke Arabic. I know a young Arab woman in her early twenties who lives only a few miles from here. Effat fled Sudan about a year ago. With the assistance of the Christian church, she found a job and settled here."

"Will she help me?"

"I don't know. Until her older sister, Hagar, arrived two weeks ago from El Obeid, her family did not know her present location. Hagar is a strong Moslem and is trying to win her sister back to Islam. Effat, however, is intent on winning Hagar's soul to the truth, to Isa, Jesus."

"I remember the quote Ellen taught me. 'You will know the truth, and the truth will set you free.' My spirit soars whenever I meditate on it," Karasa whispered.

"The Holy Scriptures states that God is no respecter of persons. Everyone is equal in His sight. *Sharia Law,* however, restricts women's rights. If a *Muslim* woman from a militant Islamic home converts to Christianity, the family suffers disgrace among the villagers. With pressure from the family, including the threat of being disowned, most *Muslims* considering conversion will recant. But if a daughter refuses to return to Islam and honor *Allah,* it's the duty of the men in her own family to put her to death. Effat's sister will be obligated to alert the family if Effat continues to hold fast to her Christian beliefs."

"How terrible," Karasa voiced sadness.

'Yes, but it is what it is," Maude stated.

"It is most likely she will not choose to go back into the hornet's nest," Karasa sounded disappointed.

"Still we will ask her. I just received an urgent message to contact her in person."

"Will you invite her to your home?"

"No. If I only extend the invitation to Effat, her sister will presume the worst. Effat works in a craft shop downtown. We'll stop and visit tomorrow morning. Now, I have a short charter about two hours out and back."

"You will leave soon?"

"Yes. The plane's loaded. You can join me, and we'll continue our chat. Of course, you'll stay at my home tonight."

"Thank you, Maude."

"Thank me when this is over. Right now, let's go deliver some cargo."

"Hope is the thing with feathers

That perches in the soul,

And sings the tune without the words

And never stops at all."

~ Emily Dickinson, poet

CHAPTER THIRTY-TWO

After the cargo delivery, Maude drove them to her two-bedroom bungalow. Designed for tropical living, the screened louvered windows let the breeze through while still giving some feeling of privacy. Once inside the residence, Maude switched on the light, illuminating the bamboo paneled front room and open kitchen. Giant fans hanging from the ceiling hummed as a refreshing breeze penetrated the open area.

"Put your things in here." Maude showed Karasa the guest room. It contained a floor rug, bed and a bureau with a wash bowl.

"This feels comfortable." Karasa couldn't resist bouncing a little on the soft mattress.

"You look exhausted."

"Yes, I am tired."

"Good night, Karasa." Maude left, shutting the door behind her.

After taking a quick sponge bath, Karasa lifted the bed covers, slipped inside and snuggled into a cocoon of warmth. Soon darkness engulfed her and Karasa entered a world of forgotten dreams.

Maude woke Karasa a little after six the following morning.

After breakfast they drove pass the City Square to Handmade Crafts, Ltd., the shop where Effat worked. Like its name implied, the shop sold a variety of items made by the local artists. The store specialized in copper jewelry, exquisite wood carvings, and musical instruments. Wealthy tourists selected one-of-a-kind pieces to display in their luxurious foreign dwellings.

When Maude and Karasa entered the shop one of the two attendants approached and greeted them.

"Maude, I am so glad to see you." The young Middle Eastern woman with her dark brown hair tied back in a twist wore a traditional kanga.

The two ladies hugged.

"Effat, this is my friend, Karasa. She would like to ask you some questions about Sudan."

"Of course."

"Could we take you out to lunch? We can talk while we eat," Maude said.

"I go to lunch from eleven until twelve."

"We'll come back at eleven," Maude said.

Once outside, they began to search for a restaurant within walking range. They found an inconspicuous place two blocks away, concealed from the main street by a wall laced with ivy. It featured an outdoor patio with covered tables. Aware of their short wait, Karasa shopped in a nearby store to purchase several personal items.

When they returned to the craft shop, Effat approached them.

"I'm ready."

"How about lunch at Edward's Fish and Chips?" Maude suggested.

"Good. I've eaten there once before," Effat said.

They chatted as they hurried to the restaurant. When they arrived a waiter greeted them.

"We'd like to sit at the table with the green umbrella," Maude pointed to a secluded table set apart from the others.

"Please follow me." He led them through the patio to a table at the far end. He placed the menus on the table. Smiling at Effat, he pulled out a chair for her and waited.

After ordering, Maude looked directly at Effat. "I received your message." Concern etched Maude's face.

"I need to make arrangements to leave Nairobi. I believe my sister will contact my brothers soon and force me to return home to El Obeid, Sudan. So, I am planning my escape. Can you take me to the airport today?" Effat inquired. "I need to purchase a ticket to . . . someplace where I won't be found."

Effat glanced at Karasa as if unsure she could trust Karasa to keep her secret.

"I will help you any way that I can, but first, please listen to Karasa's story," Maude said.

Maude explained that Karasa needed to go to Khartoum to fetch her son. Kidnapped as a slave, he would soon be released. But Maude omitted information regarding Karasa's criminal conviction. Later, it would be revealed.

"Unfortunately I planned to leave tomorrow and will not be available," Effat said.

"Actually, Khartoum might be a safer place to go because your family won't think to look for you there. When we return, you can stay in my home as my guest until we have your transportation arranged," Maude offered.

"I would prefer not to return to Sudan. *Sharia Law* governs that city. The courts forbid any Sudanese female to leave the country without the written consent of her father or legal male guardian. I have violated this decree. There will be a consequence if I return and I am found out."

Now for the moment of truth, Karasa thought.

Maude told Effat, "You and Karasa share one thing in common. You would both lose your freedom or your lives if you were taken into custody."

Maude sketched in Karasa's pertinent background information. When Maude spoke of Twangi, tears spilled from Effat's eyes. Maude also told her that Karasa had been tried in absentia and faced a death sentence.

"It will be difficult for Karasa to find her lost son because she doesn't speak Arabic. If you agree to go with Karasa, she'll have a guide she can trust. You can advise her on the appropriate role of women in an Islamic culture."

"I understand now. I will go," Effat whispered.

Karasa's mouth dropped at the unexpected turn of events.

Effat continued. "I had a dream late last night. *Isa's* light shone, and He appeared as before. He spoke, 'We are family. Each member has his own special gifts. Use yours to glorify God and to help others. A woman from Sudan needs your help.' *Isa Masih,* Jesus – Messiah, smiled at me as His light faded," Effat paused. "You must be that woman."

"God is good," Maude exclaimed.

"If *Isa* has equipped me to help, please tell me how."

"You would both be disguised in *burqa*s, but only you will do the talking once you arrive in Khartoum."

"First, we must enter Sudan without being stopped by security." Effat turned to Karasa. "Is your travel visa current?" she asked.

Before Karasa could respond, Maude said, "You won't be going in through the main terminal. I'll radio that I'm there to pick up cargo. The tower will direct me to another area. When we arrive, I'll inform the authorities that there's been a delay in shipment. This is not unusual. They expect pilots to come and go in order to eat and go back and forth to their hotels."

"But what if they board the plane and see us there?" Karasa asked.

"They never have, transporting unseen cargo is my specialty."

Maude spoke of Mr. Cafferty, the newspaper man of questionable character, who had knowledge of Karasa's son and was blackmailing her to come back to Sudan under the pretense of writing a story about a reunion.

"So now you realize this may be a dangerous mission."

"I haven't changed my mind, I'm committed," Effat said.

Effat furrowed her eyebrows and looked at Karasa.

"When you follow Mr. Cafferty back to his room, how will you get him to tell you what you need to know?" Effat asked.

Maude spoke before Karasa could answer. "After scaring and threatening him, she will leave him handcuffed and tied up in his room. He won't be found until the maid comes around the following day. If possible, she'll place a 'Do not disturb' sign on the outer door to give you even more time."

"Does this newspaperman speak English?" Effat asked.

"Yes," Karasa answered.

Effat sighed with relief. "That is good. You can follow him upstairs by yourself. I will wait downstairs in the lobby."

"Yes. It will be easier if I am alone. If he senses any hesitation, it will be far more difficult to frighten him to get the information I need. When I am done, I will return to the lobby. We will find Twangi and disguise him before bringing him back to the plane. Maude will wait and be ready to take us back to Kenya. If any problems arise, you must return to the airplane without me. You and Maude must leave immediately," Karasa said.

"What if there are guards in the vicinity?"

"You will wait a short distance away while I disarm security, tie them up, and leave them bound. I carry a gun, so if you hear gunshorts or any commotion, you must hurry back to the plane. The danger should be minimal for you."

"When will we go?" Effat smiled.

"We'll leave tomorrow morning. Can you be ready by 7:00 A.M.?"

244 ~ Kweli – the Truth Unmasked

"Yes, I can."

"One more thing, Effat." Maude's facial expression turned serious.

"What is that?"

"You absolutely, under no circumstances, can tell your sister."

"Well, what can I tell her? I can't lie to Hagar."

"Tell her that I've hired you to translate for me."

"I don't want any money to help you to free a slave."

"I'll pay you one shilling so it won't be a lie."

"Alright, one shilling it is."

"Remember, I'll pick you up in front of your home at seven tomorrow morning. Just dress like you're going to work," Maude reminded her. "I'll pack the *burqa*s."

Karasa insisted on paying for their lunch. After Effat returned to work, Karasa and Maude mounted the jeep and drove about three miles to a fashionable clothing store. They bought the *burqa*s, scarves, and sashes. Karasa's favorite purchase, the Punjabi leather slip-ons, looked stylish on her feet.

"Thank you, Maude," Karasa said. "I can't believe how well this plan is coming together."

"It's my pleasure," Maude replied as she drove to their next destination.

"Fear not those who argue

but those who dodge."

~ Dale Carnegie

CHAPTER THIRTY-THREE

Effat rented a one-bedroom apartment with most of the amenities. In the living room a Turkish area rug covered most of the polished wood floor. The walls were painted a light pastel shade of tan. The overstuffed modern-styled furniture showed little wear even though Effat regularly rested on the comfortable beige sofa after a hard day's work.

When Hagar had appeared unexpectedly, Effat invited her to stay at her place.

Now the evening sun cast long shadows as Effat arrived at her front door. When she entered, she noticed that Hagar kneeled on the oval rug and fingered her *tasbith*, Moslem prayer beads. The *tasbith* is a string of 33 beads similar to the Catholic rosary. Hagar cycled through the series, flicking each bead three times to equal 99. She softly recited one of Allah's 99 names.

"*Malik, the Sovereign,*" Hagar whispered.

"I prefer *Irahma, the Mercifu,*" Effat said as she walked past.

Hagar folded her veil and placed it in her wardrobe.

"Anything interesting happen today at the shop?" Hagar stood up and changed the subject.

"Well, the store filled early with customers, and it stayed busy all day." Effat returned to the living room.

"I guess you took a shorter lunch break."

"No. I ate at my usual time. How about your day?"

"I shopped at the market and . . ." Hagar hesitated.

Effat tensed, anticipating a barrage of criticism against the people of the book, the *Qur'an's* reference to the Jews and Christians. With disdain Hagar compared the people and their western cultures negatively to the virtuous followers of Islam residing in unpolluted communities. But the arguments never came.

Instead Hagar continued, "Supper is ready. Let's go to the kitchen."

"I smell chicken with garlic simmering in the pot. Should I serve?" Effat asked.

"No, I will bring it to the table."

Hagar has not once quarreled with me and has even declined my help. This is not like her, Effat thought. They ate the main course in silence. She noticed that Hagar wore her *taviz,* a small metal locket worn around the neck. It contained a handwritten verse of the Qur'an. A *pir,* holy man, presented the *taviz* to Hagar on her twelfth birthday. Her favorite piece of jewelry, she usually wore it only on special occasions.

Why is she wearing the locket tonight? Effat knew not to voice her curiosity aloud. She would just tell Hagar about her own plans for tomorrow.

"Tomorrow, I will leave early and meet a friend," Effat said.

"But Sunday is your day off and I need your help." Hagar looked disappointed.

"I've already promised to meet with my new friend."

"The one you met at lunch today?"

"How did you know?" Effat asked as bells of alarm reverberated in her mind.

"I have my sources. When will you leave?"

She must suspect something, Effat thought.

"In the morning," Effat replied.

"What will you do?"

"She's asked me to translate for her. It is a personal matter."

"Oh. Well, I hope you will not be long."

"After I help my friend, my work will be done." Effat hoped this vague reply would suffice.

"Work? Are you being paid for your services?" Hagar's face registered interest.

"Yes, one shilling."

"How foolish of you, that is not even enough to purchase fresh fruit for both of us."

"I didn't want any payment, but my friend insisted."

"How long will this take?" Hagar asked in annoyance.

"I don't know for sure, but it shouldn't take long," Effat answered.

"Good, I'll be here," Hagar agreed.

When they finished supper Effat helped Hagar clear the table. After wiping the table clean, Effat paused and watched with disbelief as Hagar washed the dishes.

That's strange, Hagar has not hassled me about the chores.

"Hagar, should I dry the dishes now?" Effat asked.

"*Ma'aleesh.* Don't worry about it. Just sweep the floor." Hagar did not look up but busied herself with her task.

Sweeping was usually the last chore she did, so when she finished, Effat said, "I'm tired. Good night, Hagar." Effat trudged into the bedroom.

"*al Almu Lykum,*" Hagar called after her.

"And peace be with you, too," Effat yawned.

Hagar washed and dried all the dishes before placing them back on the shelf. She cleaned the coffee carafé and prepared it for tomorrow. She treaded softly to the bedroom and peeked inside as Effat slumbered, sound asleep. When she returned to the kitchen, she retrieved a hidden pouch stored on the back top shelf. She measured the correct amount of something and added it to the brew. But Effat did not see her do this.

When she had completed her task, she picked up the phone and dialed a number from memory.

"It is time. Please arrive before noon tomorrow." Hagar breathed a sigh of relief.

In the bedroom she shared with Effat, Hagar pulled down the wall sleeper reserved for guests, hoping the creaking hinges would not wake her sister. As she lay down, her thin lips smirked and inched upward. She slowly drifted into a deep sleep.

"Most of the change we think we see in life

is due to truths being in and out of favor."

~ Robert Frost

CHAPTER THIRTY-FOUR

Karasa climbed out of the comfortable bed, still tired. She'd tossed and turned all night worrying about her family. She pondered on recent events about which she had no control. Imagining various scenarios that might turn the situation in her favor, her mind felt cluttered and her heart felt uneasy.

It's alarming how my life has changed in just a week's time, Karasa thought.

Maude served a hot breakfast and ate with gusto. But Karasa just picked at the food, putting little on her fork and delivering almost none to her mouth.

"You should force yourself to eat more. You're going to need your energy for the next couple of days," Maude counseled.

Realizing the wisdom of her words, Karasa deposited a

larger fork full of scrambled eggs in her mouth. She buttered a biscuit and took a bite, even though she still had little appetite.

The night before, they'd already washed clothes in an automatic washing machine and dryer. Karasa had marveled at these two modern conveniences. Their clothes packed, they would depart after they cleaned the dishes and tidied the kitchen.

"There's no way to contact your village, but I can radio the Andersons at the camp," Maude offered.

"Yes, maybe Jim got some word about Travis," Karasa said.

Maude checked the time before turning on her radio. She dialed the frequency to the one the Andersons monitored. Speaking into the microphone, she called the camp. After three attempts, Ellen responded.

"Have you heard from Travis, over?" Maude asked.

Maude looked at Karasa and shook her head.

"Yes, she's here with me now, over," Maude said.

"I can't say, over," Maude said. She took her finger away from the transmit button and whispered to Karasa, "She wants me to talk some sense into you. Does that include flying you to Khartoum?"

Karasa and Maude shared a conspiratorial smile before Maude returned to her conversation.

"Sorry, Ellen, I've got to go. I'll call you in a couple of

days, promise, over and out."

She cut the power to the radio even as Ellen still attempted to elicit information.

"Well, let's go."

Karasa desired to begin the journey. The events of the next couple of days would set the course for the rest of her life, and she had no idea which way they might go.

After two trips to the jeep carrying boxes of items, Maude locked her front door and they drove off. Driving through the quiet residential district, the ride to Effat's place took about fifteen minutes.

Usually punctual, Effat wasn't waiting outside her front door as planned. Maude and Karasa climbed out of the jeep and decided to investigate. Maude knocked at the door.

Hagar peeked out between the curtains before opening the door.

"Please come in," Haggar bowed. "Effat and I hope you will breakfast with us."

"Where is Effat?"

"She will be out shortly, please sit down and enjoy some hot coffee."

Maude and Karasa exchanged uneasy glances.

"Where did you say Effat was?" Maude asked in a quiet tone, so as not to cause suspicion.

"She cannot be disturbed. It is her time of the month," Hagar's eyes snapped.

Karasa turned facing away from Hagar and whispered to Maude, "Don't let her follow me."

Karasa moved toward Hagar, her face waxed with a false smile. Without warning she rushed past Hagar, pushing her roughly out of the way, and Maude stepped between to prevent Hagar from following.

Karasa hurried down a hallway in search of Effat. She ignored the banging and thumping behind her as Maude wrestled Hagar. Karasa pushed open the closed door of the small bedroom. There Effat lay bound and prostrate. Powerless, her arms and legs were tied to a bed, she had a cloth stuffed in her mouth.

Karasa raced toward the bed and removed the gag.

"I am going to untie these bonds."

"Please help me . . . Hagar tried to drug me . . . I spit it out but too late . . . don't drink the. . . " Effat eyes battled to stay open as she whispered her plea.

Karasa lifted and supported Effat, and they re-entered the main room.

With a bruised left cheek and a raised bump on her left temple, Maude knelt on the floor as Hagar pointed the blade of a small paring knife at the side of her neck.

"No, Hagar, put that knife down," Effat stumbled toward her sister.

Karasa grabbed Effat as if to offer her support. Together they advanced slowly toward Hagar.

"What is it that you want?" Karasa asked.

"You and your friend must leave. Effat stays."

She positioned Effat in front of her and moved forward.

"Trust me, Effat," Karasa whispered.

Holding Effat and circling to her left, Karasa said.

"I am ready for an exchange."

"Back off or I will use this knife on your friend."

"Your knife has a clean blade," Karasa said. "The blade of my knife is dipped in the blood of a pig. It is in my bag by the door."

Hagar's face twisted in revulsion and she glanced involuntarily at the door. As she did, Karasa pushed Effat hard in the opposite direction and charged Hagar. Hagar stumbled back, releasing Maude as she slid over a coffee table. Knocking the ceramic cups and utensils to the floor, Hagar's upper torso twisted; she landed face first upon the sofa. In the midst of the confusion, Karasa pushed the table aside with her foot and dove for Hagar's hand that held the knife. She grabbed Hagar's wrist and pulled her arm behind her back. Hagar jerked to her side and they tumbled onto the floor. Karasa's grip held firm as they rolled over. She gained the advantage with her weight on the other woman's back and pried the paring knife from Hagar's hand.

Karasa tore off Hagar's veil and held the blade tight against Hagar's neck until it drew a trickle of blood as it scratched the skin of her throat.

"Hold still. I will not hesitate to slice your ugly neck."

An angry Maude pushed herself to her knees.

"I'm pulling the phone out of the wall to disconnect it," Maude called out.

"You are too late; I have already phoned my brothers. They will be here within the hour," Hagar sneered.

"You evil hag," Karasa spit her words.

We must leave now. How do I detain her? Karasa wondered.

"Maude, bring the coffee here. That is what she used to drug Effat."

Maude picked up an unbroken cup from the floor and filled it with coffee from an urn by a chair.

"Drink this of your free will or I will pour it down your slit throat," Karasa warned. With her knee in the woman's back she pulled back Hagar's head by her hair, still holding the knife to her throat.

"No." Hagar's jaws clamped tight and teeth clenched.

"Let me do this. It's payback time," Maude's fingers pinched Hagar's nostrils closed and the fingernails of her other hand clawed at Hagar's chin to force her mouth open.

Losing the struggle, Hagar relented.

"I will drink it," the Moslem woman sputtered. It took less than five minutes for the effects of the coffee to work its magic. But it felt like they waited an eternity before Hagar's eyelids closed and hid the crimson blaze of her hateful glare.

Pressed for time, they left Hagar in a lump on the floor and helped an unsteady Effat into the back seat of the jeep and covered her. They'd sped away and rode almost two blocks when Karasa caught sight of two men riding in a brown truck going in the opposite direction. Karasa eyed it with suspicion because a canvas tarp completely covered the bed in the back.

"Slow down, Maude," Karasa said as she turned around, eyes following the vehicle. When the truck stopped, Karasa directed Maude to pull over.

Two men dressed in white chechias with black stripes, buttoned shirts and navy jeans left the truck. They paused on the walkway, looking up and down the street. The taller man knocked on Effat's front door. A few seconds later the second man joined the first.

Maude gasped, floored the foot pedal and sped toward the airport.

"Those men will have to break the window to enter the house, because I locked the front door," Maude turned to Karasa and smiled.

Karasa chuckled.

"Forgiveness is the attribute of the strong."

~ Mahatma Gandhi

CHAPTER THIRTY-FIVE

When they arrived at Maude's office, Effat still dealt with the effects of the drug. Karasa and Maude each grabbed one of Effat's arms to steady her.

"Keep Effat on her feet until I can heat this coffee," Maude told Karasa.

The aroma of the coffee filled the air, as they helped Effat sit at the table. Maude brought her coffee. Effat removed her hand from her aching head and held the cup as steady as she could with both hands.

Maude retrieved a box off the shelf and took out the first aide kit.

"Here, let me help treat your wounds," Karasa offered.

Effat spilled some of the hot coffee on the table but continued to savor the hot drink.

"Thank you for rescuing me," Effat smiled.

Twenty minutes later Effat had recovered sufficiently to move of her own accord.

"That was too close for comfort. We must leave before your brothers find us," Maude urged.

"My brothers are here?" Effat's eyes opened wide with fear.

"Yes," Maude told her. "Two men in a brown truck drove past us and parked in front of your apartment."

"How could they do this evil thing to you?" Karasa asked. "They are your own family."

"It is the way of the *Qur'an*. But I've already forgiven them," Effat replied.

"Why would you?" Karasa didn't understand.

"*Isa Masih*, Jesus my Messiah, has forgiven my sins. I can do no less." Effat's eyes gazed upward.

Karasa shook her head in disbelief, trying to get a handle on forgiving those who inflicted bodily harm and intended to take your life. But she could not.

"Karasa," Maude paused and stared into Karasa's eyes, "I have lived a long life, and this I know for sure - when you commit in your heart to trust Jesus with everything you cherish in this world, it will be your deciding moment."

Karasa could not hold her gaze and instead stared down.

"Give it some serious thought. Whatever injustice we suffer in this life is offset because God has given us the privilege to choose our destiny in the next." Maude abruptly turned to the task at hand. "Time to go." She led the way to the jeep.

The aged plane stood on the tarmac, ready to go. Maude stopped the vehicle. They unloaded their boxes before Maude parked the jeep out of sight by the building.

The extreme heat of the interior of the airplane felt as if they'd entered a large tin can left to bake in the sun. Void of passenger seats, the large unfinished cargo hold contained piles of padding material, particularly old blankets. Hemp cord and triple twined rope attached to the walls secured the stacks of wooden boxes and other cargo.

"Come with me. Only a few select people know about this. Promise me you'll never mention its existence to anyone?"

Both women nodded.

Maude walked toward the center of the hold. She lifted a section of the floor to show a hidden compartment underneath.

"Stow your clothing in there. When we get to Khartoum if there's any challenge, or anyone comes on board, you both lie down in there and pull the flooring down on top of you. Got it?" Maude asked.

"We will," Karasa said. "Does my brother know about this?"

"Yes, he does."

"He never told me about it."

"He promised he wouldn't. And I expect you to keep

your promise, both of you," Maude said with vehemence.

"Of course," both women replied in unison.

Maude relaxed and invited both women to come up front with her while she completed her pre-flight checklist. Karasa and Effat discovered that the width of the copilot seat could accommodate both of them.

Maude radioed the tower and negotiated her path as the plane taxied out to the runway. They mopped the perspiration that seeped down their faces as they waited for the plane ahead of them to take off. Two minutes later they were pushed against the back of their seat during the lift off. Once in flight, the two small fans on the instrument panel became operational. Positioned near the pilot's and copilot's seat, the fans blew refreshing cool air in their direction.

The clock on the dash read 8:50 A.M. They would arrive in Khartoum about noon. Two hours into their flight, Maude turned to Karasa.

"I want you to spell me while I stretch my legs and use the lavatory."

"But I do not know how to fly an airplane," Karasa answered.

"I'll show you. See this gauge with a little airplane in it?"

"Yes."

"See how it's on this line?"

Karasa nodded.

"As long as it's on the line we're flying level. If I push this the nose will go down and the little airplane goes below the line because we're going lower. If I pull it back the nose goes back up and the little plane comes back to the line. Now you try it."

Maude took her hands off of the wheel, held them up in the air as she vacated her seat.

"Ahh," Karasa gasped as she lunged into the pilot's seat to grab hold of the wheel.

"Okay, just hold it level," Maude stooped to look.

"Good." Maude rubbed Karasa's shoulder.

Karasa discovered that the airplane nearly stayed level by itself.

"Now, pull back the yoke and nose it up a little higher and watch the little plane in the gauge," Maude said.

Karasa did so and the airplane began to climb.

"Okay, level it off again," Maude said.

Karasa had no problem getting the airplane level again. Maude spent a few more minutes teaching her the foot controls and having her try them out.

"Look at the compass," Maude pointed at the dash. "We're on a heading of eighteen degrees right now," Maude said.

"Yes, I see it."

"Just head in that direction, and don't touch anything

else. The weatherman forecasted clear skies. You'll be fine," Maude toddled toward the rear of the airplane.

Karasa, enthralled with her new assignment, obeyed Maude's instructions.

Effat had listened with rapt attention. "Could I try flying the plane now?" Effat asked when Maude returned.

"Of course. We certainly owe you far more than that, Effat."

"Take the controls," Karasa moved so Effat could slide into the pilot's seat.

After twenty minutes Maude told Effat, "My turn." Sitting at the controls, Maude checked her gauges and prepared to descend for a landing into the Khartoum Airport.

"A work well begun is half-ended."

~ Plato

CHAPTER THIRTY-SIX

Khartoum, Sudan

In 1991 the Revolutionary Command Council for National Salvation introduced a new federal structure. Sudan was divided into nine states. In 1997 the number of states increased but Al Khartum, which includes the city of Khartoum, was still considered the most prominent and influential of all.

Magistrate Ibim Sharif supervised fifty government districts within Al Khartum, an area covering about one fourth of the City of Khartoum. In addition to his political duties as Magistrate, Ibim Sharif held the rank of Chief Law Enforcer.

After his graduation from the Sunni Islamic Legal School, his family had arranged the appointment as a present for his twenty-first birthday. In spite of his youth, he was effective and respected by the officers who worked under him. These officers didn't resent Ibim Sharif's appointment as Chief of Police. Traditionally business and government operated in this manner. A man with ability could rise through the ranks, but capability could only take you so far. The posts at the top were reserved for those with patronage. In Sudan, this was a fact of life.

The son of a wealthy man, Ibim Sharif's father owned and operated a large prosperous farm. Ibim's older brother would inherit the family's farm. As the second son his family purchased Ibim's position, and for his younger brother they purchased a commission as an officer in the army.

In addition to government administration in their districts, each of the magistrates had his specialty, such as criminal law, civil or *Sharia law*, the banks and monetary regulations, the transportation of goods, etc.

Magistrate Ibim Sharif's authority also included trade - exports and imports into the city of Khartoum. The men under the Chief of Police's command knew he showed a particular interest in human trafficking. The people of the North referred to southerners in Sudan as '*abeed*', the Arabic word for 'slaves'. The Christians and animists of Southern Sudan often referred to the northern Arabic *Muslim* tribes as '*Jallaba*', the Arabic word for 'slave traders'.

In deference to his specialty, sources from Kenya regularly informed him of suspicious suspects. It took Chief of Police Ibim Sharif's men about two hours to determine the identity of the pilot and to get a description of the incoming plane. Chief of Police Ibim Sharif detailed two men whom he trusted to stake out the airport with instructions to call him when the cargo plane arrived.

Ibim Sharif became interested in slavery because of his childhood experiences. He grew up realizing the economic benefits of slavery in running a successful farm. His father, unlike most of his Moslem counterparts, did not regard the infidels as subhuman but believed that once these mis-guided souls knew the truth about Islam, the religion of peace, they would embrace it. He provided opportunities for all slaves, his 'workers', to receive instruction in the *Qur'an*. Once a 'worker' acknowledged his faults and be-came a believer of Islam, his number was replaced by an Arabic name. They also received limited consideration. He remembered that on the Festival of *Yevmi Ashurer,* the day of sweet-soup, only the Islamic slaves shared the special dish - *Asure,* a porridge first created by Noah. His mouth still salivated when he thought of his mother's *Asure,* made with barley, corn, cracked wheat, chickpeas, sugar and whatever else was on hand.

His father adhered to the proverb: 'You reap what you sow'. He expected and received top performance from each of his 'workers'. He directed his overseer to reserve the whip for only the incorrigible. If the slave did not amend his ways, he was immediately resold in the market or given as a gift to his rivals. No official accounts were kept of slaves.

Once Ibim visited America and learned about people purchasing animal licenses. Americans kept better records on their dogs and cats than Khartoum did on their slaves. So he decided collect information to start a data base beginning with an actual numerical count. Later other pertinent information could be added.

In a case like today, he would put the fear of *Allah* into the pilot if he chose not to arrest her for transporting a foreigner illegally. The mother sneaking in to try to get back her child, he might look the other way and allow her to return home with just a stern warning. He had a child of his own and could understand even an infidel mother's desperation to reunite with her child.

"The bad news is that time flies.

The good news is that you are the pilot."

~ Michael Altshuler

CHAPTER THIRTY-SEVEN

Maude's plane touched down on the tarmac at the Khartoum International Airport. The apprehension of the travelers on board could be cut with a knife and divided in thirds.

"Go ahead and get into your *burqas*. When I stop, this plane is going to quickly heat up to 35 degrees Celsius and get uncomfortable," Maude said.

Karasa and Effat retrieved their *burqas*. Effat quickly dressed while Karasa mimicked Effat but was at a complete loss about securing her head scarf.

"Here, let me help you," Effat offered as she adjusted Karasa's headpiece.

After shouldering a bag of essential items, each held on to the cargo ropes as the plane taxied the runway.

As instructed, Maude pulled the plane up to a vacant

slot designated for those aircraft expecting incoming ship-
ments. She stopped the engines. A high chain link fence
surrounded the large paved area that held about twenty
cargo airplanes parked in a separate section, farther from
the main terminal than the passenger airplanes. About one
hundred meters from the plane, on the other side of the
landing strip, stood a single-story building with a sign: 'The
Pilot's Lounge Restaurant' in Arabic and English. Several
men entered it. To the left of the restaurant an open gate in
the fence appeared unguarded.

When Karasa approached the front of the plane, Maude
reminded her, "Remember Effat's instructions. A Moslem
woman doesn't speak to any man in public. She avoids eye
contact by looking down and always walks behind any
man. And don't show your face under any circumstances.

"We'll go over to the Pilot's Lounge. There women eat
in a separate, designated area," Maude said when Effat
joined them.

Maude noticed that both women carried shoulder bags.

"Wait. It's not necessary for you to bring your personal
effects now. We'll come back for them."

"I will just take out some money for lunch," Karasa
said.

"No, that's okay. Lunch is my treat," Maude said.

"Thank you," Karasa said as they hid their bags once
more.

Maude checked her watch: six minutes past twelve. When she opened the door of the plane she heard the last strains of the *Azaan*, the call to prayer, recited by the *muezzin* and resonating from the *minaret* or tower of the Great Mosque, *Mesjed al-Kabir*. She blocked the exit with her arm.

"We must wait until the Arabic Moslems complete their noon prayers as they bow toward Mecca. A good Moslem prays five times during the day."

When the chanting ended abruptly, Maude informed her companions, "We can leave now."

Maude climbed down the ladder last and locked the door behind her. Karasa started toward the building until Maude commanded curtly, "Walk behind me."

Karasa fell back along side of Effat. A glance around showed that no one had seen or overheard the incident.

When they entered the building, Effat touched Karasa's arm for her to follow her. She led the way into a separate seating area for women. Although not as fine as the men's section, it was quieter with no foul-smelling cigarette smoke. They sat at a table and waited for Maude to bring the food. Only three other women occupied the area, two at one table and one sat alone. Not wanting to be overheard speaking English, they sat in silence.

Maude brought a spicy rice and vegetable dish for each of them.

"How do I eat?" Karasa questioned in a hushed voice.

"You can uncover your face to eat with only women present, but leave your head covered on top." Effat added, "Just do what I do."

After they completed their meals, Maude whispered and pointed. "Effat, the phones are to the right of the rest area."

"I will call to find out where Mr. Cafferty is staying." Effat got up and ambled toward the telephones.

Ten minutes later Effat returned to her seat.

"He's staying at the Hilton Khartoum."

Maude nodded and led the way out of the Pilot's Lounge.

"After we retrieve your bags from the plane, you'll go out through that gate." Maude pointed to the unguarded opening in the fence. "Turn right and walk down Airport Boulevard up the main street to catch a minibus to the hotel."

"Karasa, remember that women sit in separate sections on public buses," Effat said.

Maude continued, "I'll spend most of my time in the Pilot's Lounge because there's no air conditioning in my plane. But if you're not back by dark, I'll sleep in my plane. The door will be slightly ajar and unlocked."

They trailed Maude to the plane.

With three meters between the women and Maude's plane, they heard the screeching of tires as two police cars came from nowhere and skidded to a stop on each side of them. The police cars had them boxed in, blocking their way to the plane. The sting, so precise and quick, caught the party of plotters unaware.

Maude's face wore a serious expression. The scarf, hiding most of Effat's face, couldn't conceal the look of fright revealed in her enormous round eyes.

Do they have a photo of me? Karasa wondered.

The Police officers, dressed in verdant uniforms and black berets, quickly exited both cars and stood in tense, attentive readiness. A young uniformed officer with his rank insignia displayed in gold on his shoulder boards took charge.

"What do you want?" Maude challenged the young officer.

The young officer ignored Maude and shouted orders. The two policemen spread out behind them as if cutting off their ability to turn and run toward the gate, while the younger one stood between them and the airplane. One officer approached Maude and spoke severely. "The Chief of Police demands silence unless you are being spoken to."

The Chief of Police turned his gaze on Karasa and spoke. Effat answered him in Arabic, in a frightened voice. As ordered, she pulled aside her scarf so that the bottom half of her face was visible. She whispered to Karasa in English, "He wants you to show your face."

Karasa considered her options before complying.

The Chief of Police asked Effat another question. Effat responded by saying her own name.

Answering another question, Effat responded, "Karasa."

If the police have a record that I'm a wanted criminal, it probably lists my warrior name. This is not good, Karasa thought. *I wish that I had told Effat to give a different name for me if anyone asked.*

A look of comprehension crossed the eyes of the Chief of Police as he stared intently at Karasa. Karasa looked down to avoid eye contact.

One thing is certain, Karasa thought, *to go anyplace with the police is the same as submitting to a slow death by torture.*

Effat turned to Karasa.

"The police have information and know why we are here. He wants to know the name of your son."

Did Effat's sister report us? Well, it doesn't matter now. For the moment I will need to play along and find some excuse to get my gun from my bag in the airplane.

"Tell him my son's name is Twangi," Karasa said.

After Effat translated, the Chief of Police asked another question.

"Did you ever fight with the SPLA?"

Karasa looked down and refused to answer.

Minutes passed slowly. When Karasa dared to peek, she felt the intensity of the man's stare as if he sought to assess the inmost depths of her soul.

"You must go with The Chief of Police," Effat looked dismayed.

The Chief spoke to his officer who approached Maude and translated.

"Are you the pilot of this plane?"

"Yes."

"What is your name?"

"Maude McMillan."

"You and this woman will remain here until you receive official permission to leave. If you try to take off before that we have orders to shoot down your plane."

Karasa felt compelled to act.

"Effat, tell him that I must have my medicine."

Karasa took quick giant steps toward the plane.

Not waiting for the translation, the policeman shouted.

Karasa did not have to understand his language to know that she had just been told to stop, but she moved faster. Watching his right hand out of the corner of her eye, she didn't see his left hand come up with another weapon pointed at her. A red dot from its laser sight marked her as its target.

The officer, standing about four meters away, fired his blunted pistol. With a popping sound two small, sharp probes attached to four and a half meters of insulated wires found their target. This powerful Neuro-Muscular Incapacitation device penetrated Karasa's clothing and delivered a high voltage, low amperage charge of electricity to stop Karasa in her tracks.

"Karasa's been tasered!" Maude yelled.

"Oww!" Karasa cried out in pain as thousands of electric volts went coursing through every nerve in her body. Her face grimaced and her body spasmed, jerking beyond her control. The .36 amp current, less than the average one amp Christmas tree light, still packed enough force to render Karasa too helpless to put her hands out to catch herself as she fell to the tarmac. Some detached part of her mind registered surprise when the police officer stepped forward to catch her and keep her head from striking the hard pavement.

Why would he do this for a criminal?

Her body still twitched without control. The hot tarmac burned her exposed ankles and hands. She couldn't even blink some particle out of her right eye.

The officer stood ready to press the trigger to relay additional charges at five-second intervals. Another policeman disengaged the taser and rolled her on her stomach. He cuffed her hands behind her back and frisked her for any weapon.

Next two policemen lifted her off the ground and carried her to the police car. They put her inside on the back seat and shut the car door.

The police car raced away after the Chief of Police entered the front passenger's seat. Except for the click and static as an officer spoke on the radio in Arabic, they rode in silence. Karasa strained to push her uncooperative body upright against the rear door so she could peek through the window. Struggling against her involuntary twitches, she tried to focus. As the vehicle passed the plane, she caught sight of an officer with his gun pointed at Maude. As Maude held Effat, tears trailed down her stoic face, falling onto the back of Effat's head scarf.

Maude cries tears for our final good-bye, Karasa observed as the pain of sadness pierced her heart.

"Some succeed because they are destined to, but most
succeed because they are determined to."

~ Anonymous

CHAPTER THIRTY-EIGHT

Khartoum, Sudan

Marco, a meticulous dresser, straightened his suit before he knocked on Cafferty's door. Cafferty eased it open and peered through the crack.

"About time, come in."

I'm enjoying myself now that the plot is afoot, Marco thought, borrowing the phrase Sherlock Holmes spoke in those detective novels.

"Good evening. The American is in his room and Lars is with him. Do you want me to watch him instead?" Marco asked, anticipating an assignment.

"No. Tell our men to watch his door in shifts. I have something that needs immediate attention."

"What do you want me to do?"

"I'm concerned with Andre Jones, one of my reporters from New Jersey."

"Is he getting curious?"

"No, just the opposite. He hasn't asked one single question about the story. That's what is making me nervous. If he has no interest in my story, perhaps he has one of his own. I want him watched. His room is next to the American's. I want you to sleep in the room down the hall with our men. If Jones leaves his room they must wake you so you can follow him."

"At what point shall I confront him, sir?"

"None, I just want you to follow and observe. I want to know where he goes. If he meets anyone I want to know who. If he talks to anyone I want to know what was discussed. Do you have a recording device?"

"Yes. It will record over an hour."

"Let me see it."

Marco retrieved a small device measuring two inches by a half inch from the pocket in his suit jacket. Cafferty examined it.

"Good, that will do. Plant it on him if he leaves," Cafferty said.

"I'll try," Marco replied.

"You'll do better than that," Cafferty answered. "He shouldn't even realize that he's being recorded."

Marco knew that he had to bring this off in order to

prove his value to Cafferty. "Yes, I understand," he said.

Marco left Cafferty's room and took an elevator down to the third floor. He entered the room and spoke to the hired men. "You will be watching the rooms of both the American and the black reporter from the <u>Asbury Park Journal</u>. If the reporter leaves you are to wake me immediately."

The men nodded. They accepted Marco as their de facto boss, an extension of Cafferty.

Marco hung his jacket carefully in the closet and glanced around the room for someplace to sleep. The beds would rumple his suit, not to mention his hair. He decided to make himself comfortable in a stuffed leather chair.

He had barely settled into position when one of the hired men whispered loudly, "The reporter's door just opened."

Marco quickly slipped his jacket back on and peeked out into the hallway.

"Jake, you come with me," he whispered.

Before entering the hall, he took out the voice recorder from his pocket and turned it on. He handed it to Jake saying, "He hasn't seen you. Ride the elevator down with him and find a way to slip this into his jacket pocket. If I don't catch up with you, follow him and tell me where he goes."

Before Jake could leave, Marco grabbed his shoulder.

"This is important. There's a big bonus for you if you

succeed."

Jake nodded and quickened his step to reach the elevator before the doors shut.

Marco peeled off down the stairway to the lobby, careful not to be seen. He caught a glimpse of his quarry exiting the hotel. Jake followed close behind. Outside the hotel, the reporter climbed into the first cab in line. Jake jumped into the second.

Marco hailed the third cab as he exited the building.

"Do you speak English?" Marco asked.

The cabbie wore a quizzical look on his face and waited.

Marco figured that money talks anyplace in the world. He took out his wallet and withdrew more cash than the man probably earned in a day.

"Where do you want to go?" The cabbie asked in English.

"I saw that man leave my wife's hotel room," Marco lied. "There'll be another twenty dollars U.S. if you follow him and he doesn't get suspicious."

"Am I doing anything illegal?"

"Am I dressed like a hoodlum? I just want to know who my wife is messing around with. Now get started before you lose him," Marco answered.

"Do not be concerned my friend. The driver of that cab is my brother-in-law."

Riding in light traffic they stayed well back in order to avoid detection, except at traffic lights where they had to close it up to be certain that they were not left behind.

Paving gave way to dirt streets.

They drove for five minute into seedier portions of town until the cabbie remarked, "Your wife has poor taste in men if her lover came from here. This is not a good part of the capital."

"Just follow that cab. When it stops and the passenger gets out, drop me far enough away to catch up, but not to be seen."

The cab continued down dirt roads without traffic signals. Marco's cab fell farther behind. The cab driver even stopped twice and turned off its lights so as not to alert the other cab.

"Stop," Marco handed the cab driver a crisp twenty dollar bill.

"Are you sure that you want to be left here? This section of the City is not safe for outsiders."

Marco paused and replied, "Wait right here to drive me back to the hotel. When I come back you'll earn another twenty."

"You got it, sir," the cabbie smiled.

Marco hurried to catch up with Jake. He wished that he wore something less conspicuous than his expensive suit. At least no street lights penetrated the dark shadows in this part of town.

Jake heard Marco coming up from behind and paused to wait for him to catch up. The man pointed. About fifty meters away from their location, Andre Jones scampered along the side of the road because there were no sidewalks. He seemed unaware of their presence.

"Did you put it into his pocket?" Marco asked.

"Yeah, I bumped him on the elevator and slipped it in. Piece of cake. What is it, some kind of a radio transmitter?"

"No, just a recorder." Marco felt magnanimous.

"I hope he doesn't find it," Jake said.

"So do I," Marco replied.

Andre turned around only once to look behind him. Marco's first reaction was to jump aside to avoid being seen, but Jake instructed, "Just keep walking."

This guy has tracked people before, Marco thought.

Andre Jones ignored them.

Andre hurried along and gained distance. A robed man stepped from an alley and together they walked a short distance before disappearing into a building about three meters from the road.

"We don't want to raise their suspicions. I'd suggest that we walk on down the street past where your man turned in and double back," Jake whispered.

"What if we're challenged?"

"I don't think that we will be. But if we are, just glance

at the guy like we're a little bit afraid of him and hurry past."

"I won't be faking it," Marco whispered.

"I will. Some tough acting raghead doesn't sweat me, but I can act like a sissy if you order it. I don't like it, but you're paying me well," Jake said.

A few minutes later the two men reached the building where Andre Jones had entered. The single story building looked identical to all of its neighbors. In the States most of these mud buildings would have been condemned and bull-dozed as uninhabitable.

A stern, unyielding man dressed in an Arabic robe leaned against a low stone wall. As they walked past the man glared at them. Marco had no trouble looking away nervously and not meeting his gaze.

They continued down the street until they were out of sight and concealed in darkness before Jake took Marco's arm and said, "Follow me."

They walked along the side of a house with no lights on and paused at the rear corner. After two or three minutes Jake led the way across the back of the house to the next, and to the next. Some had lights on and some did not. Marco kept waiting for dogs to bark, but none did.

They finally stopped behind one of the houses and Jake whispered to Marco, "The next one is the one he went into."

"All these buildings look alike from the rear. How do you know?" Marco asked.

"I counted buildings as we were walking. Didn't you?" The man said.

"Of course," Marco said, even though he hadn't.

"It doesn't look like there's anyone home in this one. Let me go in first. If it's empty I'll come out and get you," Jake said.

"What for?"

"The safest way to check out the building next door is through the windows of this one. We'll be looking out through windows that are dark. They have the lights on. That will be safer than standing on tiptoes to peep in through their windows with the chance of that bad guy discovering us."

Jake placed his hand on Marco's arm, "Wait here."

He forced open the back door and tiptoed into the building. A minute later he came back out for Marco. Jake led Marco quietly to a window. Marco could see Andre Jones in the lighted room next door, together with four or five other men in native dress. He couldn't hear the conversation across the gulf between the houses, but Andre Jones didn't appear happy. Wearing no jacket or dress shirt, he had stripped down to his undershirt. Marco wondered why.

While they watched, Andre Jones got up and walked out of sight, as one of the other men continued to talk to him.

Twenty minutes later Andre Jones came back into sight. After replacing his shirt and jacket he picked up a shoulder bag and walked toward the front of the house.

When Andre Jones exited the front of the house, a battered old vehicle pulled up in front and Jones got in. The vehicle drove away. Unfortunately they couldn't leave this house and get back to the taxi in time to follow Jones.

"I have a taxi waiting. Let's head back," Marco said.

They heard noises in the front of the house. The occupants had just come inside the dwelling. They moved as quickly and quietly as possible toward the back exit. Luckily they avoided detection and hurried away just as lights turned on.

Quietly skirting the rear of the house that Jones had entered, they continued to move through backyards, back to where the taxi would be waiting.

When they climbed into the taxi, Marco ordered, "Take us back to the hotel."

"You got it, boss. You got the money you promised?"

"You'll get it when we're back at the hotel."

"How 'bout half of it now?"

Marco didn't feel like arguing and handed it over. Elated, the cabbie pocketed the money and executed a U-turn. The driver drove three blocks before putting on his lights. They rode in silence for twenty minutes until the cab pulled to a stop in front of the Khartoum Hilton. Marco paid the cab driver the remainder of the promised money. Although Marco refused, the cabbie tried effusively to give Marco his telephone number. The driver, however, willingly agreed to write a description of the address where the meeting had taken place in Marco's notebook in exchange for a generous tip. Details about a specific location often replaced street names and numbers of residential addresses in Khartoum.

Jake waited beside the entrance of the hotel.

"Not bad. Here," Marco quickly slipped him the promised payment.

Marco hurried through the lobby and took the elevator to the third floor. He stepped into the room and asked, "Has Mr. Jones returned?"

"Yeah, he got back about five minutes ahead of you," one of the men replied.

Marco breathed a sigh of relief. Then concern etched his face. He needed a pretense to enter Andre's room. He quickly decided on a plan and gathered up some materials.

"Come with me." He called to Jake.

Returning to the hall Marco stopped abruptly.

"Jake, we have to retrieve the recording device."

As they walked down the hall they discussed their plan of action.

Andre Jones answered the door within a few seconds.

He wore a dress shirt but no tie or jacket.

"Good evening. We're here to review tomorrow's agenda. Mr. Cafferty wants your opinion about potential stories," Marco said.

"Hi. I'm Jake."

Andre Jones looked disinterested but motioned for them to come in. Marco glanced to his right. He had difficulty suppressing a smile when he noticed a jacket hanging in the closet. It resembled the one that Andre had worn earlier.

Marco motioned for Mr. Jones to follow him over to a table near a window. He sat on the chair facing the door so that Jones would face the window. Marco spread out several pictures and placed a notepad on the table.

"Take a look at these pictures. What kind of articles do you think we should aim for tomorrow?" Marco asked.

Andre Jones replied noncommittally that they should introduce Travis to his stepson. After their visit to the working farm, the next destination could be to see the *suqs* (bazaars) or other interesting the sights in Khartoum.

Jake excused himself to use the bathroom. When he entered the alcove, he paused long enough to reach into the closet and to pull out the recording device hidden in Andre's jacket pocket. When he returned to the front room, he nodded to Marco.

"Thank you for you input. Good night," Marco gathered

up his pictures and notes.

The reporter seemed relieved to see him go.

Marco hurried to the far end of the hall.

"Did you get the device?"

Jake handed it over, "Here, it's still recording."

Marco switched it off.

"Good. Now work in shifts. Stay awake all night to watch Mr. Jones's and Mr. Martin's doors, or any activity in the hall. I must run another errand."

Marco returned to his own room. Picking up the telephone receiver, he dialed Cafferty's number. Cafferty answered on the fourth ring.

"Yes?"

"This is Marco. Our mutual friend attended a meeting in the suburbs with some friends of his."

"Anything else?"

"Yes sir. I've retrieved my toy. Would you like to see it?"

"Bring it up."

The phone went dead. Before leaving, Marco took time to wash his face and hands and comb his hair. When he finished, he took the elevator to Cafferty's floor. Feeling terrific he grinned as he knocked on the door of Cafferty's suite. He had proved this night that he could deliver.

Mr. Cafferty acknowledged Marco's success. But after pumping him for information about Andre Jones' meeting, and a description of the other men, Marco was dismissed. Marco returned to his room feeling disappointed that he couldn't listen to the recorder, but delighted that he'd earned Cafferty's trust.

"He who is not everyday conquering some fear has not

learned the secret of life."

~ Ralph Waldo Emerson

CHAPTER THIRTY-NINE

Cafferty placed Marco's recorder on his desk next to a pen and writing pad with the hotel's logo inscribed on them. Using the unit's built-in counter, he'd record the position of interesting comments. He poured himself a drink, sat down and switched on the unit.

Cafferty heard Marco instruct one of his hired men to slip the recorder into Jones' pocket. He didn't perform this task himself but delegated it to his subordinates. His actions defined his resourcefulness and leadership qualities and Cafferty admired both attributes.

That young man has surpassed my expectations. His future appears promising.

The voice recorder continued to play.

Cafferty heard the reporter get into a cab.

When the reporter gave the cab driver directions and an

address, Cafferty jotted down the number shown on the counter and wrote 'address' beside it. He fast forwarded past segments with no conversation.

Cafferty resumed the recording. Andre paid the cabbie and offered him additional money if he'd wait. When the driver asked for an exorbitant amount of money, Andre dismissed the cab. Next, the reporter's footfalls were audible. The reporter's footsteps slowed.

"*al Salamu,* peace, I'm Andre Jones. I'm expected for a meeting."

After Andre's introduction, a stranger spoke. Cafferty added the location number to the pad and wrote the word 'Arabic' along side of it.

When Andre Jones' voice could be heard again, Cafferty jotted down the number in the recorder's counter.

"*al Salamu Alaykum,* Sheik Rameshwar, it is so good to see you again," Andre said.

"It is my pleasure. Our mutual friend Jaafar commends you. I've asked *Imam* Zakir to greet you," a heavily accented voice replied.

"May you be favored by *Allah,*" A raspy voice declared.

"*Inshallah,*" Jones paused. "I have wonderful news. The American terrorist, Travis Martin, is here in Khartoum. He is staying in the same hotel as I," Jones said.

"Can you approach this infidel?" asked a voice in

thickly accented English.

"Yes. More importantly I will write a front-cover story about his pending public execution for the crimes against Islam. Also, I will make certain our national stations telecast the mob chanting '*Allah Akbar*.'"

"Is this infidel being watched?"

"Yes. Three armed men accompany him at all times."

"This is of little consequence," *Imam* Kazkir replied. "Let us pray to Allah for guidance."

For fifteen minutes the *Imam* prayed in a guttural unintelligible language.

"Allah has told me what you must do. Take off your jacket and your shirt," *Imam* Kazkir requested.

"But why?"

"Our holy leader told you to take them off," an unfamiliar harsh voice commanded.

"That's alright, Abdul. We have time," the *Imam*'s voice broke in. "Andre, you can hang your jacket and shirt over the back of this chair."

Sounds of swishing fabric and shuffling of feet could be heard.

Will I still be able to hear what is being said once his jacket is taken off? Cafferty thought, anxiously.

"What now, holy leader?" Andre's voice sounded faint but clear.

"Here, put this on."

"What is this?"

"It is your ticket to paradise. Allah has chosen you to be his martyr."

"But what is in this vest?"

"Powerful explosives. As long as you are standing within ten meters of the American terrorist you will kill him in the explosion." A wicked smile slowly emerged on Sheik Rameshwar's face.

"But the people who we turn him over to would surely execute him."

"Perhaps, but we cannot take the chance. Who knows, the American government could pay enough money to buy him back. Now try on your shirt and jacket over the vest." The *imam* paused a few minutes and then added. "I cannot even tell that you are wearing it."

"But how do I detonate it?" Andre sounded worried.

"That is the beauty. You will not. All you have to do is to wear it, and at the proper time we will use a small radio transmitter, and you will be conveyed to paradise."

I have a feeling this is not what Andre bargained for, Cafferty smirked.

Cafferty was warming to this. Obviously Andre Jones had become a closet Moslem, but never expected to play the part of a martyr in this human drama.

What a fool Andre Jones is. And to think that we con-sidered hiring him to work at the Daily Times.

"I'm not prepared for martyrdom. Isn't this something that I should choose for myself?" Andre bleated.

"Some men choose greatness, while others have greatness thrust upon them," the *Imam* replied.

"What if I choose not to do this?" Andre asked.

"I suggest that you change your mind. You will not leave this city alive if you betray your faith," Abdul's surly and threatening voice replied.

"A Moslem who betrays his faith is worse than an infidel, and is hunted down and killed," a third unidentified man's voice spoke.

"As long as you will die anyway, wouldn't you rather spend eternity in paradise with sixty virgins at your beck and call?" Sheik Rameshwar asked.

"Yes, of course," Andre replied.

"Good, it's settled. Now return to your hotel. From this moment on wear this vest under your suit, any time that you leave your hotel room. If you do not, you will be treated as a traitor to Islam. You are being watched. Even in your hotel we are watching you."

"I understand," Andre replied, his voice now weak and subdued. "I will not let down our cause."

"A wise declaration," the holy man replied.

A few more instructions concerning techniques for his impending martyrdom and Andre left the house. If the *imam,* holy man, needed to get a message to Andre, someone would call him at his hotel. If the conversation included the code words 'full moon', it would alert Andre that his mentor considered the information important.

Cafferty fast forwarded through most of Andre Jones' return to his hotel, including Marco's visit to retrieve the device.

So Cafferty had a traitor in his midst - one with explosive underwear! Well, forewarned was forearmed. He continued to turn over in his mind what he should do with this traitor.

Will these men Jones met with become more dangerous to me if Jones disappears? If I were this rogue leader, I wouldn't trust all my eggs in one basket. Cafferty had to assume that this *imam* would have a backup plan in case Jones failed. *But what would it be?*

He decided to sleep on it and make a decision in the morning.

"Change is the only constant."

~ Proverb

CHAPTER FORTY

Cafferty tossed and turned. Sleep became elusive as worry steeped into the crevices of his brain. Even his usual libation of whiskey did not calm his active mind enough for slumber to prevail.

Lesser men, men who worked for a living, were merely tired in mind or muscle. They possessed no concept of the mental energy that went into a significant plot, especially a plot which would carry you to the top of your organization.

Bang, bang. Knocking came from the door.

Cafferty glanced at the clock's face which read 6:36 A.M. His body opposing the arrival of Tuesday morning, he lumbered out of bed and trudged to the door.

Maybe that's Hank bringing breakfast, he thought.

When Cafferty opened the door he gasped but quickly regained his composure as he greeted Abu al Sadir, Minister of Defense Huzang's right-hand man.

Cafferty invited him in; aware that he appeared disheveled and dressed only in his pajamas.

Abu al Sadir walked well into the room before Cafferty remembered, in momentary horror his illegal bottle of booze displayed in plain sight on his writing desk.

Due to the pressing matters of immense importance, however, the Minister of Defense wouldn't be concerned about a bottle of illegal whiskey. They shared one trait in common: both were pragmatic in their approach to life. Nevertheless, he discreetly removed the empty bottle and concealed it in a nearby receptacle.

Abu walked across the room to a comfortable stuffed chair and waved his hand over it. The gesture conveyed a request for permission to sit.

"Of course, please make yourself comfortable. I can order breakfast for both of us if you would like?" Cafferty asked.

"No, thank you, I won't be staying long." Abu al Sadir paused. "Minister of Defense Huzang told you that I speak for him?"

"Yes, he did."

"This is good."

Abu spoke English with a far more pronounced accent than the Minister of Defense whom he represented.

"Do you have the American terrorist where you can fetch him quickly, if needed?" Abu continued.

Certain that the Minister of Defense's intelligence apparatus had already gathered this information, Cafferty answered truthfully. "Yes, I do. He's right here in room 303."

"Good. What precautions have you taken?"

"He is being guarded twenty-four seven by one of my hired men. The other two men stay in a room down the hall and take turns monitoring the halls. I have also arranged that no hotel employees are permitted to enter his room."

"Excellent," Abu smiled. "How much do you trust these three henchmen?"

"They don't know who I am. They've been told that I work for an oil company. They take their orders from a man who works for me."

"Does he also work for your newspaper?"

"Yes, he does."

"If it became necessary to liquidate the three hired men, does that present a problem? You will understand why when the time comes."

"They do their job because I pay them well, but they're expendable."

"Our requirement for the American terrorist requires that there is no provable connection between Minister of Defense Huzang and the American prior to tomorrow evening. There must also be no possible connection to you," Abu said.

"You mean that I should not be seen in public with him?"

"Yes, that is correct. Also, there should not be any way to trace the airplane rental or hotel accommodations back to you or to your company."

"I've already addressed this."

"Good. Not today, but tomorrow between the hours of two and six, both you and the American terrorist and his son will be needed. This is of the most extreme importance and cannot be altered for any reason."

"I understand," Cafferty said.

Do you have also his slave son?"

"Yes, I do."

"Good. All three of you will be picked up here in this room tomorrow afternoon. You will be receiving a news story such as can make a career in your American media. I guarantee that you will be pleased with the result."

"We'll be waiting," Cafferty said.

What would be the advantage of sharing this informa-tion with Abu?

If he told Abu, the Minister of Defense might blame him for his poor choice of this reporter to accompany him. But he could think of no downside, other than a lapse of judgment. On the other hand, holding back the information would bring serious questions of trust.

Cafferty decided to confide the information to Abu.

"I have discovered a problem since our arrival here. One of the reporters, Andre Jones, is working with one of your," – Cafferty paused because he didn't want to use the word terrorist – "extremist groups."

"How do you know this?" Abu asked.

"I had him followed."

Cafferty played the pertinent parts of the recording for Abu, and showed him the address where the meeting had taken place.

"And this happened when?"

"Last evening, approximately twelve hours ago."

Abu thought this over.

"This reporter must be kept away from this American terrorist at all costs. Minister of Defense Huzang requires his presence too urgently to take any risk whatsoever."

"Today, I intended to send him on some superfluous errand just to keep him out of the way," Cafferty said.

"Good. He will be killed later."

"That's fine with me," Cafferty said. "Will you also kill the people who gave him the explosives?"

"Perhaps, but when you step on cockroaches you just cause more to breed in the walls. Besides, these cockroaches can often be useful. In this case they must be reckoned with. They should know better than to oppose the Minister of Defense. We must crush them enough that they get the message, but not so much that they hate us more than the great Satans, Israel and the United States," Abu said.

"I understand." Cafferty hid his surprise about how the people in charge regarded the extremists in their own country. Cafferty actually feared these irrational extremists.

"Where is the reporter right now?" Abu asked.

"He has a separate room down the hall from the American's."

Abu's expression showed alarm.

"How many rooms separate them?" His words remained level and calm but, 'You Fool' was written all over his face.

"There are three other rooms between them."

"Don't you know that these people can build an explosive device that can take out three rooms between and still kill the American terrorist? If this Andre Jones were simply to walk down the hall and pause outside the American's hotel door, the American terrorist would have little chance of surviving the attack."

Cafferty perceived that Abu contemplated the matter so he waited.

"Well, what ploy did you plan to use that would distance Andre from the American for the day without arousing suspicion? Assume that he has the ability to get messages to those who gave him the explosives, and believe that they will try to kill the American terrorist another way if they know he is compromised?" Abu asked.

"If I tell him that I have information that this American's wife has followed him, he would jump at the chance to approach and apprehend her."

"That will work."

Abu thought this over.

"Tell him that she is arriving by boat. I will send two of my men. You can introduce them as guides - men that you hired locally. We will take him to the waterfront, and he will spend the day watching the boats."

When the boat doesn't arrive, we will tell him that we're going back to the hotel. But instead we'll take him to the desert and leave him bound in a tent with his explosives removed and disarmed. Hopefully his *imam* will think he is in his hotel room and will not even know he has been compromised. When this affair is over, we can eliminate the reporter. Also, we'll locate his *imam* and place the fear of Allah into him."

"Should one of my men accompany Andre Jones on his fool's errand?" Cafferty asked. "My other two men can guard Travis."

"Yes, but this is not enough," Abu said. "I will send more men. They will identify themselves to yours by showing them a silver coin when they arrive. Any additional rooms on the third floor will be booked by my own men. Both room and maid service will be suspended for today and tomorrow. Necessities and food will be sent in by me.

"Sounds good."

"May I use your telephone?"

"Of course," Cafferty pointed in the direction of the phone.

Cafferty walked into the other room and quickly replaced his pajamas in order to give Abu privacy for his call. He would shower and shave later.

Abu had already completed his call when Cafferty walked back into the room.

"My men are on their way up. I would trust them with my life. They are completely loyal to Minister of Defense Huzang," Abu said.

He must have had these men standing by, Cafferty thought.

"I need to speak with your men as well, so that everyone receives the same instructions," Abu added.

Cafferty made two phone calls, and then informed Abu, "They're on the way up."

Abu settled back into the padded chair to wait, leaving Cafferty to open the door.

Abu's men arrived followed by Marco and Jake. Altogether, twelve large men crowded into the room.

Out of deference to Cafferty, Abu spoke first in English. He repeated it again in Arabic to his own men.

"Your assignment is to protect the American Terrorist at all cost," Abu said.

"From the time that we end this meeting, I want armed

men watching the elevator and the stairway doors at both ends of the hall. Two men will watch in shifts. No hotel personnel or anyone else will be allowed on the third floor. If anyone gets off an elevator or comes out of a stairway, the first man tells them that the floor is closed. If any problem ensues, the second man steps out and kills them. Any questions?"

Everyone understood.

Abu informed the men of their individual assignments. They were given instructions regarding Andre and the extremists. The extremists were the only ones who knew of a link from the reporter to the American terrorist. Anyone allowed to live must know the government's anger rages because they made the reporter wear the explosives. They could not allow anyone to think that they suspected the identity of the target.

"When you arrive at the docks, go to a location where Andre is safely controlled and cannot be found. I do not want him killed until I give the order." Abu commanded two of his men.

"Yes sir," both replied in unison.

Abu turned now to Cafferty. "Where are you taking the American terrorist today?"

"We're taking him to a farm to spend the morning touring the place and taking pictures. This afternoon we're taking him to another farm, farther from town, where he will meet his stepson. We'll return to Khartoum late in the afternoon to visit some sights. Andre planned to take pictures of the event."

"That's not a problem. Mr. Eli Mete, the reporter for the SUNA, is also a photographer," Abu said.

I have another reporter, Max Golden. His newspaper is called the Liberal Enquirer. He has no idea what is going on here. His paper specializes in sensationalism."

"A Jew?"

Abu shrugged when Cafferty didn't readily answer.

"What about your newspaper?"

"Marco, a respected reporter from the Daily Times, will cover it."

"Good. My men will provide additional security for today."

Abu turned to the leader of his elite soldiers.

"That leaves you eight men. Send two of them with the American for local security. Form the remaining men into two teams of three men each to watch from a distance. Eliminate anyone who seems too curious, and try to locate those who may be watching the reporter. They must die, but their bodies should not be discovered for several days."

"Yes, sir."

"Okay. Andre Jones must remain in his room until the American terrorist leaves. The terrorist will be escorted down the back stairs by 8:00 A.M. this morning. Two of you will meet the party at a waiting vehicle and the others will provide cover. Do not tell the Jew anything until you are on the way."

The men left the room, leaving only Abu and Cafferty behind. Cafferty was frankly surprised by all of their precautions to protect this American.

Cafferty placed his right hand on Abu's arm as he rose to leave.

"Why is this American so important?" Cafferty asked.

An enigmatic smile emanated on the corners of Abu's mouth.

"I cannot tell you now, my friend, but all of your questions will be answered tomorrow evening," Abu replied.

"Nobody can go back and start a new beginning, but

anyone can start today and make a new ending. "

~ Maria Robinson

CHAPTER FORTY-ONE

When he woke up, Travis consulted his wristwatch
he'd placed on the dresser. The digits read 6:45 A.M. He
looked out his bedroom window as the bright yellow ball of
the sun's reflection glistened on the Nile River. He washed
in the hot steamy shower, a luxury nonexistent in his home
in Kenya. Before he dressed, he strapped his Glock on his
back. He replaced his wristwatch and turned on the transmitter. Prepared to leave at a moment's notice, he paced his
hotel room in anticipation.

Will Twangi remember me? he wondered.

Tap, tap. He heard a quick knock and the door opened.

"Bringing breakfast." Lars returned with two trays.

"Smells good; it will surely stop my stomach from
growling."

Travis' stomach began to rumble, confirming his statement.

"I'm your shadow until your ride comes," Lars said.

"When will that be?"

"Soon."

As they ate in silence, Travis considered this room to be comparable to that in any above average hotel in the U.S., with only subtle differences in the art work on the walls and style of furniture.

"What's on the agenda?" Travis asked.

"You got me," Lars answered. "We'll have to wait and see."

I'm worried about Karasa. Did she ever find out about Twangi? Travis thought. Travis glanced at the inoperative phone on the writing desk.

"Hey, Lars, I need to make a phone call."

"Let's ask the boss."

Lars opened the door and looked both ways to make sure no one walked the hall. He caught a glimpse of Marco quickly entering the room down the hall.

"Let's go. He's back."

Travis picked up his backpack and followed him. When Lars opened the same door, tobacco fumes assaulted their nostrils.

"Marco, would you have any objection to me making a call home to check that everything is alright?" Travis asked.

Marco hesitated.

"No one has to leave the room, I have no secrets," Travis added.

Turning his head toward the phone, Marco gestured for Travis to go ahead with his call.

Travis' hand lifted the receiver as his heart raced. He'd determined to speak in code because their lives were at stake. He dialed the country code for Kenya, followed by the telephone number for a company that could provide a radio link to the Anderson's mission.

Ellen's voice answered the radio call.

"Hello, Ensebbe Refugee Camp, over."

Travis hoped that if he called her by the wrong name, she might take the hint that he couldn't talk freely and just get her husband.

"Ayella, this is Travis Martin. May I speak with Pastor Jim, please?"

At first Ellen hesitated, undoubtedly confused.

"Yes, I'll get him," Ellen replied.

If Ellen warned Jim that something sounded wrong and about the possibility of others listening in on the call, he'd put two and two together. Travis glanced at Marco, who raised an eyebrow.

Jim's voice sounded almost cheerful, with an edge in his voice that you would have had to know him to notice.

"Hey, Travis, how's it going?"

"This charter is running a bit long. How's everything there?" Travis asked.

"You know this camp. We get more unexpected people than we can handle every day."

Is there a double meaning there? Travis wondered:

"You been by my place in the last few days?" Travis asked.

"Yes, I had a talk with your father-in-law about the surprise party. Ellen is all excited. You know women and birthday parties," Jim answered.

"I'm looking forward to it, too," Travis lied. The fiction of a party covered what they really wanted to say, but didn't dare.

"I'm afraid that your wife tricked your surprise out of Ellen, and she knows what you're giving her for her birthday. I'm sorry about that."

Travis felt the bottom of his stomach drop out like a marine who forgot his parachute, but he showed no concern or visible emotion on his face.

Jim went on to cover Travis' lapse.

"I think that Maude is coming to the party too. It should be a real humdinger with your mother-in-law's cooking."

Maude flew a plane. So that's how Karasa would be arriving. Even if these guys heard the name 'Maude' it would mean nothing to them.

Travis felt his composure slipping, but he determined to

cover his concern by pretending his daughter had become ill.

"What about my daughter? Is she still running a fever?" Travis asked.

Jim seemed to catch on right away.

"Yes, but not high enough to be dangerous. Our wives are using wet cloths to keep it down at night."

Travis knew that Jim had mentioned his wife only to throw off any suspicion that she may have left.

It must be tearing Jim apart to be telling lies, even to save Karasa from these people, Travis thought.

Marco stood up and tapped his watch with two fingers, the signal to leave.

Travis threw out, just for good measure, "Make sure she drinks a lot of fluids and thank Ellen for helping Karasa look after her. Gotta go - see you soon."

Travis hung up the phone wishing that his lies were true.

Marco pointed at the backpack and gave Travis a quizzical look.

"Just a few sodas and some snacks from the room," Travis said.

"Would you mind if I had a look?"

"Not at all."

Travis held the bag open and Marco checked the contents. His money and extra passport were glued under the false bottom of the bag and remained undetected.

They were on their way. They left the room and descended the back stairs. Travis' feet seemed to drag in a heaviness that followed a wrecked, contrite heart. When they reached the bottom of the staircase entering a small hallway, the small group of men turned right and exited through the back door.

"The measure of a truly great man is the measure by

which he treats lesser men."

~ Anonymous

CHAPTER FORTY-TWO

The shiny black limo pulled up behind the Hilton Khartoum. The Arab driver got out and opened the rear door for Marco, Travis, the reporter with a camera, and the two other Arab men. The Arabs wore identical long sleeve hemp shirts, kaki pants, boots and white head gear with red bands. Travis suspected they were Sudanese soldiers. Even though no insignia identified the men, they conducted themselves in a way similar to the military elite of any nation, with the pride of Force Recon.

If elite Sudanese military are going along for the ride, I'm in deep trouble. Any pretense of doing newspaper articles is over, Travis thought.

Out of the corner of his eye, Travis spotted a lanky Caucasian male dressed in an ill-fitting bellhop uniform heading toward the hotel's servant entrance. Travis knew he must be Kookie, following the signal transmitted from his watch. Travis stopped in mid stride and pretended to tie his boot lace. Almost immediately a pair of strong arms grabbed each of his elbows and pushed him toward the waiting vehicle. Even though Kookie couldn't be of assistance now, just knowing Kookie waited nearby gave Travis moral support.

After he climbed into the limo he glanced out the window, but Kookie had already disappeared. Travis turned his attention to the other car that pulled up behind the limo; three Arabs dressed in civilian clothing while wearing cloth head coverings exited the hotel and got into the vehicle. The driver of the limo waited until a blue van approached and parked before starting the ignition. Travis noticed that when the van stopped, three Arabs wearing military attire exited and went into the Hilton Khartoum through the servant's entrance.

Is Kookie in trouble? Travis wondered.

The rest of the men got into another car and a van that were pulled up behind the limo.

Travis looked away when he heard his name.

"Travis Martin, I'm Mr. Eli Mete and it's a pleasure to meet you."

"Likewise."

Travis glanced at the Arab who sat beside Eli Mete. The Arab stared straight ahead without acknowledging him.

As the limo started its engines, a pudgy man of average height came running up. Out of breath, he knocked on the rear tinted window.

"Stop the car and let him in," Marco called out.

When the rear door opened, the plump, balding man clambered in and planted himself on the seat between Marco and Travis. The lush roomy interior could easily afford six people comfortable seating.

"Hi, I'm Max Golden from the <u>Liberal Enquirer</u>. I'll be helping with the interview today."

His associates greeted him with a nod.

"You must be Mr. Martin." Without warning his chubby hand grabbed and shook Travis' hand vigorously.

Travis just stared in disbelief at the enthusiasm of this misguided reporter.

Could it be that this guy had no idea what was really going on here? Travis wondered. *This guy works for the* <u>*Liberal Enquirer,*</u> *the paper that reports celebrities married to space aliens and other sensational topics. That does not speak highly of reliability.*

"Pleased to meet you," Eli Mete interjected.

Eli Mete and Max Golden conversed and exchanged information regarding their respective newspapers.

"How about a smile." Without waiting, Mr. Eli Mete snapped a photo of Travis.

"I'll take more when we get out," Eli Mete added.

Max turned to Marco and asked, "Where is that other reporter, Andre?"

"He's covering another assignment. He'll join us later," Marco replied.

"That's good," Max said, even though Travis guessed that he didn't really care.

"So how do you feel about coming back to Sudan?" Max asked Travis as he positioned his pen to take notes.

The interview begins, Travis thought.

"Rather vulnerable. If something goes wrong I have no one here who I can count on," Travis answered.

"Well, you can count on me," Max said.

Travis suppressed his desire to laugh. Instead he replied, "I doubt there's anything you can do to help." Looking Max Golden square in the eye he asked, "How are you with a sword?"

"They don't still fight with those, do they?"

The military guy sitting across from them snorted.

Travis choked off an insult about knives in backs.

"No, the Sudanese military is well armed and well trained," Travis stated.

Travis caught a flicker of surprise pass across the face of the soldier sitting across from him.

Max Golden held up a small voice recorder.

"Do you mind if I record our conversation now?" Max asked.

Eli Mete placed his camera on the cushioned seat and retrieved a small writing pad. He jotted down notes as he listened to the interview. Marco put his hand in his jacket pocket and a slight audible click of a recording device could be heard. He also retrieved a leather journal and wrote a brief entry with his Caran d'Ache gold pen.

Marco's actions suggest an alternative motive, perhaps to gain acceptance from his colleagues?

"So they hired you to go into Sudan and rescue those kids?" Max asked.

"No, nothing like that. A friend of mine from the Marine Corps saved my life in Vietnam."

"Threw himself on a grenade?"

"No, he took enemy fire and ended up crippled. He's permanently wheel chair bound. When his grandchildren were taken in a slave raid, I went to Sudan to get them back. Believe me, I wanted no part of it. But I owed this guy."

"What were his grandchildren doing in Sudan," Max asked.

Travis was warming to this guileless little guy even though he really didn't want to. "George's daughter is a Christian missionary in Kenya," Travis answered.

He purposely omitted her name.

"They were flying medical supplies to a mission up near the border. Bad weather and clogged fuel filters forced them to land across the border at the nearest airstrip."

"But how were white kids mistaken for village kids and taken in a slave raid?" Max asked.

"George's family is black."

"I thought that all missionaries in Africa were white," Max said.

"Guess not."

Eli Mete shifted gears by interjecting the next question.

"Is it true that you defiled the village *Imam* in your raid?"

Travis noticed the soldier's muscles in his arms and legs became tense; yet he remained face forward with no perceptible movement.

"No, but we faked it to look like we had," Travis answered truthfully.

"Why did you do that?"

"When we retrieved George's grandchildren there were a number of other children on the farm who were slaves. I couldn't bring myself to just take the two American children we went after and leave the others in slavery."

"Go on," Max urged.

"Well, the only way for the leader of this SPLA unit to bring back all of the children was for me and the woman I've since married to stay behind and create a diversion. We did whatever we could to make them mad enough to chase us instead of the rebels, who escaped with the children."

"Including faking the defiling of a Moslem holy man?" Eli Mete asked.

"That's right. I wanted them as mad as hornets so the enemy would track us with a vengeance instead of pursuing the kids."

Out of the corner of his eye Travis saw the soldier relax a little. Even if he'd admitted to an atrocity, Travis felt certain the soldier had been instructed not to attack him. But for some reason it felt good after all of this time to tell at least one Moslem what really happened. He didn't know why.

Leaving the city, the limo drove on desert roads as sand rose up and obscured their vision.

Max continued to ask questions about the mission. He also inquired about his current occupation and new life in Kenya.

Travis answered all the questions but wondered why this charade of an interview continued on and on.

You could've convinced me a monkey ate my lunch. Why are these reporters actually pretending to be doing their jobs? Travis wondered.

About thirty minutes out of the city they stopped at what could best be described as a small working farm. The men in both vehicles climbed out of their cars. A weather-beaten middle-aged man, his weary-eyed wife wearing a *burqa,* and three well-behaved children came out to greet them. All wore clean but much used clothing.

Two other Sudanese soldiers got out of the front of the car and walked back.

"Obviously, no slaves reside here," Marco observed.

Travis didn't argue. He knew the truth because he'd witnessed the atrocities of slavery in Sudan with his own eyes. Surely the reporters realized that neither the farm's size nor its productivity would benefit from slaves. Yet, they were expected to extol this 'sanitized' farm for their featured newspaper article.

Two Arab soldiers stayed with the vehicles while they toured the farm, walking around for an hour. One of the soldiers always shadowed Travis. The farmer spoke no English but one of the Arab soldiers translated. The farmer kept up a constant commentary, introducing them to the cows, showing them the chickens, talking about the crops they would grow when the dry season ended. The farmer strutted about and appeared proud. He did everything but introduce the cows by name.

Max asked a never-ending stream of questions, which their tour guide answered with patience that Travis envied. As Travis watched the man he became even more convinced of the man's military status.

Marco just trailed along paying special attention to not stepping in anything that would soil his Gucci loafers or brushing against anything that would dirty his suit pants. Incredibly, the man had worn a jacket and tie to a working, rural farm. When Marco began to perspire under the scorching sun, he stripped off his jacket and unbuttoned his shirt.

Their tour led them past an old wooden wagon. The wooden whiffletree where a horse would be hitched leaned against the unpainted wooden wall. A heavy looking bale of hay had fallen off and lay on the ground by the side of the wagon. Max looked about as if looking for a crane, and asked how they loaded the heavy bales of hay onto the wagon. The military man who led them around picked the heavy bale up off the ground and half swung – half tossed it up on the wagon. When he flashed Max a smile, Max appeared awed.

Travis wondered how the soldiers in sheep's clothing, especially the one who appeared as strong as a trained elephant, would react if he stretched his legs a little.

Travis spotted a device that would be towed behind a horse for plowing. Leaving the group he walked over to inspect the piece of equipment which had been left by the side of an unpainted wooden barn.

He expected to be called back to the group but heard no warnings. So he bent over and pretended to inspect the tiller's blades. The soldier brought the rest of the group over to see the equipment.

"Would you tell the farmer that I'm interested in his plow and that I plant a small piece of land in Kenya?"

The soldier spoke to the farmer, who beamed.

"Where is your horse?" Travis asked him.

Translation completed, the farmer motioned for Travis to follow. He led into the barn where he stopped by a horse.

Travis stepped up to the horse and held out his hand for the horse to smell. Reaching up, he stroked its neck just behind its ear. The farmer grinned with approval.

The soldiers obviously didn't think horses to be a threat of escape, so they would probably not bar him from access to them. Certain that Twangi had never ridden a horse; they'd still make better time on horses than on foot if the opportunity arose.

Horses couldn't cross the desert, but they could double back around Khartoum to the Nile where they could try for water transportation or a bus.The beginning of a plan was coming together.

At the end of their tour, two coolers were carried out of the trunk of the limo and placed on the ground. One contained small flatbread sandwiches. The other enclosed cooled bottled drinks in ice.

No one offered any refreshments to the farmer or his family, even though the kids' mouths drooled. Travis couldn't abide the sight of hungry children being ignored. He laid down his own food and picked out a club sandwich with his right hand. The custom in this region was to use your right hand only for eating. If anyone touched or offered food with their left hand, the item was considered tainted.

He walked over and presented the sandwich to the farmer. When no one objected, he went back and took another. Aware of Islamic customs, he didn't offer it to the farmer's wife. Instead Travis handed it to the man and gestured toward her. The farmer nodded and gave his wife the food. Her face down, Travis thought he detected a slight smile.

He moved his hand indicating the kids and the farmer bobbed his head twice in the universal motion that signified an affirmative reply. The children's eyes grew as round as melons.

Travis motioned for them to come to the cooler, and then handed each of them something to eat and drink. He waved the farmer toward the second cooler, indicating that he and his wife were welcome to have a drink as well.

This must be a treat considering their usual fare.

The soldier in charge didn't interfere. In fact Travis noticed a suppressed smile.

The second soldier, however, never strayed far from the vehicles. They might not be afraid of him petting a horse, but they weren't going to let him close to any vehicle.

Max Golden walked over to Travis and spoke softly,

his face turned away from the soldier, "That family appreciated what you did for them."

"We had plenty. I couldn't have enjoyed my own food if I hadn't shared." Travis answered in a hushed tone, in deference to Max.

"We feel free when we escape - even if it be from the fry-

ing pan to the fire."

~ Eric Hoffer

CHAPTER FORTY-THREE

About an hour after leaving the first farm they pulled up to a larger, more prosperous farm. This family estate with acres of farmland and livestock grazing in the distance gave the impression of wealth by Sudan's standards. The farm house looked freshly painted and as good in quality as the average suburban tract home in America. The soldier who acted as tour guide led them toward the farm house.

Stepping onto a small porch, the soldier knocked on a white door set in a brown painted frame. An Arab dressed in a white *jellabiya*, Moslem robe, and a *topi*, skullcap, opened the door and bowed. He motioned for them to enter the living room.

Twangi, Travis' stepson, sat on the couch next to an Arab woman dressed in a *burqa* with a veil that covered her face. She patted Twangi's hand for reassurance when

Twangi's face showed confusion.

Travis walked over and bent down to face the young man and said, "*Jambo,* my name is Travis."

Twangi stared without recognition for several seconds. Slowly a smile spread across his juvenile, melancholic face. Travis was glad that the young man still remembered him. They had only met once three years ago, and it had been terribly chaotic.

"Sadiq, Sadiq." The Arab farmer called Twangi by his Arabic name and urged him to rise to his feet.

Twangi stood unsteady as his right leg was bent slightly where a break had not been set properly. When Travis held out his hand, Twangi just looked at it with a bewildered expression.

Travis tried to hug him but fear shrouded Twangi's face and he turned away frightened.

Travis looked at Karasa's eldest son. His lack of mental clarity, unsteady gait due to an injury, the numerous scars from beatings and untreated wounds, marked him the victim of years of physical abuse. No wonder this twenty year old feared him.

I'll need time to earn his trust – if we live that long.

"I am married to your mother," Travis continued.

Twangi's eyes blinked and his left arm twitched. Travis realized this young adult didn't understand so he repeated the words in the Dinka language.

A light of recognition showed in Twangi's eyes.

"Mama," Twangi uttered and searched anxiously for his mother as he talked rapidly in Arabic, the language he understood best.

Excited, Twangi shifted his weight back and forth from one foot to the other, the way he had when Travis had first met him more than three years ago. On that occasion Travis had wanted to rescue him, but he and Karasa had been unable to.

Max Golden absolutely bubbled over with excitement as Eli Mete snapped several pictures of the event. Cafferty's absence and Marco's lack of interest in the interview did not surprise Travis.

The Arab woman served hot apple tea and sweet honey biscuits to her guests. The Arab farmer began to converse with the men.

Travis had no real plan except that if the opportunity presented itself he wanted to escape. He wore his backpack and still had the Glock tucked in his waistband at the small of his back, but he had only ten rounds of ammunition for the weapon. He had no illusions regarding his ability to shoot his way out or take control of one of the vehicles.

He wanted, however, to know how much latitude these characters would allow him.

"I'd like to take my boy outside to talk. I think with so many people, he' feeling a little over-whelmed." Travis thought that once they were outside, they could wander toward the barn and the horses. "Max, would you walk with us, and we can talk?" Travis asked.

"Yes, let's continue the interview," Max said.

If the guards were going to balk, this is when it would happen. He'd take that chance. He led Twangi slowly through the kitchen and out the back door. He faked enthusiasm and answered Max's questions. The guards did not object, but one of the soldiers followed them outside.

The ground between the back of the house and the barn had not been cleaned recently so they watched where they stepped as Travis steered them seemingly aimlessly in that direction. The two large doors at the front of the brown barn stood wide open. Travis wanted to close them after they entered, but he didn't dare. The soldier that accompanied them got a whiff of the foul odor emanating from the barn and decided to remain outside by the doors for a smoke. Once inside Travis noticed that the smaller rear barn door remained partially open, probably to allow more light and a wished-for breeze to pass through.

In the last three stalls on the right, horses munched on grains in their feeding troughs. These stalls were out of direct sight of any view from the house. Travis held his hand out to the nearest horse. The horse smelled and nuzzled his hand. Travis wished that he could feed it an apple.

A blanket and a small leather Arabic saddle hung on the

boards at the sides of each stall. The other tack, including the bridles, was stored in the rear of the each booth.

Travis began to saddle the first horse. Max appeared preoccupied, lacking concern. If Max was curious, he didn't show it. So far the Arab guard hadn't even peeked into the barn.

"When this is over, would it be alright if I visited you in Kenya?" Max asked. "I'd like to interview your wife as well. A true story about a woman who fought for years to find her children would interest my readers."

"We've only found one of them. She also has a daughter who is still in slavery, somewhere in this land of peace. But sure, you'd be welcome to visit."

Travis saddled the second horse.

"Perhaps I'll even sign up to join you on a *safari.*"

Travis' eyes widened in disbelief but he said, "It would be an adventure you'd never forget."

Travis put only a bridle on the third horse. Although not essential, Travis didn't want to leave it behind for one of the armed guards to mount and foil their attempt to escape. The limo and other vehicle weren't off-road transportation and couldn't follow them overland through the local sandy terrain.

"That settles it, for my next vacation I'm going on a photo *safari,*" Max decided.

Travis helped Twangi up onto the older and calmer of

the horses. He placed Twangi's hands on the pommel of the saddle and tied the reins from the third horse to the back of it.

Twangi sat rigid and looked frightened as if he'd never ridden a horse.

Travis held the bridle to Twangi's horse and mounted the other horse.

"Where are you going?" Max asked.

"I'm going to treat Twangi with a short ride. Would you wait here a few minutes until we get back and tell the Arab if he enters the barn?"

"Sure, I'll be right here," Max answered.

"Good, see you soon," Travis waved.

Travis rode his horse leading Twangi's out through the back door. He stayed to the right side of the barn in order to minimize his visibility from the farm house.

After riding about ten minutes, Travis looked back when he heard a faint voice calling. The Arab guard advanced and frantically waved his arms trying to get Travis' attention.

Well, now he knows I have no intention of returning, and soon the pursuit will begin.

Travis kicked his horse in the side and galloped off through a field. No crops grew this time of the year. The land under cultivation lay fallow while fields of brown grass, varying from ankle to knee high, covered the uncultivated land. In this arid region distant single shrubs stood like sentinels against their escape. He maneuvered around uninviting thorn bushes at irregular intervals that sought to snag them. The trees and leafless bushes might conceal a man, but definitely wouldn't hide a horse.

The sun's position in the sky suggested six hours of daylight remained. If they didn't get caught, they'd ride through the night back toward Khartoum. From Khartoum, he'd travel to Egypt and seek help from the American Embassy in Cairo.

As he rode, he picked up the pace. But Twangi's awkward bouncing in the saddle reduced the time he'd hoped to gain.

Out of sight of the farm house Travis stopped the horses and dismounted.

"Twangi, I'm putting you on my horse and I'll ride behind you. Maybe I can teach you how to move in motion with the horse."

Twangi answered in Arabic. Neither understood the other's language but somehow both seemed to comprehend what they were going to do.

He really hated this country with its lifeless, barren terrain. The hostility of the land seemed to have seeped over the centuries into the spirits of these intolerant people. Like their ancestors, they harbored thousands of years of unrelenting resentment toward those who differed from them.

Travis looked back at the horses' hoof marks in the sandy soil. They could be tracked on the ground but an aircraft overhead wouldn't be able to pick out their trail.

Travis turned loose the third horse. It went to graze on a small patch of brown grass. At this distance they'd be long gone before someone from the farm could recover it.

"Twangi, try to match your movements with mine and move with the horse," Travis said.

Twangi relaxed and rode with the horse's gait. Now they made much better speed and Twangi was light enough that the horse wasn't tiring much faster with its double burden than with a single rider.

Two hours later and at least twenty-five kilometers from the farm, their journey appeared bleak, with miles of yellow sand and no visible sign of habitation.

Travis heard a sound before he actually caught sight of the helicopter in the distance. A of thorn-bushes grew about fifteen meters away. He heeled the horse and raced to hide behind it.

They dismounted and stooped beside their horses and watched the helicopter. Flying in a zigzag pattern, it passed over the bushes in its line of flight. No doubt about it the plane searched, seeking to find them.

The newspaper people had betrayed him to the Sudanese government. No foreigner could commandeer a military helicopter. The helicopter would hold at least half a dozen men armed with automatic weapons. If the helicopter looped around and came back toward the farm they'd be discovered. When it took an aerial path away from their location, Travis breathed a sigh of relief.

Beads of sweat trickled down Twangi's forehead. The scorching sun began to take its toll as Travis studied the western sky. No amount of wishing would speed the sun's descent toward the horizon and provide them the cover of darkness.

Should we keep the horses or let them go?

He decided to run off the horses and continue on foot. At least when the helicopter found the horses, the soldiers wouldn't know exactly where they'd been released.

Travis slid down off the horse and helped Twangi to dismount. He freed the horses, and they trotted nearby in search of scarce grass and non-existent water.

"Yah, yah." Travis charged at them as he waved his arms in the air. The horses just stared at his bizarre behavior before continuing their quest.

Determined to force the horses to leave the area, he walked over to the thorn bush and broke off a nasty looking piece about six inches long.

"Ouch," he yelled when his hand was stuck by a thorn. It hurt. He sucked the wound, tasting his own warm blood.

He hated to do this to a horse but their own lives were on the line. He lifted a corner of the saddle on one of the horses, placed the piece of thorn bush underneath and let the saddle fall. The horse jumped up, flying into orbit.

The horse bucked wildly emitting sounds Travis had never heard before. Then it galloped off like the hounds of hell were after it.

Travis broke off another piece of thorn bush being more careful this time. He walked toward the second horse, but it kicked at him. Travis dodged to the side, barely able to keep the horse's hoof from striking his chest. Apparently it observed what he had done to the other horse and wanted no part of it.

In a second attempt Travis broke off a branch of thorn branch about four feet long. Gripping it in both hands like a baseball bat, he sprinted back. Thrusting the branch at the horse, he swiped its rear. This time it took off running. The horse stopped about one fourth of a kilometer away, turned and gave Travis a long look of disdain. Still snorting, it continued after the first horse.

"Come on Twangi, let's start walking," Travis said.

In compliance, he followed Travis in his strange shuffling gait. When Travis looked over his shoulder he made an interesting discovery. Twangi's bent leg turned his foot sideways and caused his tracks to be distinctive. This would make it impossible to confuse their tracks with someone else's.

As they proceeded toward Khartoum, Twangi made a

good effort to keep up. Travis noticed no sign of water or anything edible in this forsaken land.

In the distance an approaching helicopter could be heard. Seeing no bushes in close proximity, Travis pointed to the ground.

"Come on Twangi, we've got to lie down."

With one quick glance about for red ants Travis guided Twangi to lie on his belly beside him. They'd be safe from being spotted unless the helicopter made a direct pass overhead.

The helicopter flew to their right and out of view. If they couldn't see it, then it couldn't see them either.

"Well, Twangi, it's a good thing that we let those horses go," Travis said.

Twangi grinned back at him.

After the helicopter retreated, they stood up and Travis brushed the sand from Twangi's face. When they continued, Travis decided to move in a slightly zig-zag direction. Not a lot, but enough to mislead the soldiers if they found their tracks. It might also foil an attempt by the helicopter to bring armed men directly in front of their path.

They trudged along for another hour. The farther they got from the farm the more often Travis turned to look behind them. He knew that the soldiers from the farm would seek them. At the beginning he and Twangi had the advantage, but now the enemy had vehicles that could surpass their own speed. Twangi and he had one big advantage though; they could travel by night when darkness would hide their tracks.

Twangi, eyes half shut, labored to breathe and walked slower. Travis realized Twangi looked exhausted. He angled over to a big thorn bush and motioned to Twangi to sit under its sparse shade. He plopped himself down on the ground. Travis wiped the perspiration from Twangi's face with a cloth and retrieved crackers from his backpack and handed them to Twangi. Twangi took them with a grateful smile.

Travis sat across from Twangi and ate a snack.

"Your mother is going to be so glad to see you when we get home," Travis spoke Dinka.

"Mama." Twangi's smile spread across his face and his hands fluttered as he spoke in Arabic.

Travis continued to speak in Dinka. He enunciated each syllable of his name in a drawn out voice and repeated it several times while pointing to his chest.

Twangi furrowed his forehead as if he tried to recall some forgotten memory. As he winced, Twangi spoke in Arabic.

Travis continued his efforts to bond with his stepson as they spent time together. "I'm your stepfather. Your mother and I are married. You have a new sister back in Kenya."

Twangi's smile confirmed that he'd gained the young

man's trust.

"I can't imagine what you've endured for the past few years. You must be incredibly strong-willed just to be alive." Travis felt both sad and proud that Twangi possessed such a commendable character trait.

Twangi sensed the difference in mood when Travis spoke, and his face looked a little bit concerned.

"Don't worry, son. Trying to be free feels like Daniel in the lion's den," he paused. "That Bible story had a happy ending," Travis laughed.

They rested for about an hour before trotting off to outrace their pursuers.

"Remember, my son. The past is behind you, and you can

only learn from it.

The future lies ahead, and you must prepare for it.

But the present is here, now, and in it you must live."

~ The Leper's Book of Wisdom,

Simon the Leper

CHAPTER FORTY-FOUR

Travis considered that he and Twangi had been blessed. The moon and the stars cast enough light to continue the journey, but the soldiers would have difficulty tracking them. Come daylight, the Sudanese army would be in hot pursuit, so he'd push himself to the limits of his endurance, and a bit beyond.

Twangi's stamina had given out several hours ago. Travis wrapped his arms under Twangi's legs and carried him on his back. Twangi's hands were clasped over Travis' shoulders and in front of his chest. A canvas strap and the bulk of the pack Travis shouldered rested on top of

Twangi's thigh. Twangi was not too heavy a burden that Travis couldn't carry him for several hours. At times in the Marines, Travis had carried a pack that had weighed more than Twangi.

Twangi's grip lessened as he began to doze. Travis laid him on the ground to sleep. Travis suspected that Twangi had slept in far worse places in his past few years. Exhausted, Travis lay beside Twangi and fell asleep. About four hours later Travis woke up. He stared at the terrain, searching for any movement under the wan moonlight. He listened to the night sounds but nothing seemed amiss. Travis determined to press on.

"Twangi, time to wake up. Look at the stars—*nyotas.*" Travis pointed to the North Star. "Look, *Kaskazini Nyota.* We're going to follow that star and head northeast to Khartoum." Travis helped Twangi to his feet.

They trekked into the unknown. About one hour before dawn Travis spotted lights in the distance and angled toward them. Soon a farm house became visible, and they approached it with caution. Famished and thirsty, they couldn't go on another day without water. Twangi imitated Travis and never complained.

Travis advanced toward the house from the downwind side. If dogs roamed the vicinity, he didn't want them to get a whiff of their scents and start barking. As they crept closer, the sun rose higher over the horizon, but the flat terrain made it difficult to get a good view of the farm. A towering mound of sand would have provided a better vantage point. Too close to stand up, Travis knelt to observe the comings and goings of the people who occupied the farm.

An older man came out of the farm house and ambled to the far end of the barn. About fifteen minutes later the farmer drove a small horse-drawn wagon around in front of his home. He turned his head toward the house and appeared to be calling out. About three minutes later a woman in a *burqa* bustled out of the house toward the wagon. She had difficulty climbing aboard, but the man made no attempt to assist her.

Grooves in the yellow sand marked the trail of the wagon as it disappeared in the distance. Travis and Twangi hustled toward their destination without making any attempt to hide. If other people lived on the farm and saw them, it might arouse their curiosity but not their suspicions.

Travis felt apprehensive as he knuckled three quick thumps on the front door. No one answered. He knocked again and waited. Still no answer. Travis pushed the door and it opened.

"*Jambo*," Travis called. No one responded. Twangi reclined on a cushioned bench while Travis checked the remaining rooms. The house echoed emptiness.

Back in the kitchen Travis primed and worked an old-fashioned pump. He filled two glasses with water and returned to the living room. Twangi gulped down the cool water.

"Drink slowly, Twangi," Travis suggested in Swahili.

The young man complied, making Travis wonder if he did indeed understand a little.

Returning to the kitchen, he found some food. He brought Twangi back a piece of cornbread. He would eat later, after he checked the barn.

"*Jambo,*" Travis called out as he entered the barn holding his hands out in plain sight.

The barn gave the impression of being empty – of people anyway. A horse and a goat rested in their stalls. Three chickens squawked, scratched and roamed freely. In one corner an ancient hound dog roused from its sleep.

"Hello pup." Travis knelt on one knee and held out his hand for the dog to sniff. The dog sniffed and appeared satisfied. Travis ruffled the fur on the back of its neck. Next he inspected the draft horse who appeared healthy and in good physical shape.

A horse-drawn plow, a cultivator and other implements occupied a space across the barn. In the far corner he spotted something that might help with their escape, a small horse-drawn cart. Travis examined it closer. It resembled the surreys ridden in American cowboy movies.

Travis hauled on the traces and brought the horse out in

the open. The animal co-operated when he connected the traces and leather straps to the wagon. Ready to go, he tied the horse to a post. If they needed to make a quick escape, they had means to flee. He walked back to the house.

Travis pried opened the bottom of the backpack and removed some Sudanese money. He placed the bills on the kitchen counter to pay for the necessities he intended to take. Finding no canteens, he stuffed his backpack with jars of water. He also packed dry food and a long bladed knife.

Twangi came into the kitchen. Travis served him more the spicy *sorghum* and ate some porridge himself.

Twangi looked puzzled but didn't object when Travis dressed him in a woman's *burqa.* Travis, still wearing a waistband that secured his Glock to the small of his back, replaced his clothes with the farmer's smaller size clothing. The loose, baggy pants reached only to the calf of his legs and the collarless, ill-fitted shirt stretched tight across his shoulders. A tattered cloth skullcap covered the top of his head.

After some thought, Travis conjured an idea to dissuade anyone from communicating with him. Using the knife, he cut strips from a piece of cloth and wrapped them around his neck. He didn't have a mirror, but hoped his handiwork would pass as a bandage.

If anyone spoke to him or asked him a question, he would point to the bandage and brazen it through with a surly attitude.

Turning to Twangi, he asked, "Well, kid, how do I look?"

Twangi's face, not visible below the eyes, voiced a little chortle when he lifted one hand and pointed at Travis' bandages.

He stuffed his own clothing into the remaining crevices of his backpack.

Travis motioned to Twangi to follow him out the door and to the barn.

Travis stowed the bag behind the seat and released the horse's bridle from the post before climbing up into the cart.

They left, following the ruts in the yellow dirt toward the general direction of Khartoum. Travis urged the horse on. He wanted to cover ground but had no intention of overtaking the farmer who'd recognize his own stolen horse and wagon.

They rode less than an hour before coming to a dirt road. Travis turned north, concerned he'd encounter local traffic.

At about 9:00 A.M. they passed another farmer and his wife in a small horse-drawn wagon. The farmer called out something in Arabic, but Travis shook the rein and his horse trotted faster. After gaining some distance, he slowed down.

Soon he covered enough distance to come along side a wagon drawn by two horses, containing several burlap bags of grain. One of the two Arab farmers waved with both hands raised and called out to him as he passed by. Undaunted when Travis gave no response, the farmer increased his speed and overtook the cart. It sped ahead about a quarter kilometer and turned around to span the entire width of the road, blocking Travis' path. When Travis slowed, one of the men dismounted and reached for his horse's bridle forcing it to stop. The farmer patted the horse as if it were familiar to him. The horse responded by nuzzling him.

The taller Arab farmer approached Travis, and grabbed him by the front of his shirt. He pulled him off the cart allowing him to tumble to the ground. Speaking in Arabic in a hostile tone of voice, he pointed to the horse.

"Sifa, Sifa."

He pointed to the cart and shouted out again in a stern voice and pointed a finger as if in accusation. The other Arab farmer moved closer, into Travis' face. He shook his head vigorously back and forth, shouted loudly and waved his arms about wildly.

Travis pointed to his bandages and made grunting sounds. But his actions only seemed to increase the man's fury. The farmer who had pulled Travis off the cart quickly snatched and tore away the bandages. Detecting no scars or injury, the farmer's face became a massive scowl as rage overtook him. He stared at Travis and made a motion as if he were cutting off his hand with a sword. This worried Travis because he knew that was how they dealt with thieves in this country.

Next the man looked up at Twangi appraisingly. An evil smile curled his lips, as if he still believed Twangi to be a woman in a *burqa,* and he anticipated what enjoyment they would have once Travis was out of the way.

Still furious about the deception, the tall Arab farmer turned and shouted something to his companion. The second farmer ran to their wagon, reached in, and snatched out a machete. When Travis caught sight of the weapon, he raised his left hand to signify surrender, but with his right he reached behind his back and curled his fingers about his Glock. As fast as lighting strikes, he drew the gun and shouted in Dinka.

"Get back or you're dead."

He cocked the gun.

The Arab farmer raised both hands and moved back three steps. When he heard the other man with the machete racing up behind him, the leering, evil smile returned and he lunged, his arms outstretched. Travis aimed and pulled the trigger. The bullet hit the man in the center of his chest, knocking him backward.

The other Arab farmer sped up and bounded over his

comrade, the machete raised high over his head. Travis shot him point blank while he hovered in midair. The man's body spun once before he dropped to the dirt in a dead, twisted heap.

The gun shots had spooked the horse. It reared and kicked in fright, but Travis got hold of its reins and managed to calm it. After reassuring Twangi, he bounded up to the top of the larger wagon and glanced up and down the road. He needed to be assured that no one had witnessed the incident or traveled in their direction.

Satisfied, Travis jumped down off the wagon. He grabbed one of the dead men by the wrists and dragged the body off the road into a shallow ditch. He threw the second body into the ditch to join the first. Anyone coming down the road wouldn't see the dead bodies unless they dismounted and walked out into the field.

Again Travis mounted the wagon and looked in both directions. Good, still no witnesses. He drove the wagon off the road and about one hundred meters out into the brown grass. He set the brake on the wagon and jumped down. Running back, he kicked some dirt over patches of splattered blood on the ground.

"It's okay, son, I've hidden the bodies." Travis voiced no remorse as he climbed back into the wagon.

Twangi frowned, pointed at the other wagon in the field and spoke in rapid Arabic.

"I'm hoping that if someone sees that wagon they'll assume the driver hid out of sight behind the wagon to relieve himself."

Twangi's eyes widened and darted as if searching.

Travis straightened out their cart and sped on down the road. In the next ten minutes they passed two wagons.

They traveled about five kilometers at a fast rate until the horse began to tire.

Travis pulled over. He took out a large mouth container of water and let the horse drink.

"It's alright, Twangi, we're safe now." Travis returned to the cart and helped Twangi remove his *burqa*.

"Here, have a drink of water." Travis handed Twangi, who had been sweating profusely under his head gear, a small jar of water. Next they shared some bread. Travis looked anxiously in both directions and wondered how fast news traveled in this rural area.

They returned to the road. The closer they traveled to the city, the more the traffic increased. Within the next half-hour they passed people on foot, on horseback, and in a variety of horse-drawn vehicles. Twice motorized vehicles sped by, the second one, a military jeep driven by non-uniformed officers. Travis looked away.

A loud whirring sound could be heard in the distance. Shortly afterwards a helicopter flew overhead following the road's path as if conducting a search. Travis thought briefly of leaving the road and cutting overland, but decided that the tracks of a horse-drawn cart going through the arid, barren land would draw more attention than just one more horse-drawn conveyance on the road.

They continued to move with the traffic, but in ten minutes the helicopter returned.

"Well, Twangi, it's flying lower and slower this time."

Twangi covered his eyes and watched as it flew over.

"One of the most important keys to living a happy life is

to clearly identify your core values. You must decide

what

matters most."

~ Mac Anderson

CHAPTER FORTY-FIVE

The helicopter flew down the road again. Resembling a distant dragonfly, it turned to the left and started a large arc back the way it had come as if circling them.

Travis watched until it flew almost out of sight to their rear before it crossed back over and completed another loop in the opposite direction, coming up on their right.

"Twangi, we might be in a tight place soon. Just keep your chin up and we'll get through it somehow," Travis snapped the reins to hurry the horse.

Speaking Arabic, Twangi touched Travis' arm and pointed directly ahead. In the distance a fast moving vehicle kicked up dust and sand.

As the source of the dust drew closer, the sweat that trickled down Travis' back had nothing to do with the heat of the sun.

Brakes screeched and a black limousine emerged from the obscuring dust. The limo swerved in front of them and blockaded their path. Two men with automatic weapons burst from the vehicle as red lasers fixed on Travis' head and heart.

Even if he pulled his Glock he couldn't shoot both of them before they fired at him, and probably hit Twangi as well. Travis would have rather died here fighting than be captured and tortured. He restrained his urge to pull the polymer pistol for Twangi's sake.

As if to seal his fate, four more soldiers rushed from the rear of the limo. Speaking in Arabic one of the soldiers handed his weapon to the officer in charge. When he advanced forward, immediate recognition occurred between him and Travis.

Is this soldier bent on revenge because he's been reprimanded for allowing us to escape?

Travis glanced at Twangi as he kept his hands in plain sight. He showed fear on his face, but also an inner strength. Travis wished he could tell Twangi's mother, his wife, of his pride in this young man.

Travis decided not to resist whatever the soldier intended to do. The man's muscular arm reached up and grabbed Travis by the front of his shirt. Lifting Travis over his head, he smashed Travis hard onto the ground.

Bruised and with the wind knocked out of him, Travis was otherwise undamaged. The soldier continued the assault and kicked him savagely in his side. Bright flashes flooded his vision before his eyes closed in pain. He heard the leader bark a command in Arabic. He expected another kick. Instead, the first man knelt beside him, turned him onto his stomach and pinned his hands behind his back.

Why did the leader order the beating to stop?

Whatever the reason, it gave Travis some needed relief.

The soldier felt the Glock at the small of Travis' back and held up the pistol for the others to see. Someone made a caustic remark, and they all laughed.

The helicopter landed, kicking up sand that stung the eyes and penetrated the mouth, the nose, the ears, and other body parts previously unconsidered. Even as the rotors cycled down, Travis couldn't stop coughing. Two of the men picked him up and tossed him like a sack of grain through the empty door of the helicopter. Another brought Twangi, slung over his shoulder, and set him in through the door. Twangi sat next to Travis and put a hand on his shoulder.

Travis still struggled for breath while Twangi tried to comfort him. In these few seconds their roles reversed.

"Its okay, Twangi, I'll be alright. You will, too. Just do whatever they say to do."

Twangi remained stoic and kept his hand on Travis' shoulder.

Definitely a superior young man, Travis thought.

"The patient in spirit is better than the proud in spirit."

~ Ecclesiastes 7:8

CHAPTER FORTY-SIX

As Karasa rode in the back of the police car, the affects of the taser began to wear off and she slowly regained control her arms and legs in spite of their jerky motions. She sat behind a secure glass shield separating the front and back seats.

The police car drove past double-story buildings in a quiet residential area of Khartoum. At random intervals small family-owned shops squeezed between and separated apartments built of local clay bricks with wooden roofs. The dirt lane appeared well maintained and provided a smooth ride, but the oppressive atmosphere that permeated this place felt as if a black widow spider crossed over her foot in the dark.

Karasa expected to be taken to a police station or a government building. But instead the police car pulled into an alley and followed its twisting turns for almost a quarter of a kilometer to an isolated one-story residential building.

Invisible from the road, this secret, unofficial detention facility claimed dubious fame as the 'Ghost House'.

*Is this a place of non-stop private torture and a slow
death in the name of Allah?* Karasa wondered.

Two officers hooked her arms and half-dragged her into
the building.

I'll kick one of them where it hurts, Karasa decided.

Before she could act on her plan another officer stepped
in front of her, taser pointed and ready to fire. Karasa didn't
want to repeat that experience.

The officers led her up three steps and in through a
doorway. A blast of hot air greeted them; it felt as if someone just opened a huge oven door. The first officer flicked
on a ceiling fan and raised one small, narrow window while
the other two officers ushered her into an open room.

Once inside, the officer unfastened Karasa's handcuffs.
The man held up his hand with five fingers spread apart. He
kicked open a bathroom door and reached in to switch on a
single light bulb that hung from the high ceiling. He turned
and grabbed Karasa by the arm, pushing her in. He closed
the keyless door behind her.

A foul smelling stench assaulted Karasa's nostrils. She
walked to a corner farthest from the door. On the floor an
open hole contained a pot about twenty-one centimeters in
diameter. Next she made her way to another corner and
used a rag and the water in a wash bowl lying on the wood

floor.

Karasa looked in the direction of the door and listened to voices speaking a language she did not understand. She heard shuffling sounds of feet coming nearer.

As promised the door opened five minutes after she had entered. An officer, standing three meters away, aimed his weapon at her. He motioned for her to come out into a small windowless room with a single heavy metal armed chair. Two officers tied both her arms and both legs securely to the chair with rope. In the corner, a wood plank one-half meter wide and two meters long rested on top of a wooden box and extended at an angle to the floor. Rolls of twine and twisted rope and two large gourds filled with water lay on the floor next to this contraption. Implements of torture adorned a nearby wall and shelf, but no one reached for them to torment her. Instead, all the officers left. One policeman positioned himself in front of the closed door. She could see the back of his head through the door's small opening. Lined with iron bars, it measured approximately twelve centimeters by six centimeters.

About three hours later the Chief of Police walked into the cell, followed by a man Karasa recognized, the interpreter. He shut the cell door behind them.

Will this man now play the role of interrogator?

Karasa wouldn't have to wait long for her answer.

"Even though I walk through the valley of the shadow of

death, I will fear no evil, for you are with me."

~ Psalm 23:4

CHAPTER FORTY-SEVEN

Before the helicopter took off, a soldier forced Travis, hands still bound behind his back, to the floor. He placed his knee and all of his weight on Travis' legs just above his knees. It hurt like hell, but it also guaranteed that Travis couldn't kick the man while he tied his ankles together.

Another guard pulled Twangi's *burqa* off and replaced it with a full-length hooded poncho with a drawstring around his face. The opening in the front was partially closed by the draw string, and Twangi resembled the fabled one-eyed Cyclops. With Twangi's face nearly concealed, his identity could never be determined.

Wearing a similar hooded poncho, Travis discovered he could see out through the small opening if he moved his head just right. He abandoned any hope of escape. These guards displayed the character and conduct of an elite troop, equivalent to U.S. Green Berets.

How do I, a common criminal, rate a helicopter and the attention of specialized soldiers to carry out a simple execution? Travis wondered.

Twangi was his main concern now. If he had to give his life for something, then let it be for that. The loud noises echoing from the helicopter prevented Travis from talking with Twangi.

The flight lasted twenty-five minutes before landing on a small, enclosed military base in the desert.

A jeep pulled up on the left side of the helicopter by the open door. Two soldiers jogged up, pulled Travis out and dumped him with haste into the back of the jeep. They deposited Twangi next to him.

"Don't worry, Twangi. It's going to be alright."

Twangi remained silent.

Four elite soldiers from the helicopter piled into the jeep and hung on while the jeep drove at high speed to a concrete building near the outskirts of the camp. Here soldiers waited to carry Travis into the building. To Travis' surprise they eased him into a sitting position on the floor near a rear wall. The soldiers untied his and Twangi's hoods to reveal their faces. Both took a deep breath of fresh air.

Two men with automatic weapons stood guard near the door. Travis tried to talk with them.

"Hey guys, what is going on?"

The soldiers stood motionless and would have reacted more to the sound of a mosquito buzzing near their ear.

"I wish that your mama could have seen you again," Travis looked at Twangi.

"Mama," Twangi whispered as a little smile pulled at one corner of his mouth.

Travis knew his time was short and it felt good to hear Twangi's voice.

They sat for about fifty minutes before Travis heard noises outside. The soldiers stiffened to attention as foot-steps approached the building.

The door opened and one of the soldiers called them to attention. The soldiers stood, no slouch in their posture, their backs ramrod straight. A General flanked by four sol-diers entered the building. The General wore more gold medals and colored ribbons than there were spots on a leopard. There's an expression in the Marine Corps that 'a general makes his own uniform'.

Major General Ahmed sauntered over to Travis, his personal guards holding weapons in readiness. He signaled his guards to leave the building. In one accord they backed out through the door, defending their general as long as they were able.

Major General Ahmed pulled out a semi-automatic pis-tol and pointed it in Travis' face.

"You led us on quite a chase. Your bizarre behavior almost distroyed some very important plans of mine."

"What do I have to do with your plans?" Travis asked.

"Your destiny intertwines with my future plans of advancement, so let's not disappoint President al-Bashir. We must not be late for such a major event, the beheading of a terrorist. Most important, it will be broadcast on National Television," Major General Ahmed answered.

"You can't stop me from making a statement in my defense on National Television," Travis stated.

"In fact I can," snorted The Major General. "You won't be able to speak at this event. I will explain that only the removal of your tongue stopped you from blaspheming *Allah*. This allegation will be accepted by the authorities."

Travis realized that he could do little to thwart the general's plans, so he didn't verbalize his intended insult.

Instead he said, "Your argument is with me. This young man had nothing to do with it. Let him go – he can do you no harm."

"Why should I take any chance for the sake of a slave? By the time you are beheaded, his body will be fed to the crocodiles in the Nile."

Anger flooded Travis' body and he surged against his bonds, but it accomplished nothing except to bring a mocking laugh from General Ahmed.

The Major General reached down as if to pat Travis on

the cheek in what was meant to be a patronizing gesture.

Travis tried to bite his hand but missed.

The Major General pulled back his other hand holding the pistol as if to smash Travis with it, but he stopped. Instead he stood and with force kicked Travis in the groin.

Travis never saw it coming. An intense pain washed over and through him. He heard himself scream as if from outside of his body. He curled into a fetal position in agony.

The soldiers returned and watched their prisoners with focused attention, their automatic weapons ready.

Unable to lift himself from the floor, Travis waited for the intense pain to subside.

"Ambition is pitiless. Any merit that it cannot use it finds

despicable."

~ Eleanor Roosevelt

CHAPTER FORTY-EIGHT

Minister of Defense Huzang's security phone rang and he picked up the receiver.

"The message I have is urgent." Lt. Colonel Arok Mekki related the pertinent details.

An outstanding loyal supporter, Colonel Mekki worked on President al-Bashir's staff. Because of his proximity, the Colonel often overheard confidential information relevant to current affairs. After his brief conversation with the Colonel, Huzang summoned Abu.

"Colonel Mekki just informed me that our president expects more than the public execution of the American terrorist. He's determined to avenge Major General Ahmed for his folly three years ago. Most of all, the president is livid about this terrorist's recent escape attempt. Even though the American has been recaptured, he holds General Ahmed responsible for the blunder."

370 ~ Kweli – the Truth Unmasked

"Why does he do this?" Abu questioned in disbelief.

"His all-consuming power corrupts him completely, but it must be dealt with through our parliamentary system. Now we must address a more pressing problem."

"Has our president gone mad?" Abu asked.

"Our president is angered by the military victories of the SPLA. He's troubled by the aid to the resistance from the Western nations and our African neighbors. He's also found out about our private meeting with Dr. Garang at the café in Juba. He considers that brief but unplanned contact with the enemy and the follow-up meeting as insubordination. So I. too, have not escaped his wrath – I may be going to Kobar . . . indefinitely."

"The situation appears hopeless. What can we do?"

"We must remain positive and pretend to proceed as planned. The president must never know, however, that we've been warned. We will make the necessary preparations and take the proper precautions."

"What can we do on such short notice?"

"First we'll initiate a new course of action. Colonel Isam is due to arrive by helicopter at my residence on the outskirts of Khartoum in less than five hours."

Huzang tore off a sheet of legal paper and started to jot down ideas and draw diagrams. Abu and Huzang spent forty minutes deep in discussion, finalizing and coordinating their movements.

"You must intercept Major General Ahmed, and tell him that I need the following items from his arsenal." He pointed to the list and continued. "But do not reveal the truth about why our plans have changed. He may do something fool-hardy and jeopardize all of our lives.

"We race against time. I'm leaving the office immediately. Go now. Even if you don't complete everything that's required, you must meet me at my place by one-thirty this afternoon. Understood?"

Abu bowed to his master.

Huzang grabbed Abu by the shoulders and said, "If anything happens to me, I just want you to know that you're a good, strong man. Your loyalty is unmatched."

"I'm just doing my job, sir." Abu's face flushed as he turned to go.

Both men left the city, traveling in different directions.

"Far better it is to dare mighty things, to win glorious tri-

umphs, even though checkered by failure, than to take

rank with those poor spirits who neither enjoy nor suffer

much, because they live in the gray twilight that knows

neither victory nor defeat."

~ Theodore Roosevelt

CHAPTER FORTY-NINE

Travis tried to reassure Twangi. Although neither understood the other's language they communicated by signs
and gestures.

At the appointed time the guards approached and pulled
the hoods back over their heads. The soldiers tightened the
draw strings and tied the openings. Travis and Twangi
could only peek through at a small pinhole of scenery directly in front of their heads.

A broad-shouldered soldier picked Travis up, carried
him out and dumped him into the back of a military truck.
He heard Twangi being place next to him.

"It's alright Twangi, I'm here," he said.

Twangi's breathing had become laborious, and he didn't reply.

The truck sped away. Over the sound of the engine Travis heard the three soldiers' distinctive voices in close proximity, speaking in Arabic.

Travis couldn't see out of the rear because the truck's canvas top was drawn closed and his sense of direction became disoriented. When he felt less jostling, Travis assumed the truck drove on a paved road.

Are we getting close? Travis wondered.

They drove almost an hour before the truck pulled up to a stop. Feet shuffled and metal clanked before the tailgate dropped. Travis glanced out and viewed a sliver of an oasis in the barren waste. A few meters away stood a wheeled canvas-sided affair, like janitors might use here to empty trash cans in offices. It seemed out of place here. With the sun's shadow almost directly under the cart, he reasoned that the time was about 12:30 P.M.

One of the soldiers pulled back the hood of Travis' robe, put a cloth gag in his mouth and tied it behind his head. Another soldier withdrew a stun device with two metal electrodes at the end and held it before Travis' face. When the two metal electrodes were pressed against flesh and the button pushed, the victim received an electric shock that completely disabled him for several minutes. The guard pressed the button to demonstrate and a brilliant lightning arc jumped between the electrodes. The meaning was clear that if Travis made any noise or attempted to draw attention, the device would be used on him. Next the hood was pulled back up and tied. Several hands lifted his body up and into the conveyance. He felt Twangi placed in beside him. A large cloth now covered and concealed both of them.

The wheels on their canvas conveyance vibrated with vigor as they were pushed up several ramps, into a building and down a hallway. The cart pushed through a door and into a small storage room under the stairwell of the main reception room.

After disengaging the cloth casing, strong arms lifted Travis bodily out of the cart and laid him on the floor against a wall. The soldier removed the hood and untied the gag. After his eyes adjusted to the light, Travis noticed Twangi next to him. But his brain registered disbelief upon seeing Kookie. Hands and ankles bound, he sat propped up with his back against the wall about three meters from him.

"Sorry they got you too, Mate," the Aussie said. "I didn't tell them nuthin."

"I knew you wouldn't," Travis replied. "I'm afraid that you got yourself in a bad situation, though, by trying to help me out."

"Can't be helped," Kookie said. "Is this your boy?"

"Yes, this is Twangi."

Turning to Twangi, Travis said, "Twangi, this is our friend Kookie. He helped us."

"At least I tried, Kid. Doesn't look like I did too good a job, but I'm pleased to meet you."

"He only speaks Arabic and a bit of Dinka he hasn't forgotten," Travis said.

"I have a bit of Arabic," Kookie replied.

Over the next few minutes Kookie and Twangi conversed in Arabic.

Kookie turned back to Travis to relate the details, but the guard shushed him.

Kookie put a finger to his lips.

"We'll have to whisper so the heathen won't object. Twangi already knew that you had married his Mum, and about you being his new step-dad and all. I filled him in on his new baby sister. He wanted to know about his other sister who was taken as a slave in the same raid. I told we didn't know anything about her. He doesn't either."

Kookie added, "You don't have to worry Mate, I didn't tell him anything about his Mum."

"What about her?" Travis' words almost caught in his throat.

"Oh, blimey, you didn't know?"

"Didn't know what?"

Kookie's expression turned somber.

"It's about the Missus. She followed you here."

"How do you know?"

"I wondered about hiring that old woman pilot who had flown you about before, but by the time I tracked her down, your old lady had already hired her. So I took a commercial flight to Khartoum. I called your missionary friend from here. He'd gotten a radio call from the old lady pilot. She said that your wife had been arrested at the airport in Sudan, and that her plane remains boxed in by police cars and she's not allowed to leave. Sounds like your wife may be a goner, too. Sorry, Mate."

Travis felt desperate. Longing to rescue his wife, the love of his life, he couldn't even help himself. As if hearing the final ding of the death bell, the realization hit him that neither of them would ever see their little daughter again. He took some comfort in knowing that in their absence his sister-in-law would raise Tamara as her own. George Mitchell would arrange for his extended family to settle in California, and his little princess would receive the advantages of an American life.

"Maybe Karasa got away?" Travis said.

"You want hope, Mate, or the truth?"

"The truth."

"That old pilot woman said they hit your wife with a high voltage taser, and handcuffed her while she lay on the ground. The officers carried her to a police car and drove her away. She hasn't been seen since."

"Did she say police car, or military police?"

"Civilian police, but I don't see where that's going to make too much difference. I'm sorry to be the one to have to tell you this, but I thought you should know."

"Yes, but it's difficult to accept."

Travis hadn't felt utter despair for many years, and now it covered him again like a shroud. This time both his and Karasa's fate seemed sealed. He felt that his death would accomplish nothing. He would have broken down if he had been by himself, but he'd remain strong for Twangi.

"I don't want him to know about his mother," Travis said.

"You got it, Mate."

Travis shifted gears, "How did you get picked up, Kookie?"

"I haven't the foggiest, Mate. I went through customs okay. After seeing you escorted into the limo, I returned to the Grand Holiday Villa for my bag. Without warning, the Sudanese soldiers just scooped me up off the sidewalk and locked me in a holding cell on an army base. I was brought here a couple hours before you were."

Kookie paused and continued.

"Mate, did you know that Winston Churchill once stayed at this historical hotel? The Grand Hotel Villa is like a step back in time with its colonial style architecture and wonderful atmosphere. Now, that's class."

"No, I didn't. At this moment I don't find that fact entertaining either."

"Never, never, never, never give up," Kookie paused. "You know Churchill's famous quote."

Travis rolled his eyes, sighed in exasperation and suppressed a smile.

The guard shushed them again and motioned with the butt of his weapon that he'd hit them if they didn't shut up. They both glared at him but kept quiet.

"God, grant me the serenity to accept the things I cannot change; the courage to change the things I can, and the wisdom to know the difference."

~ Serenity Prayer

CHAPTER FIFTY

The Chief of Police spoke in Arabic and the interpreter translated.

"I am Officer el Durman. This is Chief of Police Ibim Sharif, chief of the fourth and largest precinct of Khartoum. You will be held here until tomorrow because someone important has requested to speak with you."

"Who?" Karasa asked.

The interpreter passed on her question. The young Chief of Police stepped closer to Karasa. A shadow passed behind the man's eyes as he stared intently at her. Then he shook his head indicating that he wouldn't reply.

The Chief of Police spoke again to the interpreter.

"Chief Sharif says to tell you that a rumor of your husband's arrest has been hushed up. We have been unable to find out anything else. What do you know of this?"

"Nothing."

"There is also reported that he conspired with the Western authorities, possibly with American criminals, to enter our country illegally. Most disturbingly, he's suspected of aiding the rebels in the south to gain access to important military security documents here in Khartoum. Still another memo claims that his own country has betrayed him, because he is wanted for war crimes against our nation. What is the truth?"

"I do not know," Karasa replied. She hoped her blank facial expression wouldn't reveal her inner turmoil. Her thoughts drifted. She imagined an overgrown jungle of despair whose vicious vines were determined to constrict her heart and strangle the essence of her life.

The Chief of Police Ibim Sharif eyed her shrewdly, frowning in displeasure. He spoke and the interpreter translated.

"Chief Sharif says that your feelings are written on your face. You cannot hide them from a trained police officer. You have less than one day to tell us all you know or there will be serious consequences."

"I know nothing."

The Chief of Police turned and left abruptly. Officer el Durman stayed behind.

"It is best if you talk now. Your husband's time is short,

and he will be executed if he is involved in espionage."

He paused. "If you change your mind, I will be guarding the door and will hear if you call out."

The interpreter left and stood at his assigned post.

Karasa had consoled herself that at least her daughter would have her father to raise her, and now it appeared that she would be an orphan. No longer in control of her emotions, she heaved and sobbed until the front portion of her *burqa* flattened, drenched with tears.

When Karasa looked up she couldn't see the guard who had been posted outside her door. Hearing the song of the crier, she realized the evening call to prayer had begun. She heard the muffled voice of a man repeating words in Arabic. Fifteen minutes later he came into the room.

"Are you ready to tell us what you know?" asked Officer el Durman.

Karasa shook her head.

"I will untie your right hand so that you may eat. One of my men will be here soon with food."

In the quiet that followed, they heard the front door creak open.

"Well, dinner has arrived." The officer paused. "It will go better for you to speak to us. The NIF military will not be as patient as Chief Sharif."

Karasa's eyes widened in fear as two soldiers dressed in military fatigues and dark green berets stormed into the room with weapons drawn.

Officer el Durman spoke in an even voice. "We were just speaking of your NIF Forces, Lieutenant al Nilian."

"Officer el Durman, my Captain has full jurisdiction here, and I'm following orders. This is a military matter, step aside," barked Lieutenant Berat al Nilian.

"No, Captain al Kadesh is not in charge of this investigation. Chief of Police Ibim Sharif commands this precinct of Khartoum. Our department is investigating an illegal, domestic matter. This is in compliance with criminal law. At this time it doesn't entail national security."

"Put you hands in the air, now!" the Lieutenant Berat al Nilian commanded.

Officer el Durman raised his hands slowly. Hoping to catch Lieutenant al Nilian off guard, he rushed forward.

The Lieutenant blocked his charge and swung the butt of his weapon. With one strong blow to the head, he knocked the policeman out cold. He found el Durman's handcuffs and bound the officer's hands together.

The other soldier kept his weapon pointed at Karasa until the Lieutenant motioned for him to position himself near the door. He sidestepped to his left, still pointing his weapon in her direction.

Lieutenant al Nilian came and stood before her. He took out a man's handkerchief and attempted to cover her mouth. Karasa clawed at him with her free hand. With one sweep the Lieutenant grabbed her wrist and twisted her right arm behind her back. A sharp pain jabbed her shoulder's socket.

"One sound from you and I will rip it off!" the Lieutenant hissed in his strong accent.

To prove his point, at random intervals the Lieutenant exerted painful pressure and alternately eased the stressful hold. The torture increased in duration and intensity, becoming almost unbearable.

Relief came when they heard a short squeaking sound coming from the front room. The Lieutenant eased his grip and turned sharply. He pointed at the door, and spoke a hushed command in Arabic to the soldier.

* * *

About five minutes earlier the policeman had stood outside the residence. He carried food intended for their evening meal. About to knock for admittance, he stopped short when he noticed that someone had jimmied the lock. Marks on the side of the door suggested that the entry had been compromised. He pushed the door open and stepped inside. Shifting the heavy pot of lamb stew to his right hand, he pulled his taser from his left hip.

Seeing an armed soldier storm into the living room, the policeman tasered him. The soldier jerked and stumbled to the floor, unable to stop flailing. The policeman pulled the trigger again, then knelt and struck the twitching man hard on the side of his head with the butt of the taser. The soldier went motionless. The policeman dropped his taser and hurried to the wall next to the interrogation room. As he flattened his body against the wall near the door, he shifted the pot to his left hand and released the strap on the holster for his pistol with his right thumb.

"Your chances of success in any undertaking can always

be measured by your belief in yourself."

~ Robert Collier

CHAPTER FIFTY-ONE

When Lieutenant al Nilian heard the commotion in the front room, he released Karasa and moved to join the confrontation. The NIF Lieutenant swung the door open and paused briefly. As the Lieutenant stepped over the threshold and advanced forward, the policeman pulled his gun from its holster. Not having enough time to fire his weapon, the policeman swung the heavy pot of food by its crescent metal handle. The metal pot cut into the Lieutenant's right cheek, bruised his forehead and caused him to be off balance.

Greasy lamb stew spewed down the Lieutenant's uniform as he stumbled sideways, landing hard on his left knee. Twisting around to face the policeman, the Lieutenant fired wildly as he fell backwards onto the floor. The single shot grazed the top of the policeman's scalp, plowing a furrow through his flesh and knocking him back against the wall. Eyes shut; he slumped to the floor with his chin resting on his chest.

The Lieutenant hobbled over and bent down to examine the unconscious man. Satisfied the policeman could do no further harm, the Lieutenant walked over to his partner who lay stretched out on the other side of the doorway. Unable to revive him, he staggered back into the adjoining room to complete his assignment.

* * *

Aware that the clamor and commotion bought her precious time, Karasa brought her aching right arm around and began to finger the rope on her left wrist in an attempt to loosen it. She succeeded and quickly pulled her left hand free. But when she heard gun fire, it startled her into a frightful stillness with her eyes fixed on the open door.

The Lieutenant, minus his black beret, limped into view.

Karasa gasped as the Lieutenant approached her emitting an aroma of spicy lamb stew. Portions of the stew mixed with the blood that covered his right cheek and the right side of his shirt. The slimy mixture trickled down his fatigues and spotted the floor as he walked. His face cut and bruised, he continued to hobble toward her.

Karasa regained her composure and resumed untying her right leg.

"Stop! Sit up or I'll shoot."

The NIF Lieutenant cocked his pistol.

Karasa slowly slid back in her chair, keeping her eyes on her enemy.

The captain reached for her head covering and tore it away from her face, sputtering in hate. "You disgrace Islam by wearing this Moslem veil. We know who you are. You and the American are wanted for crimes against our nation."

He reached in his unbuttoned shirt pocket and retrieved an official looking document and a pen.

"You must sign this confession before you will be released."

"You will not release me."

"Still you must sign, or it will not go well with you."

"Why should I sign, you will kill me anyway."

"Yes, we both know how this will end. But this is a legal document and your signature is required."

Karasa stared straight ahead in silence. The soldier put the paper aside. With the full force of his opened hand, he slapped her hard several times. The right side her face slammed into the chair's metal back, bruising her cheek. A hard slap to her mouth followed and forced her teeth to bite into her lips. Blood trickled from her mouth.

"Sign, and I will stop hurting you."

When he received no response to his second request, he reconsidered.

"We will have no more bloodshed here. There are other places to administer punishment more effectively. But I must have that signature now."

The soldier lunged at her and grabbed both her arms, pulled them back and over her head and forced her head between her knees. He retied her arms. Pressing against her legs to restrict any movement, he retied both feet together.

"You look thirsty. I will bring you to the corner where you will drink."

The Lieutenant half carried and half dragged Karasa and placed her on a slanted board with her head near the floor. He bound her to the plank. She lay at an angle with her feet raised higher than her head.

"Do you know what this is?"

Karasa shook her head side to side.

"This is not torture, but you will know panic and fear." He paused for effect. "The fear of drowning. When you can no longer bear the pain, you must shout the word 'Allah', and I will stop." The Lieutenant smiled a malevolent grin.

"Nod your head if you understand."

Karasa nodded her head.

He quickly seized a soiled terry towel and covered her face. Next he picked up the gourd and proceeded to pour water over her face in small, quick amounts, pausing after each splash. The cloth became thoroughly drenched.

After six splashes of water and fifteen seconds of agony, Karasa tried to breathe but found it nearly impossible. With her mouth closed the water forced its way into her nostrils. She opened her mouth to breath. She coughed out water that entered her mouth and gasped for air. Still unable to breathe, water continued to fill her nose. The splashes now felt like a steady, relentless stream. Unable to control her body movements, Karasa's left hand began to shake.

Time stood still as her mind entered an abyss of despair. Her brain plunged into chaos and became unable to function as its repeated request for oxygen had been emphatically denied. Pain gripped her chest as it heaved. Her heart beats thumped louder and louder, demanding air.

My heart beats too fast, and I am frightened.

Plunged into turmoil, she lost control of her outer extremities, her legs and arms shook and trembled out of control.

Breathe, breathe, her brain urged, but it only throbbed with dizziness and disorientation.

Would it ever stop? She had no concept of how much time had passed or how much longer she could endure this torture. Reality seemed illusive as the anguish and misery of suffocation consumed her. Karasa agonized as the relentless assaults of water persisted. Exhaustion overwhelmed her as she fought to breathe.

I will die. Unable to endure the pain and convinced she would surely succumb to death by drowning, Karasa panicked. Through clenched teeth and thinly separated lips, she sputtered the word, '*Allah*'. Obtaining no relief, Karasa in desperation spat the word again.

The Lieutenant removed the dripping wet cloth and untied the twine across her chest that held her to the board and moved her to a sitting position. Eyes wide with terror, Karasa's stomach retched convulsively, spewing its meager watery contents out of her mouth. It puddled beneath her chin and down her *burqa*. She heaved, taking in great gulps of air. She could not seem to get enough life giving oxygen into her lungs.

My only desire is to breathe normally again.

"Do you want another drink?" The Lieutenant mocked.

Karasa slowly shook her head back and forth.

"Will you sign now?"

Karasa moved her head slowly up and down.

He turned to face her and said, "We will go back to the chair." He bent and reached over to unfasten the twine that stretched across both her legs.

As she looked past his shoulder she caught a glimpse of movement behind him.

Her legs now dangling over the side of the board,

Karasa tried to stall for time.

Karasa pleaded. "Wait, I must rest a moment to catch my breath." She paused, "My heart races."

"We go now," the Lieutenant shouted, showing no mercy.

"If you untie my legs, I will walk with you."

"I do not think you will walk with me willingly, and you may even try to escape." He hissed and clawed his fingernails into her upper arms and pulled hard.

Now in a standing position, Karasa turned and elbowed him hard under the rib cage, forcing him to fall backwards. Stumbling on top of the Lieutenant, they sprawled in a tangled mess with him holding her down. Her bound hands reached for his thumb and pulled hard. He shrieked in pain. She kicked furiously with her bound legs to free herself.

Forcing his body weight on top of her legs to restrain her, he regained control and pushed her hard. Karasa's head struck the floor with a thump. Head aching, she felt her strength diminishing as she attempted to sit up again.

Without warning, her enemy jerked and slumped back onto the floor, thrashing uncontrollably.

What happened? Karasa wondered as she lay back on the floor.

Officer el Durman, hands cuffed in front of him, pressed his taser to the NIF Lieutenant's back. He repeatedly pulled the trigger at intervals to administer disabling electric charges and to force the Lieutenant into submission.

Karasa used her elbow to scoot away to safety and to avoid being battered by the lieutenant's flailing. She remained on her side, struggling to loosen the twine around her wrists. Her wrists became bloody when the knots tore into her flesh as she pulled at the twine to stretch it. She forced her right hand through a small loop. Repeating the process several times, the opening got wider each time until she freed her right hand completely. She brought both hands in front and pulled off the loosened twine from her left wrist. She rose to a sitting position with knees bent and used both hands to untie the bonds at her ankles. With determination she stood up and hurried to grab a sharp knife from the shelf.

The electric charges became less effective and died altogether as the Lieutenant gained partial recovery. The officer dropped the useless weapon and reached for his holstered pistol. This action proved cumbersome due to the handcuffs. As he struggled to retrieve the weapon, the pistol slipped to the floor. He reached to grab it but Lieutenant al Nilian kicked the pistol away. The Lieutenant rose to his knees and jabbed the officer in the chest with his elbow. The officer fell back to a sitting position but quickly recovered and lunged toward the gun.

The Lieutenant had revived sufficiently to draw his

own weapon and stand erect.

"Don't touch it or I'll shoot," the Lieutenant shouted as he held the weapon with both hands in an attempt to steady it.

When he caught a glimpse of Karasa near the shelf, he turned and jerked his head. "Get over here," the Lieutenant commanded. He watched as Karasa did as directed.

Taking advantage of the distraction, Officer el Durman again bent down to retrieve his gun.

The Lieutenant cocked his pistol and fired. The officer fell backwards, blood oozing from his right side.

Karasa acted on instinct. Using the knife concealed behind her back, she rushed forward and slit the Lieutenant's throat with one skillful, reflexive action even as he still held his gun pointed at his victim. Arterial blood gushed and painted the nearest wall, the floor and the occupants with crimson splatters. His dead weight slumped onto the floor as a puddle of scarlet blood pooled and matted his hair.

I did what I had to do. He deserved to die.

Karasa knelt by Officer el Durman, who held his hands over his right side as blood oozed from between his fingers and onto his shirt. Assessing the damage, Karasa sprinted to get the wet towel. She pressed it into the wound, hoping to prevent the loss of more blood.

An almost inaudible creak of the front door broke the

eerie silence that had invaded this creepy place.

Officer el Durman looked at Karasa and put his index finger to his lips. He rose cringing in pain and tottered toward the opened door, gun ready.

The person behind the door barked a command in Arabic. The interpreter breathed a sigh of relief and responded. Chief Ibim Sharif rushed in. The chief spoke in Arabic as he unlocked the handcuffs and examined el Durman's wounds.

"Yes, it seems that Lieutenant al Nilian came for dinner, and the dinner is on him. But he will not live to tell about it," the interpreter said.

Officer el Durman turned toward Karasa and said, "The Lieutenant intended to shoot to kill. You saved my life."

"Now, please drop the knife to the floor. This is now a crime scene."

Karasa did as directed.

The Chief of Police reentered with a plastic glove, took the Lieutenant's weapon from the floor and walked back into the front room.

Bang.

The gun fire startled Karasa but not the officer. The Chief of Police reentered the cell.

Returning without the pistol, the Chief of Police and his officer continued to talk in serious, rapid tones and seemed to momentarily forget about Karasa as they conspired.

The Chief of Police returned to Karasa and brought her back to the chair. He picked up the veil from the floor and gave it to the interpreter.

"Put this back on but don't conceal your face." The interpreter said. He waited for her to make the necessary adjustments.

"What did the Lieutenant want?" the interpreter asked.

"He wanted me to confess my crimes against Sudan and sign a paper."

The Lieutenant spotted a piece of paper on the floor, picked it up and showed it to Karasa.

"Is this the document?"

Karasa nodded in the affirmative. The officer spoke to the Chief, who put the paper into a zippered pocket.

"You cannot remain here. You will be taken to a safe house," the interpreter informed her.

The Chief of Police handcuffed her and both men escorted her to the front room.

They stopped in front of an opening in the wall. The Chief of Police reached in and retrieved a large burlap bag.

"Climb into this body bag so that we can transport you without raising any suspicions," Officer el Durman spoke while the Chief replaced a panel to conceal the opening in the wall.

After Karasa climbed in, the Chief of Police tied it so that only her head showed. After carrying the unconscious officer out of the house, the Chief of Police returned and carried Karasa outside, leaving the crime scene intact.

He unlocked the trunk of the police vehicle and placed her inside.

"Why are you doing this?" Perplexed, Karasa looked at Officer el Durman.

"My fellow officer and I need immediate medical attention. While we are in the Emergency room, you must be hidden," Officer el Durman replied.

The trunk lid slammed down over her head.

Karasa tossed and bounced at every bump in the road in the nearly pitch blackness. As her eyes began to adjust, she noticed shafts of light coming through tiny holes. Even though they emitted no noticeable breeze, they provided assurance that she received needed oxygen. Sweat poured off her and the bag became drenched with perspiration as the temperature in the closed trunk began to rise. When the police car stopped, she could hear a commotion and audible voices. Soon a coverlet of silence lulled her to sleep.

About forty-five minutes later she awoke, startled by the slamming of a door and starting of the motor. This time she rolled and bounced with more intensity as the speed increased. The police car turned, slowed and stopped.

Karasa waited for about ten minutes, uncertainty mounting with each passing minute. Finally the Chief of Police raised the trunk lid and carried her into a small kitchen area of a building. He removed her from the canvas bag and placed her in a chair. He pointed to a cup of water and a bowl of overripe fruit on the table. With his right hand he gestured that Karasa should drink and eat.

Karasa reached for the glass. Although tepid, she drank its contents in one gulp. But she ate the fruit one bite at a time to savor its sweet taste.

When she had finished, the Chief of Police al Sharif brought her to a room with a mattress near a wall. On the wall and floor were shackles for her hands and feet. Karasa lay face up with her hands cuffed together above her to an iron railing. Her wrists, still raw from the twine, bled from the chafing. Her feet were attached to metal ankle bracelets with chains that were fastened to the floor at the foot of the bed. Almost immediately she began to squirm and rub her back against the mattress, trying to get relief from the itchy bites.

Bedbugs? It is probably the least detestable thing that has happened to me today.

Alone and stretched out on a mattress, she heard the engine of the vehicle start and then soon fade into silence.

Even at night, the temperature in the bedroom seemed never to drop below 28C. Alone and bound in the stifling heat, Karasa felt vulnerable but refused to allow her mind to entertain thoughts of despair. Her only companions, darkness and gloom, encased her like a cocoon. Bruised, aching, and exhausted, she fell into a fitful sleep. Once she woke up in a haze, her mind reeling with distorted images. Overwhelmed for a time, she finally dozed off. When she woke again darkness still surrounded her, but her mind cleared and pressing thoughts returned.

Who is this important person I will meet tomorrow? she wondered. Several horrific possibilities crossed her mind. But realistically she could conjure only two probable scenarios. She would be handed over to a general in the National Islamic Front for public execution, or sold and shipped off to be enslaved by a wealthy, old Sheik residing in a foreign country.

Whatever will be, will be, but I will not go down without a fight. Again, exhaustion compelled her eyelids to flutter shut and sleep to resume.

"The greatest friend of truth is Time,

her greatest enemy is Prejudice,

and her constant companion is

Humility."

~ Charles Caleb Colton

CHAPTER FIFTY-TWO

As each guest arrived at the Minister of Defense's residence on the outskirts of Khartoum, a uniformed waiter ushered him into a sitting room. The elderly household butler had reported ill today; his first absence in thirty years.

John Cafferty and Marco Allende entered together at 1:55 P.M., five minutes before the appointed time. Shortly afterwards Eli Mete came by taxi. Finally Max Golden, arriving in his own vehicle, bustled up to the entrance.

When all of the guests were present, a servant announced that afternoon tea was now being served in the dining room. Each person waited to be escorted to his seat. The waiter filled goblets with either mango juice or water. The guests who preferred a hot drink could choose from

Arabic Coffee or Arabian Mariamia Tea. They helped themselves to an elaborate assortment of freshly baked breads with jams, fresh fruit and pastry.

"Gentlemen, thank you for coming to take part in this historic event. The American terrorist and another conspirator have been captured and are being guarded. Soon they'll be transported under the watchful eye of the president's top commander to our maximum security prison. There they'll be publicly executed for the crimes committed against Sudan. This event will be televised on our local stations and on *Al Jazeera.*"

"Will we witness this event?" asked Eli Mete.

"Yes, you'll be flown there by military helicopters. Afterwards you'll return here for a final briefing. All newspaper accounts will synchronize. I believe the modern term is 'slant', but each of you will get an exclusive story and photos."

Dr. Huzang continued. "Please enjoy your refreshments. I must coordinate with my associate, Mr. al Sadir. I shall return."

Dr. Huzang entered his private office where Abu waited.

"General Ahmed's elite guards are positioned in strategic places, including the posting of two armed guards at the front and back entrances," Abu said.

"Did you give them the silencers to place on their

weapons?"

"Yes. They were instructed to allow only Colonel Isam and his personal guard to enter the residence," Abu informed him.

"Good. When the General arrives, we must inform him of the change in plans," Huzang said.

After a brief discussion of several crucial matters, Huzang walked to the stairwell to address the guard stationed beside the door. "Open the door."

Inside, Travis, Twangi, and Kookie sat bound, leaning against the walls.

Huzang's face displayed a mixture of emotions, as if his feelings had been mixed in a blender and sprayed across his features.

"The NIF Commander will arrive shortly. Mr. Martin, you will be taken by helicopter to your final destination… to appear before the President of Sudan for sentencing and execution."

"What about Twangi?" Travis asked.

"He'll remain here for now and will be disposed of later. Now, Abu will remove your ankle bonds."

The guard unholstered his taser devise and covered them with the weapon as Abu ordered the men up and out.

"Close the door," Huzang ordered.

Looking at Kookie, Huzang informed him. "Your fate will be different. The Israeli Mossad agent will be killed outright during an attempt to escape captivity."

Travis turned to Kookie, "Mossad? You said you were a Baptist."

"I said I was raised a Baptist. I converted when I married an Israeli. An explosion during a rocket attack in a shopping district killed my wife. I couldn't see any better purpose for my life than to work to protect the innocent and prevent further assaults."

"Be quiet!" Abu commanded.

Gags placed over their mouths and tied tightly behind their necks insured no further communication.

Again a soldier demonstrated the device that could incapacitate them with an electrical shock. He motioned for them to follow Abu into the reception area.

Bam! The front door opened with such force it hit the wall and bounced back into Colonel Asmath's face. The Major General entered, accompanied by the Colonel's four elite guards. After assessing the situation he ordered, "Guard the criminals."

One guard flanked each enemy's arm and the other guard, positioned behind Travis and Kookie, held an automatic weapon at the small of their backs.

"Thank you, Major General Ahmed. Have your men follow Abu and bring these terrorists into the sitting room. We'll wait for Colonel Mohammed Isam there."

The sitting room, festooned with heavy tapestries on the

walls and ornate gold leaf about the ceiling suggested a British influence in the décor. The ornate furniture and detailed handmade carpets, although ancient, were probably worth a fortune.

"Major General, post a guard at each of the doorways," Dr. Huzang ordered.

The General did as instructed.

"General Ahmed, we must discuss several important changes before —" Dr. Huzang stopped in mid-sentence.

The deafening sound of automatic gunfire just outside the front and back doors paralyzed his tongue. He became speechless.

The Major General and Colonel Asmath turned abruptly and reentered the reception room. Abu raced in the other direction through the kitchen.

"Get down; on the floor now," Abu yelled at the civilians around the table as he charged the rear door.

Dr. Huzang ignored the commotion behind him and hurried after the Major General. As he stepped over the threshold, he caught sight of Colonel Mohammad Isam and his personal guard with their guns drawn.

"You're coming to Kobar with us," the Colonel ordered.

"Yes, of course I'm coming with you. We're cooperating on this mission," the Major General answered.

"Drop your weapon now," Colonel Isam commanded.

"No, I have seniority here. I leave for the ceremony in full uniform."

"If you don't disarm, I have orders to shoot."

"Who gives these orders?"

"My commander and chief, President al-Bashir."

"You can't do this," the Major General sputtered in indignation.

"I carry his orders with me," Colonel Isam held up an envelope stamped with an official seal. Once again he secured the document in a zipped pocket.

"There are witnesses."

"Dead men don't talk. On the count of three. One . . . two."

Major General Ahmed and his body guard drew their weapons, but their holstered pistols were no match for the guard's automatic weapons. Blood splattered where the two officers dropped to the floor, dead. Hearing gunfire, an elite guard ran past Huzang into harms way. He lost his life in the exchange of gunfire while wounding the Colonel's officer in the upper arm.

Four more soldiers under the Colonel's command rushed the residence with weapons ready.

"Wait! Hold your fire," Colonel Isam ordered.

The Colonel pointed his weapon at the Minister of Defense, standing on the threshold.

"The president requests the honor of your company.

You will be coming with us."

"That's not in our original agreement. President al-Bashir exonerated Major General Ahmed and requested that this operation be initiated without bloodshed."

"There's been a change of plans."

"Your orders were to bring the terrorist and his coconspirator to Kobar. They're waiting in here." The Minister of Defense said in a controlled voice as he backed into the sitting room.

Another elite guard grabbed Dr. Huzang's right arm and forcefully pulled him away toward the kitchen door.

Colonel Isam and five of his men stormed the sitting room with guns drawn.

"Freeze and drop your weapons, or I'll shoot the Minister of Defense," the Colonel ordered.

"The president has ordered my assassination too?" the Minister of Defense asked in disbelief.

"No, he prefers that you change your residence temporarily to Kobar."

All the Major General's elite guards did as commanded, except the guard closest to Huzang. He positioned himself as a human shield.

"Move away or you will die."

Huzang's self-appointed bodyguard fired, killing the Colonel's personal guard. Return fire struck his forehead, instantly lobotomizing him. Blood splattered the nearby

408 ~ Kweli – the Truth Unmasked

walls and into the face of Dr. Huzang. Responding without hesitation the Colonel pointed his gun and fired point blank. Dr. Huzang jerked violently as he took two shots in the chest. The force propelled him back into the kitchen. Abu, racing back through the kitchen, dove and caught the fallen Minister of Defense.

. Together they fell onto the floor with Abu's arm and hand supporting Dr. Huzang's head.

"The Minister of Defense is dead!" Abu knelt at his master's side.

As if on cue, an impossibly well-timed and perfectly choreographed and coordinated ballet ensued. Dressed as the elite officers they were, the performers stepped out from behind the heavy draperies as if moving to the time of music only they could hear. Weapons moved to shoulders in perfect unison and fired as if the deafening sound originated from a single source. In the finale, Colonel Isam and his four soldiers shook violently and spasmed, each moving erratically to his own personal dance of death. Mortal silence and fatal stillness followed.

Unharmed, the five elite officers of Major General Ahmed rushed from the room and canvassed the grounds outside. Gunfire ensued followed by silence. Five officers returned. The hostile exchange ceased in seconds. In the blink of an eye everything had changed.

* * *

Meanwhile in the kitchen Max had taken charge.

"Under the table!" Max ordered everyone after Abu had disappeared toward the rear entrance.

Kneeling under the table, Max positioned a chair in front of him and pulled out his automatic revolver.

"You know how to use that weapon?" Marco whispered in disbelief.

"Yes. Not another word. Cover your head with your hands and be still."

Everyone complied, heads face down. Interspersed with movement and gunfire in the other rooms of the house and outdoors, the twenty-minute ordeal caused more extreme anxiety and uncertainty. Without warning a gasping sound and feet thumping in the kitchen caused immediate alarm.

"Mr. Cafferty!" Marco's eyes widened with fear.

John Cafferty lay face up on the floor panting as he clutched his chest.

"I can't catch my breath. I've got this unbearable pressure, like an elephant sitting on my lungs," Cafferty whispered breathlessly as his face distorted in pain. He gave one final gasp before lying quite still.

"Marco, go to him and undo his shirt buttons and try to administer CPR. It looks like a heart attack," Max commanded.

Marco scooted to Cafferty's side and administered CPR.

"He's not responding. I think I'm losing him," Marco stammered in desperation.

Before futher assistance could be administered, an explosion of intense gun fire erupted and everyone scampered under the table for protection. When it stopped, Max hurried to examine Cafferty. Max couldn't find a pulse or detect a heartbeat. Cafferty had stopped breathing. Several more attempts of CPR did not prevent the inevitable.

"Cafferty is dead," Max stated the fact.

Abu still knelt beside Dr. Huzang. Max went over to examine the Minister of Defense and felt for a pulse.

"His pulse is weak and his breathing is shallow. He might make it," Max informed them.

The Minister of Defense fluttered his eyes and motioned for Max to come closer. He whispered in his ear and collapsed. Max retrieved a piece of paper from the Minister's pocket and turned to Abu.

"He needs immediate medical care," Max ordered. "Get a medical kit, extra bandages, and attend to him."

"Yes, of course. I'll also phone Dr. el-Sheikh, the Minister's personal physician," Abu replied.

"Guards," Max called out. "Carry the Minister of Defense to a private room. Follow Abu."

"Everyone has his own specific vocation or mission in life:
everyone must carry out a concrete assignment that demands fulfillment. Therein he cannot be replaced, nor
can his life be repeated, thus, everyone's task is unique

as his specific opportunity."

~ Viktor Franki

CHAPTER FIFTY-THREE

Max Golden instructed the civilians and two servants
to join him in the reception room. When he passed through
the blood-stained sitting room, he noticed Travis and
Kookie laying on the floor unharmed. Max ordered the officers to pull them to their feet and accompany them. The
other officers swept the grounds again to secure the area
and returned.

One of the soldiers discovered Twangi and brought him
into the sitting room.

"Untie their hands," Max ordered, pointing to Travis
and Kookie.

Travis kneeled in front of Twangi and grabbed each of his shoulders and smiled, "Twangi, everything is going to be alright."

"Mr. Mete, go with the General's men and take photos of all the men who have died, including Mr. Cafferty. But do not disturb Prime Minister Huzang at this time. He's fighting for his life."

Mr. Golden pushed a button on a speaker telephone on a desk and dialed a number from a scrap of paper in his pocket. Almost immediately a low, baritone voice answered.

"Hello."

"Mr. Haile. This is Max Golden, member of the Mossad. The Minister of Defense is in critical condition and can't talk now. He asked me to make this phone call," Max's voice resonated with authority. Now a dignified professional replaced the former buffoon.

"Is he going to live?"

"I'm afraid the chances are not in his favor."

"Sorry to hear this. May I speak with Mr. Cafferty then, please?"

"That's not possible. Mr. Cafferty is dead. He died of an apparent heart attack."

"This is indeed tragic. Let me speak with Mr. Allende."

Max motioned for Marco to come forward and take the phone.

When Marco just stood flabbergasted, Max suggested, "Speak to him."

"It's me, Marco Allende. I'm an eyewitness to this horrific event and will report the highlights of the entire story."

"You saw nothing," the voice from the speaker phone said. "You'll be instructed on what you saw, so you can write about it. Do we understand each other?"

"Yes, sir."

"Good, there'll be a promotion waiting for you when you get back. You work for me now."

"Yes, sir. I will not disappoint you.Mr. Haile!"

"Mr. Golden," the voice continued, "is my man safe?"

"I've made arrangements to get him out of the country and back to the United States. He'll be leaving now."

Max motioned for one of his agents. "You'll drive Mr. Allende to the airport," he ordered. He retrieved a small envelope from his pocket.

"Marco, here's your airline ticket. You'll have just enough time to return to the hotel to pack your personal items and the company's office equipment. The next flight for the U.S. leaves in two hours."

When Marco and the Mossad agent left, Max returned his attention to the speaker phone.

"Thank you, Mr. Golden," the voice on the speaker phone said, "but there is just one other person I need to talk with. Is Travis Martin there?"

Travis took a step closer to the speaker phone, unsure why the publisher of the entire newspaper took an interest in him. "I'm here," Travis said.

"I would like to ask you one question. You owe me at least that much for springing you, so to speak."

"Go ahead."

"Who are you that the Cappa de Tutti Capi of the entire northeast Mafia takes a personal interest in you?"

"What?"

"Do you really need me to repeat my question?"

"No, I heard you. I have no idea. As far as I know I've never even met a mafia person."

"Sure, I hear you. If you can't tell me, that's alright. Just tell the Don that I kept my end of the deal and that the guy who shafted you has been dealt with. Let him know you're safe. Can you do that for me?"

Travis hesitated and replied, "I promise that I'll tell him the next time I see him."

"That's good enough. Is Max there?"

"Yes. I'm here."

"Good-bye. It's been a pleasure doing business with you," Mr. Haile said. With a click, he hung up the phone.

Max Golden faced Kookie. "Your cover was blown when you visited the Hilton Khartoum, so I arranged to have you arrested."

Kookie looked startled.

"Why?"

"I knew that Huzang would make arrangements with the local authorities to have you here when I needed you."

Now Kookie looked angry.

Max didn't seem to notice and called the two servants to his side. I want you to meet Addis and Rumbek. They're working in Khartoum incognito and speak fluent Arabic. Most importantly these men have contacts with rebel sympathizers at the ports. They'll transport you to your ship. The foreign freighter will provide safe passage into international waters.

Travis and Kookie, still guarded by two men apiece, stepped forward and joined their new escorts.

"Travis, you and Twangi will wear your hooded robes. Kookie will dress in the traditional Arabic *dishdasha* and *turban*. You must leave immediately before the local authorities arrive. Once aboard the ship, you'll go directly into your cabin and draw the curtains. I'll have sharpshooters watching the ship with orders to kill if you're seen on deck or in a porthole window. Do we understand each other?"

"Yes," Travis and Kookie said in unison.

"Truth is certainly a branch of

morality and a very important one to

society."

~ Thomas Jefferson

CHAPTER FIFTY-FOUR

"Let's talk. I have a few questions I need answered," Max said to Eli Mete when he returned to the reception area.

Max took a seat across from Eli.

"How well did you know Mr. Cafferty?"

"Today was my first encounter with him. Why do you ask?" Eli inquired.

"I'll ask the questions," Max said. "Did you hold a grudge or extreme dislike toward the American based on your political or religious beliefs?"

"No. I only know that he's the editor of a U.S. newspaper and that he died of a heart attack."

"Let's talk about that incident. You sat next to him at the table. Did you notice anything unusual before his fatal heart attack occurred?"

"No."

"Let's cut to the chase. Why did you tamper with his coffee?"

"I don't know what you're talking about."

"You waited until Cafferty was distracted and emptied green powder into his drink."

"Yes, it's true, but I didn't think anyone noticed."

"You concealed this slight of hand with your napkin but some of the residue fell onto the table. Now empty your right pants pocket of its contents and hand me the empty cellophane pouch."

Mete did as requested and Max examined the small pouch with care.

"Our lab can detect even the minutest particles and determine their chemistry. I believe it will verify that this pouch contained poison leaf. The plant is native and grows in the Savannah and other semi-arid places in Africa."

"Yes, the main ingredient is gifblaar, poison leaf. I purchased it from a local pharmacist. Once ingested it produces cardiac arrest in humans," replied Eli Mete.

"I still don't understand your motive. Why did you do it?" asked Max.

"I shouldn't be alive today. Just before my scheduled execution at Kobar, I was released. Mr. Haile's influence rendered the impossible, possible. So when he asked me to return the favor, I agreed. Mr. Haile told me that Cafferty plotted to take control of the newspaper industry. Mr. Cafferty intended to write a featured international story after arranging for Mr. Haile's early retirement."

"So, Mr. Haile believes in the Proverb 'An eye for an eye and a tooth for a tooth'."

"Yes."

"Except that Mr. Haile planned a first strike, and asked you to execute it."

"Yes," Eli Mete confirmed.

"You've committed premeditated murder, and it's a crime punishable by imprisonment or death. Why shouldn't I hand you over to the proper authorities?"

"I'm willing to take full responsibility for my actions and pay the consequence."

"That's good to know. But I believe you're a resourceful young man with a bright career ahead of you. That opportunity is possible if you'll consider supplementing your present employment. It's an opportunity of a lifetime. Interested in hearing my offer?"

"Yes."

Max presented his proposition as Mete listened intently. Due to time restraints, their conversation ended in short order but would be continued later.

"You'll remain here and talk with the local authorities when they arrive. You'll also report the events we've discussed to your superiors at the <u>SUNA Newspaper</u>. Do you have any further questions?"

"No, I understand."

"Good. We'll keep in touch."

"How will I find you?"

"I'll contact you."

"When you know that everything matters — that every

move counts as much as any other — you will begin living

a life of permanent purpose."

~ Andy Andrews

CHAPTER FIFTY-FIVE

"Thank you, Dr. el-Sheikh, for coming on such short notice," the Minister of Defense said.

"I'm always on twenty-four hour call for my most famous patient. Now you must rest."

Dr el-Sheikh nodded at Abu al Sadir who carefully pulled one pillow from beneath Dr. Mansoor Huzang's head to allow him to recline.

The guard knocked once and opened the door to permit Max Golden entry.

"How is the Minister of Defense?" Max whispered to Dr. el-Sheikh.

"He must rest now, but he'll recover."

"Max my eyes rest, but I'm awake," Dr. Huzang spoke faintly.

"I've made the phone call you requested, and now I'm taking my leave. I had a concern about your condition," Max said.

"Dr. el-Sheikh successfully removed the two bullets."

Max Golden walked over to examine the bullets on a tray on the dresser.

"Just as I suspected, a bullet proof vest saved your life."

"Yes, it did. An informant from the president's staff warned me about the two detrimental revisions to the ceremony. Unfortunately for Major General Ahmed, I wasn't able to convey our change of plans before the arrival of Colonel Isam. If the General had remained in the sitting room where our elite guards were hidden and prepared for action, it might have saved his life," said Dr. Huzang.

Dr. el-Sheikh's face registered alarm. "This information does not leave this room!" the doctor said sternly.

"Of course, your secret is safe with me," replied Max Golden.

The door burst open and Captain al Kadesh entered, followed by a guard attempting to restrain him.

"Captain al Kadesh, you're disturbing my patient," Dr. el-Sheikh said. "He sleeps now and must not be disturbed."

"President al-Bashir is concerned that the event previously scheduled has not yet occurred. He's also upset by the dispatch his office staff received that reported gunfire at the Minister of Defense's residence."

"That is correct. Dr. Huzang was shot twice in the chest. He'll require complete bed rest for some time. You must lower your voice now, or you'll wake him."

"President al-Bashir has ordered me here to seek answers to his questions. I will wake Dr. Huzang now."

"That's not necessary. Eli Mete, a representative for the <u>SUNA Newspaper</u>, should be able to answer most of your questions," Max suggested.

"Is he here now?"

"Yes."

"Good." The Captain turned to face Dr. el-Sheikh. "President al Bashir wants a full report regarding the Prime Minister's injuries and medical treatment."

"Of course, I will send it by courier as soon as possible."

"I'll speak with the newspaper reporter now," Captain al Kadesh left with haste.

When the door shut again, the Minister of Defense uttered a faint but audible sigh of relief.

"Mr. Golden, Abu will escort you to your vehicle so you are not drawn into this investigation."

"Thank you, Dr. Huzang. I wish you a speedy recovery," said Max Golden as he turned to leave. His mission accomplished, he left the estate.

"The firmest of friendships have been formed in mutual adversity, as iron is most strongly united by the fiercest flame."

~ Charles Caleb Colton

CHAPTER FIFTY-SIX

When Travis, Twangi and Kookie entered the waiting van and were safely on their way to the port, one of their escorts began to speak.

"My name is Addis. Neither my companion nor I can reveal our true identities. We can tell you that we're secret operatives of the SPLA. We work in covert action with Northern Moslems who sympathize with our cause. We also pass military information to our men in the battlefields when possible."

"Well, keep up the good work, Mates."

"Why are you helping us?" Travis asked.

"We know what you did to help one of our own. Karasa being reunited with her only son is something we want to be a small part of," the SPLA rebel replied.

"Yes, that is something I wanted, too," Travis agreed. Travis didn't want to reveal to his benefactors that what they both desired seemed like a remote possibility.

After they were driven to the docks in a passenger van, they followed two soldiers up the gangway and boarded on an ancient and decrepit tramp freighter.

"If you had to attribute any color to this ancient tub, it would be rust," Kookie said.

A deck hand wearing worn clothing and tattered shoes met them at the end of the plank and led them to a designated cabin.

When they all entered the cabin one of the soldiers motioned for them to sit. The crewman addressed them in halting, heavily accented English.

"This ship will take you all of the way to South America. You must not get off or even poke your noses out of this room during this voyage. Your meals will be deposited outside of your door. Wait until the hallway is clear to fetch them and wait until the hallway is empty to place your dirty dishes back out for collection."

"Won't this raise a lot of suspicion in the crew?" Travis asked.

"It's not uncommon. They'll just assume you're criminals who have paid the captain well for a safe passage and escape."

"He's right, Mate. It's done all the time," Kookie

added.

"My bag is gone. We have no money, passports or identification," Travis told him.

"Once you get off in South America you are no longer any of our concern and are free to leave," the crewman smiled.

"How long will the trip take?" Travis asked.

"I have no idea. It depends on what cargo we pick up and where it needs to go, but probably no more than three weeks," the crewman replied. "Any questions?"

With no response, the crewman and soldier left the room and locked the door.

"I'm sorry, Mate," Kookie said. "I know how you must feel about your wife being in these blighters' hands. If we ever return and find a way to go back for her, I'll be right at your side. But if we leave now, the surprise will be back on our side. Right now, they know exactly where we are, and they're holding the cards.

"Could you have walked away and left your wife behind?"

"Not if only my life was at stake. But if I had children, they would come first. She would tell you to get her son to safety."

"I know." Travis stared at the floor as if in deep concentration.

I can't sacrifice Twangi's life for a possibility near zero of finding or saving Karasa. She might even be dead, Travis thought.

With this revelation, a wave of depression dampened Travis' mood. Without Karasa by his side, his future appeared bleak.

"Baba," Twangi reached for Travis' hand.

"Son," Travis nodded with affirmation. "We're going to make this work."

"I seldom end up where I wanted to go, but almost always

end up where I need to be."

~ Douglas Adams

CHAPTER FIFTY-SEVEN

Karasa woke up to the sound of noises from the front room.

It must be morning because the sunbeams shine and dance on the threshold, she thought.

The morning passed slowly. Karasa silently prayed to God for peace and the fortitude to accept whatever fate dealt her. Twice her captors came and allowed her to sip water with her bonds still secured. Twice the *muezzin* called the faithful to prayer. About mid-afternoon, Karasa heard the noise of a car's engine and her whole body tensed. The car doors opened and closed. The front door opened and voices greeted the visitors as they entered. A police officer entered the bedroom and unbound her hands and feet. He replaced the handcuffs and led her to the chair in the kitchen. Here Chief of Police Sharif waited, accompanied by a young Moslem woman carrying a baby. She wore a *hijab*, a Shayla wrap and long garment that covered everything except her hands.

Is this young Moslem woman the important guest the Chief spoke of? Karasa's eyes squinted as she turned this thought over in her mind.

The Chief of Police stood aside as the young woman approached Karasa and sat opposite her on the other side of the small rectangular table.

"Good day," the woman addressed her in Dinka.

Karasa felt astonishment flush her face as her mouth dropped and her eyes rounded in curiosity.

How is it that this Moslem woman speaks Dinka? Karasa wondered.

"I was told that you had a boy named Twangi taken as a slave. How long ago did this happen?"

"Eleven years ago."

"Was he your only child taken?" The young woman continued to speak in the Dinka dialect.

"Why should this matter concern you?" Karasa questioned, speaking in Dinka also.

"Please, answer my questions, and then I will tell you everything."

Karasa considered this before answering. "The slave raiders took my son Twangi and his younger sister Nayeela."

"What was your given name?" the young woman asked.

"My parents named me Jamala."

The young woman sighed and the young Police Chief stepped forward and remained at her side, his hand on her shoulder as if to steady her.

"I am Nayeela."

Nayeela removed the veil covering her face.

"Nayeela?" Karasa gasped. "You are alive . . . and well?" Karasa did not trust her eyes and her ears.

Nayeela said something to the Chief. He hesitated before approaching Karasa and removing the handcuffs.

"I asked my husband to release my mother's bonds," Nayeela said in Dinka.

A flood of emotion washed through Karasa's heart. She stood and stepped toward her daughter, taking her into her arms. She couldn't hold back her tears of happiness. Nayeela, overcome with joy, welcomed the embrace.

They just stood and held each other for several minutes.

"Here, I am called Orpah. This is your granddaughter, Adiva. Her name means 'Gentle'. And this is your son-in-law, Ibim."

Hearing his name he nodded to Karasa.

"He is Chief of Police in this quad of Khartoum, and he comes from a respected, wealthy and influential family."

"How did you come to be married?"

"I was purchased by his family. Being two years

younger than Ibim, we grew up together as playmates and became constant companions. Ibim taught me to read Arabic. When Ibim reached adolescence he could have taken me as his mistress, but his feelings would not allow this. He told his parents that he wished to marry me, and they approved. For a wedding gift, his parents presented me with legal documents of freedom and citizenship. We've been married now for nearly two years.

"You were forced to convert to Islam?"

"No, I embrace the religion of peace. I am a *Muslim* because that is what I wish to be. Islam and the teachings of the Prophet *Muhammad* are what I believe."

Karasa struggled with a new emotion of sadness mixed in with her happiness. *She is found, yet she is still lost.* But she determined to trust God to work in her daughter's heart, and perhaps those of her in-laws through her.

"Everyone makes choices about what they believe. I am saddened by your decision, but I respect that it is yours to make. Most of all I thank God that He has protected and cared for you when I could not. Please remember that all good things come from God."

"Yes, mother, I will. Are my grandparents well?" Nayeela asked.

"Yes, they are well, and so are your Uncle Jeshi and Aunt Ayella. And you have a new little sister. We have all moved to Kenya to escape the fighting and the genocide of our people."

"I know that my father was killed in the raid. I have heard that you have a new husband who is a white man. Is he good to you?"

"Yes, he cares and provides for us. Is your husband good to you and Adiva?"

"Yes, mother, I love him with all my heart."

"Have you ever found your brother?"

"No, and my husband has helped me to search for many years. We have never been able to locate him.

"I have to know something, mother. My husband says that you and your new husband defiled a *mosque* and an *Imam* when you attacked our country three years ago. Is this true?" Nayeela asked.

"We blew up a *mosque,* but we did not defile either it or the holy man. But we did make it look like we had."

"Why?"

"We had to get the soldiers to chase us so that your Uncle Jeshi could get away with slave children we were trying to rescue. We faked what they saw so that they would be angry enough to chase us instead of the children. It nearly cost us our lives."

"You were brave, mother."

Karasa's son-in-law came over, whispered something to Orpah in Arabic, and hurried off into an adjoining room.

"Mother, there is a problem. I had hoped we would

have more time to visit but there is a rumor of an attempted assassination at the Minister of Defense's residence. We don't know many details yet, but we must take you to the airport, and you must depart before the airport officials discontinue all flights."

"What a beautiful young woman you have become, and I will always cherish this time with you and Adiva."

Karasa kissed her daughter's cheek and her granddaughter's forehead. Her smile remained even after she fastened the veil that covered her face.

"We must leave now," Orpah said as two strange Arabic men approached them.

Each man sported a black mustache and goatee. Dressed in the attire of the Sharia Desert nomads, they wore *chechia* head coverings and multi-colored long flowing *chechai* robes. *Babouches* protected their feet. They escorted the women outside and into the rear seats of an unmarked car. Two police cars with the men loyal to the Chief of Police flanked their unmarked car ahead and behind.

Karasa noticed that her daughter showed no apprehension regarding the Moslem men who sat in the front seat of their vehicle. So Orpah and Karasa continued to share on their way to the airport as if making up for lost time. Karasa also delighted in caressing Adiva.

"You are happy here, in this place?" Karasa sought affirmation.

"Yes. Perhaps I can best explain by sharing a poem. An Arabic poet describes the meeting of the Blue and White Nile as the longest kiss in history. And at the site of this eternal kiss lies the city of Khartoum. So, here I am at home, and I, too, feel loved."

The Moslem sitting in the front passenger's side turned and spoke in Arabic.

I recognize that voice, thought Karasa but she remained silent.

Orpah nodded and turned back toward Karasa.

"Please listen carefully to these instructions. You cannot tell anyone that we have met or what happened to you here in Khartoum. Most of all, no one must learn how you got away. Any rumors regarding our relationship or your escape could cost our family imprisonment or our lives."

"I understand. I would never do anything to put you in danger."

"I know you wouldn't."

Karasa had to broach the subject.

"Nayeela, do you know anything about my husband?"

Orpah looked down before answering. "My husband just received a private message confirming that the Minister of Defense was shot twice and his wounds might be fatal. The American terrorist is the prime suspect because he was seen in the vicinity of Dr. Huzang's residence. He can do nothing to help him. Mother, I'm afraid that you may be a widow again. I am sorry."

Tears flowed from Karasa's eyes, and she began to sob.

Orpah put an arm around her mother as she shared what little additional information she knew. Based upon rumor, some details seemed contradictory.

"I love you, Mother," Orpah hugged her.

"Always remember that I love you, too," Karasa returned the embrace.

When they reached their destination, the first patrol car continued to proceed to the main terminal of the Khartoum International Airport. Their vehicle veered and passed through a less conspicuous entrance and made a beeline to a lone cargo plane. The police cars stopped some distance from the plane, blocking the opened side gate that led into the commercial section of the airport. One policeman got out and stood guard.

Karasa looked from under the hood of her garment and saw Maude walk down the plane's ramp and onto the tarmac. She appeared apprehensive as she waited for their unmarked car to pull up. One of the Arab nomads who sat in the front climbed out of their vehicle.

"Listen to your orders," the Arab commanded in English. "You have cargo – the body of an unknown person, being sent for burial. Get ready to load it and take off at once. Ignore any calls for delay from the tower. Understood?"

Maude nodded her head.

The other Arab opened the car door and handed a canvas body bag to Karasa's daughter as he spoke in Arabic.

Karasa looked into the eyes of the man who spoke but felt no fear.

"Mother, I will help you into this canvas bag. It will conceal you. It is for your own protection and for ours."

Karasa slipped into the oversized body bag. Orpah pulled the bag over Karasa's head and tied the cord loosely to make a small breathing hole at the top.

One of the men threw the bag over his shoulder. Karasa couldn't see anything as he climbed into the plane and placed the body bag onto the metal floor.

As soon as the Arab left, Maude closed and locked the side door of the airplane. Effat ventured out from where she had been hiding, behind some crates.

"The police have ordered us to leave immediately," Maude told Effat.

"What's in the canvas bag?" Effat asked.

"It's a dead body," Maude shivered, shaking slightly.

"Karasa's?" Effat questioned in shock.

"Get me out of here," a muffled whisper pleaded.

The women exchanged glances, knelt down and untied the cord and helped Karasa out of this oversized sack.

Maude gave Karasa a quick hug.

"We must take off. Effat, care for Karasa's needs." Maude hurried to start the engines.

Effat reached into her own shoulder bag for a bottle of water and offered some to Karasa.

Karasa wanted to rush after Maude and take one final look out the window for a glimpse of the ones she held dear, but she wouldn't risk it. Instead she sat, hidden from view, waiting for take off. Effat sat quietly beside her.

Maude spoke to the tower on the radio, to alert them of her intentions.

Karasa listened to the radio chatter from the tower.

"Wait, we have a crisis, you must come around. Over."

Maude ignored the request and continued to taxi down the runway.

"We have a red alert, you must return to the airport, now! Over."

Again Maude ignored the request, and pushed the throttle wide open to accelerate, and as the plane's speed increased she brought back the yoke. The plane eased off the runway and into the air. When the plane stabilized, Karasa and Effat joined Maude.

"Were you harmed?" Effat asked, as they sat together in the copilot's seat.

"No, I was detained but released." Karasa couldn't reveal the truth. She desperately desired to protect her daughter and her daughter's family. Besides, her scratches and bruises were hidden by her *burqa* and veil. Maude and Effat asked more questions, but she remained evasive.

"It was a case of mistaken identity. The authorities confused me with another wanted criminal. After interrogating me, they decided to let me go," Karasa explained.

Maude looked at her sideways. Karasa knew that Maude did not believe her but would not press the matter. Maude would assume she had a good reason for withholding the truth.

"Did you find Twangi?" Maude asked.

"No."

"What about Travis?" Maude questioned.

"That's why the tower tried to prevent your departure," Karasa said. "I overheard hushed whispers of an assassination attempt on the Minister of Defense. Much is not known, but Travis matches the description of the American at the residence. The military under the command of one of their generals stormed the area and gunshots were fired. The president's elite team took charge and locked everything down. They took no prisoners. So Travis must be . . . dead . . . That is all . . ."

Karasa burst into heaving sobs. Her grief found no comfort.

Effat placed her arm around Karasa's shoulder and silently prayed as Maude flew the cargo plane back to Nairobi.

"The truth is the most beautiful thing in the world; it's un-

changing."

~ Jeremy Matthews

CHAPTER FIFTY-EIGHT

The vigil service for Travis and Twangi would soon commence. Hopefully this event would bring closure. Because their bodies had not been recovered, both were assumed dead. Karasa, overwhelmed with grief, wept softly since entering the church. Now Tamara, her young daughter, began to cry.

George Mitchell, too, mourned for his friend. He sat in his wheelchair at the end of a pew in the chapel of the Holy Name Catholic Church. George, a Methodist, had never before graced the interior of a non-Protestant Cathedral. He noted the similarities: stained glass windows depicting scenes from the life of Jesus, carpeting running up the three steps to the sanctuary. But the church held an opulence not found in his family's simpler place of worship. Its magnificence, however, neither enhanced nor detracted from the holiness of this place. A similar spiritual presence that George associated with his own church prevailed here as well.

His eyes fell on the back of Karasa's head. She waited with her family in the first pew for the service to begin.

It's a miracle they're here at all, George thought. He had called in favors from the U.S. State Department to contact the embassy in Nairobi. He had used all of his government connections, lawyer expertise, and a couple of monetary bribes to pull this off. But he'd willingly jump through all the hurdles again to get Karasa and her family brought to the United States from Kenya.

The family adjusted well to their new community and had begun to settle in. Some of their new friends had even accompanied them and were seated in the back rows of the chapel.

Just before the service, George had made one more call to his son-in-law, Jim Anderson, a missionary in Kenya. Sadly the news coming out of Sudan was sparse. Jim only mentioned that someone named Rocco would fly back into Nairobi tomorrow and that Karasa would understand.

The organ played a hymn, commencing the ceremony. The music had an enthralling affect on Tamara, who calmed down. Father Gabriel entered the sanctuary and walked over to Karasa to comfort her. Afterwards the priest proceeded to the pulpit for the introductory rites and the meditation, a reading from the Holy Scripture. A brief homily followed. While Father Gabriel commented on the family's reflections of Travis' life, George's emergency cell phone rang, momentarily distracting the congregation.

Only two people had this number - his wife Betty and his secretary. Betty sat next to him on the pew, hands folded and head bowed.

George retrieved the slim silver phone from his belt and flipped it open. In a low voice he said, "Can this wait? The service has already begun!"

"Believe me, Boss, you'll want to take this call. Hold on, I'm transferring it to you right now. It came in collect a few minutes ago," said Marge.

George heard a clicking sound.

"George, are you there?"

George almost fell out of his wheelchair.

"This had better not be a practical joke." He raised a shoulder to hold his phone to his ear and zipped to the rear of the church.

"What are you talking about? Listen, I need some help. Twangi and I, along with another friend, are in Rio de Janeiro. We don't have plane tickets, passports, or even money to buy us something to eat," Travis spoke in desperation.

"We'll work that out," George said. "But we thought that you were dead."

444 ~ Kweli – the Truth Unmasked

"We can talk about that later, but not on an open line. What's going on with my daughter, and with Karasa's family?"

"I pulled some strings and Karasa and her family are all here in California," George answered.

George hadn't noticed his voice growing louder with excitement. He glanced around. Some people were giving him reproachful looks for his disrespect at this solemn occasion.

If they knew what I knew they wouldn't glare, George vindicated himself.

"Did you say Karasa – and her family?" Travis' voice, two decibels higher, shouted with accelerated excitement.

"I'd heard that she had been arrested. I thought that she was dead."

"Likewise," George said. "You're interrupting your own funeral."

"Is Karasa there?"

"Just a minute. She's sitting about fifty feet away from me, crying her eyes out."

Travis and Karasa will both soon discover an eternal truth – that whatever the sacrifice, love is the greatest gift of all, George smiled.

Every pair of eyes, including those of the priest, followed George as his arms pushed the large wheels and he whirled around the corner of the front pew, stopping directly in front of Karasa. She glanced from George to Father Gabriel who had just completed his eulogy and intended to conclude with a final prayer. Instead he raised his eyebrow, nodded in affirmation and blessed the people in the sanctuary with the sign of the cross.

"Special delivery! Someone wants to speak with you," George Mitchell fairly shouted as he held out his hand.

Karasa reached out to take the phone.

"You will know the truth and the truth will set you free."

~John 8:32 NIV

Glossary

This story takes place in the countries of Kenya and Sudan. Swahili is the language of choice throughout Africa. The Christian and animist tribes in Southern Sudan also speak their own distinctive dialect. Northern Sudan is dominated by Moslems who speak Arabic. Below are some foreign terms used in *Kweli, the Truth Unmasked.*

Word	Language	English Translation.
Abeed	Arabic	slave
Allah	Arabic	God
al Salamu Alaykum. (es sa –LA-moo ALAY- kum)	Arabic	Peace be with you.
asante (ah-SAH-nty)	Swahili	thank you
baba (BAH-ba)	Swahili	daddy
burqa	Arabic	woman's knee length dress
dishadasha	Arabic	man's robe
Imam	Arabic	holy man

Word	Language	English Translation
Inshallah	Arabic	If Allah wills it, it will happen
Isa Masih	Arabic	Jesus, Messiah
jallaba	Arabic	slave trader
jambo (JAH-mbo)	Swahili	hello
jellabiya	Arabic	Moslem robe
jihad (je-HAD)	Arabic	war by Moslems against unbelievers
jihadist	Arabic	Moslem warrior
jubba	Arabic	an unbuttoned knee length jacket
kanga	Swahilia	woman's colorful cloth garment
karasa (KAR-a-sa)	Swahili	a mongoose
Kaskazini Nyota	Swahili	North Star
kwaheri (kwah-HAY-ree)	Swahili	good-bye
kweli (k -WAIL -le)	Swahili	truth
kurta	Arabic	man's dress jacket
Ma'aleesh	Arabic	Don't worry about it.

Word	Language	English Translation
mama (MAH-mah)	Swahili	mother
matatu (mah-TAH-too)	Swahili	minibus
mimi panda ku	Swahili	I love you
mosque	Arabic	church
muslim	Arabic	Moslem, true believer
nyotas	Swahili	stars
Qur'an	Arabic	Koran, the book of Islam
riika	Swahili	friend
rooibos tea (roy-boss)	Swahili	reddish colored herbal tea
safari	Swahili	journey or hunting expedition
salwar kameez	Arabic	a man's dress suit
Sharia Law	Arabic	civil law
simba (SEE-mba)	Swahili	lion
thingira.	Swahili	a man's round, thatch-roof hut

Word	Language	English Translation
topi	Arabic	skullcap

turban	Arabic	a cloth headdress worn by men
uhuru (oo-HOO-roo)	Swahili	freedom
ugali	Swahili	cornmeal porridge
Yevmi Ashurer	Arabic	Day of Sweet-Soup

Holiday that commenmrates Noah emerging from the ark.

22469385R00245

Made in the USA
Charleston, SC
20 September 2013